LISA McKENDRICK

BONNEVILLE BOOKS ™

AN IMPRINT OF CEDAR FORT, INC.
SPRINGVILLE, UTAH

This is a work of fiction. The characters, names, incidents, places, and dialogue are products of the author's imagination and are not to be construed as real. The opinions and views expressed herein belong solely to the author and do not necessarily represent the opinions or views of Cedar Fort, Inc. Permission for the use of sources, graphics, and photos is also solely the responsibility of the author.

ISBN 13: 978-1-4621-1553-2

Published by Bonneville Books, an imprint of Cedar Fort, Inc.
2373 W. 700 S., Springville, UT 84663
Distributed by Cedar Fort, Inc. www.cedarfort.com

LIBRARY OF CONGRESS CATALOGING-IN-PUBLICATION DATA

McKendrick, Lisa, 1965-
Letters to my future husband / Lisa McKendrick.
  pages ; cm
ISBN 978-1-4621-1553-2 (acid-free paper)
1. Young women--Fiction. 2. Mate selection--Fiction. 3. Man-woman relationships--Fiction. 4. Chick lit. I. Title.
PS3613.C554L48 2015
813'.6--dc23
                2014033313

Cover design by Kristen Reeves and Michelle May
Cover design © 2015 by Lyle Mortimer
Edited and typeset by Melissa J. Caldwell

Printed in the United States of America

10 9 8 7 6 5 4 3 2 1

Printed on acid-free paper

To my husband, Rich,
who sits high atop my list of essentials.

chapter 1

WHEN I WAS five, I thought choosing a husband meant deciding who you wanted to build Lego castles with for your Barbies, so when my dad said he couldn't marry me, I crumbled. Knees collapsing, I fell to the floor and cried my eyes out. "Wh-hy?" I asked. "Why won't you marry me?"

He bent toward me and wiped away tear after tear. His skin was rough, but his touch gentle. "Because, sweetheart, I'm already married."

"So!" I sobbed.

"To your mommy," he said.

"That doesn't matter!"

"It does in certain circles," he said, the corners of his mouth edging upward, like he was about to laugh. Laugh! What was funny about the man I'd chosen refusing to marry me? What was funny about my five-year-old world coming to an end? If there was one thing I hated, it was being laughed at. Heartbroken and humiliated, I did the only thing that seemed reasonable. I kicked him, or tried to. My legs beat the air, but I couldn't make contact.

Dad scooped me up, despite my best efforts to be un-scoopable, and sat me on his lap. "Someday, my love, you are going to meet a wonderful man."

I folded my arms in protest. "No, I won't!" I said.

Dad patted my ringlets. I hated my ringlets. They were a Saturday-night torture my mom insisted on, pulling and wrapping my hair around "soft" curlers that made sleep impossible. "You'll want to hold his hand."

"Punch his face!"

"And give him a kiss."

"A kick!" I corrected.

"And spend all your time with him."

"Never!" I cried. "I hate that poopyhead. I hate him, Daddy!"

"But why, honey?" asked Dad.

"Because he's not you," I said, choking with emotion. "He'll never be you."

Dad didn't say anything for a moment. He just let me cry on his shoulder until my chest stopped heaving and my tears slowed to a trickle. In some ways, that only made things worse. No one was ever going to be like my dad. Snuggled against him, I tried to picture my future. It was going to be dull, that was for sure, especially with Mr. Poopyhead in the picture. More boring, no doubt, than the Little Miss Manners tea parties my mother forced me (and my ringlets) to attend once a month. Sucking in deeply, I sighed as the fight I still had in me began to fade like air from a leaky balloon.

"It's hard to see right now, my love," Dad said softly, "but he's coming. One day your future husband will walk into a room and steal your heart."

"Then the policeman will put him in jail," I said, my face pressed to his shirt.

"I don't think so."

"Why not?"

"Because he'll be a good man."

"He'll never be as good as you, Daddy."

Moving me off his shoulder, he looked me in the eye. "No, my love," he said, "he won't be as good as me; he'll be better."

I blew a raspberry, spraying him a little. It was my way of telling him that was impossible, but according to my dad it meant I wanted to be tickled. Dad dug his fingers into my ribs and I laughed and laughed, until all thoughts of my future husband left me and I was happy again.

Later that week, Dad came into my room just as I was going to bed. "I have an idea," he said, sitting on my bed and rubbing his hands together the way he did when excited.

"What is it?" I asked, my arms wrapped around my stuffed elephant, Jasper.

"Sophie," he said, "you love me because you know me." I looked at him, eyes wide, waiting for him to say more. "And the problem is, right now you don't know your future husband, so it only makes sense you don't love him."

I moaned at the mention of this mystery man and slumped into my bed. "This is going to be the boringest talk ever," I said and covered my face with Jasper.

"Hear me out, Sophie," said Dad, gently pulling Jasper away. "I'm just trying to explain that once you get to know him—"

"I don't want to get to know him!"

"But once you do, you'll love him too."

I rolled my eyes.

Dad waited a moment and then cut to the chase. "I'd like you to write him."

"Who?"

"Your future husband," Dad said, tucking a few strands of hair behind my ear.

I scowled. "I don't even know that dumb man."

"That's okay. You're not sending the letters in the mail. I want you to keep them in here," he said, handing me a book like none I'd ever seen. Covered in tooled leather, the design on the front was of a town far different from the one I knew: Mesa, Arizona. Buildings sat squashed together on either side of a river, and spanning the river was a bridge covered, oddly enough, with shops. Above it all, stars sparkled in a cloudless sky. The book was locked shut, and dangling from a string was a small but heavy key whose jagged teeth alone could open it.

"This is for me? Oh, Daddy! Did you get it at Target?"

Dad smiled. "No, honey, someplace far away that I visited on business. Promise me you'll use it to do what I said—write letters to your future husband."

"But why, Daddy?" I asked, lying back on my pillow, my new book in my hands.

"Letters can help us get to know a person. Right now you don't know who your husband will be, but as you write letters to him, bit by bit, you'll figure out what you want him to be like—*who* you want him to be."

I yawned. "Did you write letters to Mommy?"

"No," he said, tucking me in. It was just one word, and I was just five, but I thought I detected a twinge of something, possibly sadness.

My door opened, and I did my best to hide my new book with my little arms. "Honestly, Howard, what is taking so long?" asked my mother.

Dad kissed my forehead and stood up. "Just having a chat with our Sophie."

"It's been a long day. We've earned some alone time," said Mom, leaning on the door frame, her hands on her slender hips.

"Good night, sweetheart," he said, turning off my light. "I'm off to spend some alone time with your mother. Although how we'll accomplish that together, I'm not sure."

"You know perfectly well what I mean," said Mom, her icy tone melting a little as my father stopped to kiss her cheek as he walked by. My kisses didn't soften my mother, nor did my tendency to slouch.

"Good night, Sophia. Try not to wet the bed," said Mom, sounding certain that she was going to have to wash my sheets in the morning.

"Good night, Mommy," I said.

As soon as my mom shut my door, I switched on my lamp, a large ballet slipper with a pink shade on top meant to inspire me to become a graceful dancer (so far, it wasn't working). I put the key into the book's lock and turned, springing it open. Then I took out a pencil and wrote my husband a letter.

Der Futur Husbun,
Go away!
Sophie

All my early letters were like this, really just hate mail to the man of my dreams. Sporadic and spiteful, they made it clear I was still bitter that my father was already taken. As I grew older, the letters lost their sourness. The boys at school started looking cuter to me, and my dad, noticeably balder. Then, practically overnight, I made a startling observation: most, if not all, of my brother's friends were cute enough to be in a boy band! But there was just one who was lead-singer gorgeous, one who barged through the kitchen door without knocking and helped himself to whatever was in the fridge, one who made me scream, not out of annoyance—as everyone assumed—but like an overwhelmed, adoring fan. And that one was Hanno Olsen.

Hanno, like my brother George, was four years older than me. He lived down the street from us and made popping wheelies look so natural and effortless that it seemed to me the only way a bike should be ridden: one wheel on the ground, the other in the air. And so I tried it and broke my arm. But that was part of Hanno's appeal: this sense that he got to play by his own set of rules. By the time I turned ten, my letters to my future husband were drippy pre-teen ramblings to Hanno, filled with gushing blow-by-blows of our encounters (*You looked at me, then I looked at you, then you grabbed your napkin, and you looked at me again!*), reviews of his latest haircuts and T-shirt choices, and, at times, long deliberations about what we should name our children. They were unguarded and innocent, and they came to a screeching halt after I came home and found my mother, scissors at her side, sitting on my bed, my book open in her hands, and the leather strap meant to seal it shut cut in half.

"Mom!" I cried, my face flush with horror. "What are you doing?" I rushed toward her and tried to grab my book, but she quickly stood up and hid it behind her back.

Tears stung my cheeks and I made another futile attempt to snatch it from her.

5

"We shouldn't have any secrets between us, Sophia," she said, her words as smooth as her pencil skirt. "A mother needs to check in and make sure her daughter isn't doing anything regrettable. It's my job, Sophia."

"To break into my book?"

"Well, I couldn't find the key," she explained while checking my standing mirror to make sure nothing about her was out of place. "Parenting is full of difficult choices," she continued, smoothing a few strands of her brunette bob with a book-free hand, "but you shouldn't be so upset that I saw your little love notes. I'm your mother, Sophia, the one who changed your diapers and fed you a bottle, for heaven's sake." She spoke impatiently, like I was four and trying to pour my own glass of milk. "What I don't understand is why you never told me about this," she said, taking my book out from behind her back and offering it to me. I yanked it from her and clutched it to my stomach. "I thought it would've come up in one of our mother-daughter talks."

I shrugged, though what I wanted to do was scream that if anyone should have told her, it was her husband, and the fact that he'd chosen not to was proof she was nosy.

Mom picked up the scissors. Head tilted, she studied me for a moment, as if not looking at her daughter but a puzzle, the kind where the pieces are exasperatingly small. "I honestly don't know why you're so put out, Sophia. I think it's sweet that in second grade you found Henry and Cole so cute," she said, making me wonder if it was possible to die from embarrassment. "Of course, in the long run neither one would likely be tall enough for you." She said this, as she always did when talking about my height, with an unmistakable note of censure. "But your ongoing interest in Hanno Olsen . . . I must admit is a surprise, considering how much you two bicker."

The answer was no, death by embarrassment wasn't possible. She had mentioned Hanno, and I was still breathing.

"Yes, Hanno's tall and handsome, but he's an unreliable sort. Definitely not one to entrust with your future."

Words. I wanted to hurl them at her. Mean, ugly words—the kind the kids on the bus said. But nothing came. Like a pileup on the freeway, they'd all collided in my throat, making it impossible to speak. So instead, I threw my book against the wall.

"Sophia," said Mom, her tone disapproving, "don't treat your things like that."

"You ruined it," I sobbed through gritted teeth.

"You can still write in it, Sophia. In fact, I hope you do."

"Never!" I shouted, tears streaming and fists clenched. "Never, ever again!"

As upset as I was, this didn't stop her from bringing up one of her favorite complaints about me. "You're looking taller," she said, disappointment softening her voice. I looked at the carpet, frowning and huffing. "If you grow too tall, it won't be my fault. Grandma Stark will be to blame. Regardless, you shouldn't slouch. Even less likely than a tall girl finding a husband is a slouchy one."

I didn't say anything, and not for the first time when it came to my mother, I wished I wore hearing aids, the kind you could shut off.

"Well," she said, "you know I love you so I'll go make dinner now. Remember, Sophia, no secrets." She shut my door, and as she did, something inside me shut her out of my heart. Not that I ever told her. It was my secret.

chapter 2

TEN YEARS LATER

A TOURIST BUS PASSED, engulfing me in exhaust, and though I coughed and waved my hands in front of my face, the truth was those fumes made me feel sophisticated. No longer was I in Mesa, Arizona, home of the three-foot churro at Gas and Go. Thanks to Grandma Stark, or Gram as I liked to call her, my hometown was thousands of miles away, and I was traveling through Europe. She had paid for me to go, though my mother had been against it. "It's misspent generosity," she had complained to my dad. "If she wants to part with thousands, why doesn't she help us redo the kitchen?"

But no matter how sweetly (or unsweetly) my mother approached the subject, Grandma Stark remained uninterested in kitchen make-overs. "You work on your kitchen, and let me work on Sophie," she had said, making my mother turn on the heels of her classic black pumps and storm out of the living room.

"She thinks I'm not ready to appreciate Europe, Grandma," I said, sounding like this might sadly be the case.

"Nonsense," said Gram, her brown eyes narrowing.

"I'm not very good at art appreciation, Gram," I said. "To be honest, I don't get the point of benches in museums. Everything I want to observe about a painting, I can see as I walk past it."

Gram tutted. "I'm not sending you there to stare at paintings, Sophie."

"Then why?"

Gram looked me in the eye, which was easy enough to do. Just as my mother had feared, I had grown to be every bit as tall as my paternal grandmother, a "highly unmarryable" five feet eleven inches. "My dear Sophia," she said, "you need to grow."

"Not according to Mom," I said, frustration uncorking inside me. "If I grow another inch she says there won't be two men in the whole world who will want to marry me and my size-ten feet! Maybe," I said, more to myself than Gram, "the Chinese were on to something when they bound feet . . ."

Gram's eyes sparkled with repressed laughter.

"What?" I asked.

"I meant grow inwardly," she said, giving me a nudge.

"Hmm," I said, not agreeing or disagreeing with her and definitely not asking her to explain further. Call me crazy, but I'm not a fan of hearing a list of my shortcomings.

"But not to worry," she said, putting her arm though mine, "we all have a few kinks to iron out."

Across from where we stood, a large antique mirror was hung over my mother's beloved white couch. We looked at our reflections. We were so similar: same height, same brown eyes, just the years between us adding differences. "I went to Europe when I was your age, and it changed me," said Gram, speaking to my reflection.

"How?"

"Well, for one, I fell in love."

I turned to her. "What? With whom?" I asked.

"With Paris."

"Oh."

Gram winked. "You were hoping I was about to mention *some-one*, not someplace?" she asked.

"Of course not," I said. "City crushes are so interesting."

"Sorry, there is no European summer fling to confess," she said, a hint of laughter in her voice. "The only man waiting for me beneath the Eiffel Tower was selling postcards. And as I've told you before, I met your grandfather at the DMV." Gram took my hands in hers, making a flutter of worry pass through me. Her knuckles seemed to be getting larger. "Go to Europe," she urged. "No more silliness about whether or not you deserve it. Enjoy the incredible scenery, the delicious food, and the chance to walk past a few paintings."

I sighed. "Fine, I'll go to Europe and spend your money."

Gram smiled. "Good. And Sophie, don't let your mother's worries about your stature become your own. You're beautiful exactly as you are. Some lucky young man, when the time is right, will recognize that."

It was the sort of thing she always said to me, but I never got tired of hearing it. "Thanks, Gram," I said.

"And keep in mind, my dear, all you need is one."

"One what?"

"Just one man in the entire world to fall in love with you and your size-ten feet."

Gram had been right; I did need Europe. I needed the crowded trains, the gorgeous cathedrals, the cobblestone streets, not to mention my mother being six "thousand" plus miles away. The tangled knot of tension, self-consciousness, and worry that usually pinged and ponged in my stomach when I was around cute boys had, over my several weeks abroad, shrunk considerably. It was still there, making me talk a little too fast at times or laugh a little too loud, but settled in next to it and slowly crowding it out was a new confidence I felt about myself. It made me stand taller, wear sandals with or without shaving my big toes (my mother would die), and roll my eyes dismissively when Italian men whistled at me (even though deep down I felt like shouting "Thank you!"). Yes, I had needed Europe, but according to the Italian businessman who sat next to me on a train, the only city that mattered was the one we were speeding toward—Florence, Italy.

"Until you see Florence, *La Firenze*," said the businessman, his accent thick but his English comprehensible, "you have not begun to live, or"—he leaned forward conspiratorially—"to love."

Across from me, my friends Gina and Marie stifled a laugh. *Awkward!* I mouthed to them, then smiled at the businessman and scooted as far away from him as I could without appearing rude. He wasn't a creepster; I could tell that. Just a friendly guy with a missing upper molar who happened to love, love, love the city where he worked.

A sign indicating that we'd just entered Florence whipped past. "Looks like my life has just started," I joked. "Quick, someone call my parents and tell them it's a girl!"

While Gina and Marie giggled, the businessman, who clearly had no concept of respecting personal bubbles, leaned forward a little more and continued his ringing endorsement of Florence. "Even the air in my city is special." He sniffed. "It's like wine."

If all the guys in Florence wore as much cologne as he did, then I could understand why the air was debilitating. Head beginning to throb from aftershave overload, I leaned back a little more. "Well, since I don't drink, I guess I'll have to remember not to breathe once I get there," I said, trying to make him laugh.

He didn't, but his blank stare was killing Gina and Marie. They covered their mouths and leaned on each other.

The train was slowing and my friends (still giggling) were grabbing their backpacks, but the businessman wasn't finished. "And the sounds of my city," he said, hands cupped together and shaking for emphasis, "are not noise, but music."

I stood up slowly because it seemed less rude than standing up fast. But either way, it was time to go. "Okay," I said, grabbing my backpack, "so the air is wine and the noise pollution Mozart. Good to know," I said, not completely hiding that I was finding this conversation ridiculous.

"You will see," he said, blasting my personal bubble to smithereens by giving me a peck on each cheek, "Firenze is the city of love, and it will be your city . . . of love." I let the weirdness of that moment settle over me as I walked out of the train behind him. It was absolutely the strangest thing that had ever happened to me, until the next morning, when I ran into Hanno Olsen.

You expect to see a lot of things when you visit Italy: ancient architecture, gorgeous scenery, priceless works of art, but not your childhood crush. Definitely not your childhood crush. Yet there he was, Hanno Olsen, sitting on a stone bench in Piazza Duomo, unaware of me (as always) and reading an Italian newspaper.

"What are you doing?" asked Marie as I veered away from my friends.

"I'll catch up with you later!" I cried and, like a moth to the hypnotic blue light of a bug zapper, headed for Hanno.

It had been five years since I last saw him. Five years since his (hasty) wedding in his parents' backyard to Jenny Mayfield, his high school sweetheart. Accompanied by a local cover band and whispers, all eyes had been on Jenny's stomach that night as they'd danced their first dance as a married couple.

"There'd have been no fanfare back in our day!" one old lady had said to another near our table.

"To be sure!" her friend had said, clucking her tongue disapprovingly.

"You put the cart before the horse and I say punch and cookies should go out the window."

"And hiring a band! They only deserve the radio."

"Positively scandalous."

But the scandal of Hanno and Jenny having to get married was nothing compared to the news that they didn't—*have* to, I mean. Fearful of losing Hanno, Jenny had lied about being pregnant, and when she finally came clean during their Hawaiian honeymoon, she lost him anyway and tearfully returned home alone, a situation, incidentally, that was referred to later by Teddy Watson, a twelve-year-old deacon in our ward, when asked to give a talk on honesty.

I gulped though my mouth was dry. What should I say to him? "Hello"? "Long time, no see"? Each step closer to Hanno made my heart beat faster. In some ways he looked exactly the same. His swimmer's body was still stripped of any unnecessary fat, his thick blonde hair still just long enough to gather into a hair band, which at home had usually been one of my hair bands that he'd taken from my room without asking. A jolt of annoyance for his petty theft flashed over me. *Come on*, I told myself, *it was just a few (hundred) hair bands.* But the problem was that it wasn't just hair bands. It was Halloween candy, Easter candy, the last egg roll in the fridge from Ling Guini's, the best Chinese/Italian place in the valley. Hanno was always taking our stuff. MY stuff. *But*, I reminded myself, *it's been five years.* Five years! I should be happy to see him. And I was happy to see him. But, childish though it was, I was also irritated, which occurred to me, as I stepped in front of him, was perfect. Because when it came to Hanno, those two emotions usually duked it out inside me, and so, despite his chiseled jaw and sun-kissed skin and gorgeous blue eyes, I would have no problem being myself.

"Nice fur ball hanging off your face," I said, pointing to the soul patch he'd grown sometime since he'd twirled Jenny around a rented dance floor in his parent's backyard.

Squinting, Hanno looked up. I waved as his face split into a grin revealing teeth white enough for a toothpaste commercial. "Sofa!" he cried, standing up and hugging me. "Sofa, Sofa, Sofa!"

I hated it when he called me that, but still I closed my eyes and melted for a moment. He smelled of soap, a touch of aftershave, and his cheek was scruffy against mine. It was absolutely magical until he tried to make me wet my pants. Lifting me off the ground, Hanno hugged me tighter and tighter, and then started to shake. Just the sort of thing he and my brother George used to do to me, especially when I was cranky.

My eyes popped open from the pressure. "You are so immature!" I cried, squirming and trying to break free. "Stop it!"

"But it's so good to see you!" he cried, shaking some more.

"I swear, Hanno, that if I have to go back to the hostel to change my pants, I will kill you!" I cried.

Hanno kissed my cheek, and then, setting me on the ground, let go. "I love it when I bring out your homicidal tendencies."

"You're such a dork," I grumbled, giving him a shove.

An old man sitting at a nearby café shouted something at us in Italian, making Hanno laugh.

"What did he say?"

Hanno grinned. "He thinks we're having a lovers' spat."

My mouth fell open and I shook my head. "Tell him we're not!" I cried, pummeling him (lightly) with my fists. Hanno shouted at the man in what sounded to me like fluent Italian. The man shouted in return, and they both laughed.

"What? What'd you tell him?" I cried, sounding a tad desperate.

"I said, of course we're having a lovers' spat. This is Florence, the city of love!"

"What's with this place being called the city of love?" I asked.

"There's gotta be a reason," he said, smiling.

I cupped my hands around my mouth. "We're not in love!" I shouted to the old man. "We're just old friends from Arizona!"

"Kiss!" he cried, as did the tables sitting near him. "Kiss! Kiss!"

"Okay, I'm going to assume those people don't understand English," I said.

"It's either that or they just really want to see us kiss," said Hanno.

I shoved Hanno in the arm and our little audience cheered, making me feel oddly like a cowboy in Tombstone, Arizona, where every day at noon you can see the Old West come to life with a shoot-out on Main Street. I could almost hear a tour guide saying, *Florence is the city of love. Over to your left we have a young couple engaged in a lovers' spat. Notice the playful way she just slugged him in the arm. Oh, to be young and in love! As we move along, please take a moment to note the baptistery doors.*

Hanno waved at our onlookers and then put his arm around my shoulder, which I didn't attempt to shrug off. Yes, he was obnoxious, but can you say childhood crush? "Let's relocate," he said softly in my ear.

"Kiss girl!" cried the old man as we walked away.

I covered my mouth and mumbled, "Don't you dare."

Hanno moved his hand from my shoulder to my waist. "Don't worry," he said. "I never kiss on demand." He grinned, making me feel a prickle of undeniable disappointment.

We walked along a winding street away from the crowds of

tourists and hordes of vendors selling leather goods. "Where are we going?" I asked, though to be honest it didn't matter. I was with Hanno!

"To get some breakfast."

"But I've already had breakfast," I said, continuing to walk in step beside him.

"What'd you have?"

"A granola bar."

Hanno pshawed. "That's calories, not breakfast."

"Look, I only have one day to finish seeing Florence, and so breakfast had to go."

"Breakfast had to go," he repeated, incredulous.

"Yes," I said. "I'll admit it was hard at first, but now it's a relief, sort like shoving a grand piano from the cargo hold of an airplane." My stomach growled exposing me as a liar. "Sort of."

"Sofa," he said, stopping and turning toward me. "Let me show you Florence, and we'll begin with breakfast." Hanno gestured toward a bakery close by where baguettes were stacked in the shop window like firewood.

"First of all," I said, "I am not a piece of furniture, so there's no need to call me Sofa."

"I don't know, I'm pretty sure I've sat on you before," he said, a smile playing on his lips.

My hands flew to my hips. "Only so George could grab the remote from me! Not your classiest moment."

Hanno took one of my hands in both of his. I told my heart not to flutter; it didn't listen. "You've caught me on a rare day off," he said, tugging gently. "Come on, Sophe. Let me show you around."

I bit my lip and looked up, like I was mulling over his offer. "But there's Skeen, my tour guide," I said.

"Will he freak?"

"Not at all, but I really like his flag, the one he waves around to make us follow him like sheep. Do you have a flag?"

"Nope."

"Potential deal breaker."

Hanno tugged again, as if it were necessary. My answer was going to be yes. I just liked stringing him along. "We'll see all the requisite stuff you haven't seen yet, I promise. And then I'll show you the real Florence, my city."

"It can't be your city," I said. "It already belongs to a business-man who buys aftershave by the gallon and has a morning com-mute." Hanno tilted his head and gave me a puzzled look. I didn't elaborate, but instead took a deep breath. "Fine," I said, "you can show me Florence. But don't leave out any of the important stuff."

"I promise you'll see what's important," he said. Then he hooked his arm through mine (gulp) and we headed for the bakery.

I'm the kind of person who likes to stick with a good thing, so had it been possible to eat foccacia for breakfast for the rest of my life, I would have been game. Fat yet airy bread drizzled with olive oil and layered with a smattering of Parmesan flakes. It was delicious, filling, and, surprisingly, just as portable as a granola bar, which turned out to be a good thing since Hanno wanted to motor through the "requisite" stuff.

The thing about tourist attractions is they attract tourists, so it would have been stupid for me to have expected to flit around Flor-ence all day with Hanno while never running into my travel group, but what can I say, sometimes I'm awesome at stupid. As soon as we stepped inside the Duomo (our first stop), there was Skeen, his SeeEuropeNow! polo shirt stretched to capacity over his gut and his orange-and-white striped flag hovering angel-like in the dusky cathe-dral. My heart sunk a little. So much for it being just the two of us. A middle-aged woman with a floral scarf and a laser pen, acting as our guide for the cathedral, was pointing out to our group some of the Duomo's features, but according to Gina and Marie, gothic archi-tecture and fourteenth-century stained glass were far less interesting than the sight of me walking toward them with Hanno, especially when, after they waved to us, he reached out and held my hand.

I knew what he was doing. He was trying to shock my friends, and it worked. As we walked toward them, their mouths fell open. Still, for a moment, I soaked in the feeling of his warm hand clasped in mine, luxuriated in the thought of it being real: Hanno and me together in Italy. And then I started pulling away.

"You're such a dork! Let go!" I cried, but quietly, because after all, we were in a church, even if it was a tourist trap.

Hanno didn't let go until after, standing in front of Gina and Marie, he kissed my captive hand and flashed them a blindingly white smile. "Hi, I'm Hanno," he said. "And you two must be Sophia's friends."

"I'm Gina," said Gina, tugging her shirt down, a nervous habit of hers meant to conceal the weight she wanted to lose.

"And I'm Marie," said Marie, shaking Hanno's hand as vigorously as you would a can of spray paint.

"Nice to meet you," he said in a professional sounding tone that made me think of how handsome he looked when he wore a suit.

Gina blushed. "Nice to meet you," she squeaked, the filtered cathedral light glinting off her blonde hair.

"Real nice," said Marie, her dark eyes locked on Hanno in a way that made me wonder if his good looks had the power to hypnotize.

I thwacked Hanno in the side, like it had been super annoying to have had such a handsome guy refuse to let go of my hand. "Sorry I took off earlier, but I saw *this* guy," I said, poking Hanno, "and couldn't believe it. I mean, we're both from Mesa!"

"I want to be from Mesa," said Marie dreamily.

Hanno coughed politely. "Well, like I said, it's nice to meet you both. Sophe, I'm going to go look around." We watched Hanno walk away, his head tilted up to better take in the massive domed ceiling.

"Rugged yet gorgeous," sighed Marie. "I love rugged yet gorgeous."

"Seriously, how is it you wander off and come back with a model?" asked Gina.

I rolled my eyes, as if they were exaggerating Hanno's good looks, which they weren't. "He's just an old friend," I said, opting to skip saying "of my brother's," because I liked the way they were looking at me, like I was the luckiest girl in the world. "Hanno wants to show me around Florence today," I said, feeling my resolve to let him do so start to slip. "Do you think Skeen will mind?" I asked, gesturing toward our leader, who at that moment was picking a scab on his arm. The orange-and-white flag drooped unnoticed at his side.

"You're kidding, right?" asked Marie.

"I hear he left four kids in Switzerland last year," said Gina. "They drank goat milk to survive."

It was true Skeen Skarvegard wasn't gunning for employee of the year. His job, as he saw it, was to wave a flag, show up at the next destination, and smoke whenever possible. No friendly chatting, no dogged determination to memorize our names, and certainly no clucking around like a nervous hen doing head counts.

"He won't care," continued Gina. "He doesn't care about anything. Probably has something to do with where he's from. I hear the drinking age there is eleven . . . or was it four?" She rubbed her chin, trying to remember.

"Go!" cried Marie. "Don't worry!"

But I couldn't help but worry. Partly because I'm really good at it and partly because, though Hanno was my brother's friend and had probably spent more time at our house while growing up than he had his own (even weaseling his way into more than one family trip to Lake Powell), I knew my parents—my mother especially—wouldn't have approved.

I could see her, arms folded, sighing while looking upward as if in imploring heaven for the patience to deal with her silly daughter. *Sophia,* she would say, *don't be ridiculous.* But what was so ridiculous about Hanno wanting to spend time with me? I was no longer a gangly kid with food stuck in my braces and Hanno was, well, no longer married. *Your pulsating heart, Sophia. When you fall in love you hand it over. Is Hanno good-looking? Yes. Fun? Of course. But is he trustworthy? Do I have to bring up Jenny Mayfield or the fact that you've neglected to shave your big toes?*

He was tricked! I wanted to cry. *She tricked him!*

I sighed. My mother was thousands of miles away and I was arguing with her. What was the point in that? All that mattered was Hanno was here, and he wanted to be with me. Me! Who cared what she would have thought of it. This was, after all, the woman who wouldn't let her husband change the oil at home for fear it might stain the driveway. She was a control freak. An opinionated control freak, who, every time she looked at me, spotted something that needed fixing.

Sneaking up from behind, Hanno laid his chin on my shoulder, making my skin erupt into goose bumps. "You ladies okay if I steal her away?" he asked.

"Take her!" cried Gina.

"I'm game if she's not," said Marie, again looking in danger of being entranced by Hanno's good looks.

Her forwardness seemed to bring out a need in Hanno for a throat lozenge, and he coughed again.

"I'll see you later then," I said as Hanno slid an arm around my shoulder and pulled me away, leading me through a throng of tourists, toward the Duomo's exit. Passing Skeen, I wondered if his ever-present frown of indifference would, at the sight of me leaving with Hanno, transform into a look of concern, or possibly outrage. It didn't. (However, one eyebrow did lift slightly with mild curiosity.) I took a breath, drinking in that perfect moment—the airy cathedral, Hanno's arm around me—and wondered how anything could ever top it.

We stopped before leaving the Duomo to look at the bust of a long-dead pope. A Japanese toddler strapped into a stroller whose cutting-edge design made it appear ready to tip over stared at us, his eyes wide with what looked like amazement. And why shouldn't they be since he was looking at the happiest girl ever? I wanted to jump up and down, punch the air with my fists, and shout "I'm with Hanno! Hanno LeGrand Olsen!"

But, of course, I didn't. All that would have done was guarantee Hanno mercilessly teasing me and an armed security guard escorting me to the exit. I could never tell him how much he'd meant to me—the lump that as a little girl would rise in my throat when he'd walk into our house, the heartfelt letters I'd written to him growing up, declaring him my future husband, and the silent tears that had slid down my cheeks the day he exchanged vows with Jenny Mayfield. He couldn't know how much I cared for him, not if the day wasn't going to be super awkward, and if I—it seemed crazy to think it—was ever going to stand a chance with him. So I pulled myself together and shrugged off his arm. "You're such an idiot," I muttered.

Hanno leaned in and kissed the top of my head. "But today I'm your idiot," he said, his breath warm against my skin. "Come on," he said, grabbing my hand, sounding eager. "I want to show you the Gates of Paradise."

I'm already there, I thought, the edges of my mouth curling like the Mona Lisa's. *I'm already there.*

chapter 3

$\mathcal{F}$OR A GIRL who had decided to ditch her travel group for the day, I was seeing an awful lot of them. In fact, it seemed like I couldn't escape them. The Uffizi Gallery, Accademia Gallery, Ponte Vecchio, the Palace Gardens: everywhere we went—EVERY-WHERE—there was Skeen's orange-and-white flag fluttering in the wind, as if frantically waving hello. We even stopped for lunch at the same panini street vendor in Mercato Centrale. Marie still managed to make Hanno cough as we chatted in line, waiting to place our orders. It wasn't until we started ducking in and out of shops that the orange-and-white flag and my friends' furtive looks faded from view.

We spent the afternoon hunting souvenirs, Hanno excitedly dragging me by the hand into a store when he considered it one of Florence's best and dragging me out if, according to him, I'd stayed too long. Hanno's playful touches—his hand on my back while I leaned forward looking at a case of silver jewelry, his arm around me as we walked—were constant, and though I feigned indifference, each one made my heart nearly burst with happiness. A part of me, the part that needed to grow up, wanted to shake him by the shoulders and demand he define our relationship. Were we now boyfriend and girlfriend? Did he want to date exclusively? And, considering we lived thousands of miles apart, how were we going to handle major holidays? *So immature*, I told myself. *Just relax and enjoy the moment.*

As the afternoon slipped away and the sun sank lower on the horizon, Hanno dubbed himself my shopping serf. Arms laden with my purchases, he leaned against the counter and sighed, waiting for me to decide whether or not to buy a leather purse. "I don't know," I said and bit my lip.

"Get it," said Hanno.

"But it's my grandmother's money," I said, turning the bag over, examining it again.

"Right," he said, a note of exasperation in his voice, "and I think that today it's safe to say you've worked through your reluctance to spend it." He held up all my purchases as evidence.

"Which is precisely why I'm hesitating," I said. "I've already spent too much."

"Fair enough," he muttered, then walked to the sales clerk, placed my packages on the ground, and, saying something in Italian, pulled out his wallet. The bag was mine. He bought it for me before I could protest or fully consider which color I was more committed to, tan or black.

"You're indecisive, Sophe," he said, when at dinner I mentioned yet again that he should have let me pay. "If I had, we might still be there deliberating." A waiter set two long-stemmed glasses on our table, talked briefly with Hanno, and left. "Don't take this personally," said Hanno, twisting the stem of his glass between his fingers, "but you buy a purse like the fate of the world is depending on your choice." Hanno put a finger to his chin, pretending to be in deep thought. "Tan, we live; black, we die. Or is it black we live and tan we die? What is it?" he cried, shaking his hands at the ceiling in frustration. "What is it?"

"Very funny," I said just as the waiter reappeared, a white cloth draped across his forearm and a bottle of wine cradled in his hands. He sliced through the bottle's disgustingly old wax seal with a small knife, giving us a smug look as he did. Then he uncorked the bottle and filled both glasses. I looked at Hanno, waiting for him to correct the waiter, to tell him that he'd made a mistake, and that I was just going to have water, but he didn't, and the waiter, after getting the okay from Hanno, rushed off again. "Maybe I should introduce myself," I said. "I'm Sophie Stark, your long-time neighbor and member of your ward. The girl you watched get baptized in the Nelsons' pool, and yeah, I don't drink wine."

"Sophe," he said.

"Not even when it's ceremoniously poured by an Italian waiter." I wanted to say to him, *Are you kidding? You really think I'm going to cave, chuck the Word of Wisdom just like that? My young women leaders were way too good at role playing the just-say-no moment for me to not get this right.*

"It's not just wine," he said, picking up his glass. "It's an experience, Sophe." Hanno moved his wrist in gentle circles, admiring the dark liquid as it turned. "Marticello, 1974," he said, then put the rim near his nose and took in a big whiff.

"From what I hear, the conventional approach is to drink it."

Hanno smiled. "I told you, Sophe, it's an experience, and one that should be savored." He took a sip. "Mmm," he said, then smacked his lips softly. "That's glorious."

"Yay for you," I said, folding my arms, as if to better stand my ground. Because I was going stand my ground, right? The trouble wasn't the wine; the trouble was Hanno. Just looking at him pull a hand through his hair made me feel weak.

"Sofa . . ."

"Not my name," I said, feeling irritation strengthen my resolve a little.

"Sorry," he said, the candlelight dancing in his blue eyes. "Sofa with complimentary love seat."

I picked up my fork, threatening to throw it at him.

"Careful," he said, his hands out in front of him, "you've already wounded me once." I knew what he was referring to, the one time (one time!) during a game of darts when one of my darts had ended up stuck in his thigh. Stunned, he had let the dart stay there for a moment, stuck like a pin in corkboard, while he alternated between staring at it and me.

I could actually feel embarrassment singeing my ears, turning them bright red. "You were practically in front of me!" I cried.

"I was behind you," he said, running a hand across the table-cloth, smoothing out a crease.

"I said practically," I muttered and slouched a little in my chair. As mortifying as it was to have Hanno bring up my terrible throwing skills, at least we were off the subject of wine, or so I thought.

"Come on, Sophe," he said, sliding the glass toward me. "I don't think you know what you're passing on. Marticello is a local vine-yard that's been producing wine for so long, it claims the original vines were brought over by the Apostle Paul when he visited Rome. The soil is so rich, the grapes bulge to perfection, giving the wine an unparalleled bouquet." Again, Hanno edged the glass toward me.

An experience, possibly a once-in-a-lifetime experience—enjoy-ing a glass of wine in Italy with Hanno Olsen, wine that was, when you got right down to it, made possible by an ancient prophet of God. How bad could that be? My fingers curled around the glass's stem, and all at once I felt a little wobbly, like instead of solid earth beneath me, there was nothing but a tightrope, and beyond that, no net to catch me. I had never *ever* been tempted by wine, and so in my young women's meeting role plays I had been plucky and resolute when turning down offers. But no role play had ever involved Hanno or how much at this moment I wanted to please him, to see him smile.

I pulled the glass toward me, so close that now I could smell it. "Tell me more about this so-called experience," I said as that sensa-tion of toes desperately gripping a tightrope returned to me.

"Well," said Hanno, a note of victory in his voice, "after the harvest, the grapes are crushed by the alabaster feet of Benedictine monks."

It was like a CD stuttering and skipping, revealing an undeni-able flaw. "Huh?" I asked, wrinkling my nose.

"The monks methodically stomp—"

"No thanks," I said, sliding the glass away from me just as our waiter reappeared. "I don't want this," I told him flatly, pointing at the wine. "Could I get some water? *Wa-ter.*" He looked like I had just asked if I could punch his mother in the face but managed a brief nod.

The waiter made to reach for the glass, but Hanno put up a hand to stop him. Though they spoke in Italian, I understood that Hanno was telling the waiter he'd drink my glass of wine, news that made the waiter brighten considerably.

"What changed your mind?" asked Hanno as the waiter hurried off.

"Alabaster feet," I said with a shudder. "First of all, eww. And secondly, I try not to drink anything that's been stepped on." Hanno opened his mouth, ready to convince me otherwise, but I got there first. "And that's final, even if you tell me it's pasteurized by nuns."

"Fine," said Hanno, raising his glass as if in a toast. "But you're missing out." Then he tilted the glass and drank deeply.

"Well, this Sofa with ottoman can deal with it," I said, slumping a little in my seat as I thought how nice it would have been to make him smile. But why did making him smile have to involve alcohol? And why did alcohol have to involve feet? Maybe if my mother hadn't made me so hyperaware of my own feet, I wouldn't have minded pulling an errant toe hair out of my beverage, but there was no way. No matter what, I wasn't going to be persuaded to wager a sip of Marticello, and this realization made a sliver of guilt wriggle uncomfortably inside me, because I knew doing the right thing shouldn't have depended on whether or not I had a foot aversion.

Rushing from the kitchen, our waiter returned to our table and handed us our menus, taking a moment as he did to subtly sneer at me. I wanted to say, *Dude, get over it. I'm not drinking the wine*, but I didn't speak Italian and he was already walking away, muttering under his breath. I looked at Hanno and rapped my knuckles lightly on the table. "But one thing bothers me," I said.

"What's that?" he asked.

"Just because I'm choosing to pass on the 'Marticello experience'"—I made quotes in the air—"you think I'm a kid, just a dutifully obedient Mormon kid letting life pass her by."

Our waiter returned with my water. It was small and without ice, and he placed it on the table with just enough force that it sloshed a little onto the tablecloth. "I don't think of you as a kid," said Hanno, handing our menus to our waiter and letting him know we'd take the manicotti. "Though I have to admit," he said, taking another sip of Marticello, "that you suggesting Michelangelo should have sculpted David wearing shorts wasn't the height of maturity."

I pointed a finger at him as he sipped his wine. "That's exactly what I'm talking about! You skew things because you think of me as a kid. Anyone with eyes could tell you that nearly all the statues in this town don't meet a minimum clothing requirement. And I'm not going to lie that it's a little unsettling, but that doesn't make me a kid!"

Hanno took another drink, then dabbed his mouth with a cloth napkin. "I told you I don't think of you as a kid."

"Yes, you do."

"Really, I don't," said Hanno, a smile tugging at the corners of his mouth. "Not since you forgot to lock the bathroom door on the houseboat at Lake Powell and I saw you wearing nothing but soap in your eyes."

Sliding down my chair and hiding under the table seemed like a good option, but shock and embarrassment had paralyzed me, so I sat there, mouth open, making a low, almost imperceptible moan of agony. I knew exactly what he was talking about. I was fifteen at the time and it was the last Lake Powell trip Hanno made with my family before marrying Jenny Mayfield. After a long day on the water, I had gone in the bathroom to take a shower, figuring I'd try my mom's new shampoo. It promised to make hair luxuriously smooth and that during its production no animals were harmed, so I figured how bad could it be? BAD! While rinsing, a tiny amount slipped into my eyes, stinging like a maniacal nurse administering vaccinations to my pupils, leaving me temporarily but most definitely blind. I tried flushing my eyes with water, but the stinging only got worse, so pulling back the shower curtain, I fumbled my way toward the towel rack, and as I did, the door opened, just a crack, stayed open for a beat, and then shut. I had convinced myself it was my mother, and had blocked the moment from my mind—until now.

Hanno was saying my name, trying to get me to look at him, but

I couldn't. Impossible! All I could do was look at my backpack on the floor and wish I'd thought to pack a snowsuit with goggles. No amount of clothing seemed too extreme to wear at the moment, even if doing so would have no doubt convinced our waiter that I was the biggest weirdo to ever walk into his restaurant. But that didn't matter; all that did matter was shielding myself from what felt like Hanno's X-ray vision.

Hanno sipped his glass of Marticello. "Sophe," he said, "don't be upset. All the nude statues we've seen today, I've only said to myself once, no twice, *Hey, that looks like Sophie.*"

I let out a groan just as the bread arrived. The waiter, interpreting this to mean that I'd seen better bread, grumbled as he walked away. A voice in my head, sounding vaguely like my grandmother's, said, *What kind of man has fun at a young woman's expense? Walk out. You don't deserve this.* The trouble was, my mother was inside my head too. *For heaven's sake, Sophia. Don't be ridiculous! Hanno is not for you!* And that made me want to dig in my heels and stay put. Because what she was really saying was, *Sweetheart, compared to Jenny Mayfield you have the feet of lumberjack.* Okay, so I wasn't top-of-the-cheerleading-pyramid material like Jenny, compact and cute, but was it impossible to assume that Hanno could find me beautiful? To my surprise, I quickly got my answer.

Hanno reached across the table and grabbed my hand, pulling me, as he did, out of my reverie. "Don't be embarrassed. You're beautiful, Sophe." Hesitantly, I looked up. "And I should know. I've seen the whole enchilada."

Go! Kick him first, then go! cried Gram as Hanno, leaning back, let go of my hand and chuckled. "I'm just kidding!" he said, reaching for my wine glass now since his was empty. "But not about you being beautiful. I'm dead serious about that. You've grown into a beautiful woman."

I had to agree with Gram. Only a jerk would humiliate a young woman for the sake of a few punch lines, but hang on a minute . . . he thought I was beautiful! Gram tried to tell me that it was just the Marticello talking, but I wouldn't let her get a word in edgewise.

Hanno thought I was beautiful! Happiness and anger converged inside me, mixing into a frothy, volatile concoction. So whether attempting to be playful or not I wasn't sure, but I swung my leg and tried to kick Hanno. I missed and hit the underside of the table hard, making it jolt just as the waiter set down our manicotti. Startled, then annoyed for having been startled, the waiter glared at me and left.

"What was that?" asked Hanno.

"That was meant for you," I grumbled, scooping piping hot manicotti onto my plate.

"Why?" asked Hanno, his low voice rising in a note of true surprise.

I stabbed my pasta with my fork. "You keep bringing up stuff to embarrass me, even though I haven't brought up once your twelve-hour marriage to Jenny."

Hanno's gaze looked far away for a moment. He smiled, but for all its typical flashiness it looked a little tired. "Sophe, come on. I was just having some—"

"But now that we're talking about it," I interjected, "I do have a few questions for you." That was an understatement, but I was trying to sound casual.

Hanno raised his glass. "For courage," he said, then took another sip. "All right, Little Miss Nosy. Fire away."

Timing is everything, something every strolling violinist should realize. Of course, the one that came over to our table didn't, and so just as I started to ask Hanno, just as I had scraped together enough nerve to ask the one question I was dying to know the answer to—if he had missed me as much as I had missed him—some dude in a black-on-black ensemble jutted his violin toward us and started to play. And as silently as it came, my nerve scattered like confetti in the wind.

"So," said Hanno, "what was that you were saying?"

Stepping up to the brink of honesty and then pulling back felt as disorienting as the view from the top of a skyscraper. I cleared my throat and rubbed my forehead, trying to steady myself. "Uh, well . . . why haven't you been back to Mesa since your wedding day?" It wasn't a question that made my palms clammy, but still, I was curious about the answer.

Hanno didn't pick up on my inner wobbliness, and I wondered for a moment if that bothered me. "It hasn't been on purpose," he said, cutting his manicotti. "One thing just led to another. Jenny and I had booked a rafting trip down the Hawaii river. When she left, I figured I might as well enjoy it. So I went and became friends with Hoki, our guide. At one point he asked why I'd shown up for the honeymoon package alone, so I told him, and by the end of the day he'd offered me a job. I will admit that going back to Mesa just then didn't appeal to me, so I took it, and that job led to another, which took me to a rafting gig on the River Ganga in India, then on to Portugal where I studied architecture restoration, and finally here, Italy. We're working on a cathedral in Prato where I live, testing the strength of the outside pulpit, seeing if we need to reinforce . . ."

Pulpits, I thought as Hanno rambled on about his job. *Who cares about pulpits?* Like an impatient reader, I wanted to skip ahead. "That's nice," I said, cutting him off. "But what about Jenny? Do you guys stay in touch?

Hanno drained the last of the Marticello from my glass. "No," he said in a clipped way that made me wonder if the question bothered him, but just for a second, because, after all, he was the one who had said "fire away."

"Did you know she's married again?" I asked. Hanno chewed his dinner and nodded, his eyes fixed on the salt and pepper shakers. "His name is Clay," I continued. "He's not much taller than she is, but he's in medical school, which according to my mother is an acceptable substitute for height, so the good news is their cake won't fall, most likely anyway."

A thin stream of steam escaped as Hanno cut into his manicotti again. "What cake?" he asked, glancing at me as he did.

"Their *cake*," I said, as if that explained everything. "You know, their marriage, their compatibility as a couple. As much as you were over at our house, you never heard my mom talk about her relation-ship recipe theory?"

"If I could," he said, motioning to the waiter for another glass of Marticello, "I never heard her at all."

I should have been high-fiving Hanno in agreement. After all, no one found my mother harder to take than me. But hearing Hanno say this made me feel protective of her. She had always gone out of her way to be nice to Hanno, feeding him, giving him rides, even making him a quilt for his sixteenth birthday. She deserved a little respect, but at the moment Hanno was leaning back, head tilted, and he was staring lovingly (lovingly!) at me, so somebody else was going to have to stick up for my mom. I was currently busy. "She likes to say that just like baking a cake from scratch, two people falling in love requires certain essential ingredients."

Hanno held up a finger to tell me to wait while he finished chewing. "So," he said after wiping his mouth with his napkin, "what are these essential ingredients? A smidge of patience, a cup of honesty . . . the sort of attributes the Relief Society ladies are fond of painting on wood?" The note of derision in his voice surprised me like a little zap of static electricity. But he was gorgeous, so I let it go.

"No," I said. "More like ski slope nose, straight teeth, flawless complexion—that sort of thing."

He took a moment to stretch, and I took a moment to notice his tan and well-muscled arms. *Gulp.* "So, according to your mom, mar-riage is for the beautiful," he said.

"Well, not exactly," I said. "She just thinks that when it comes to love, there's a recipe."

"Take two gorgeous people, heat, and stir."

I bit my lip. "Not exactly," I said, "because if an essential ingredi-ent is missing, there are substitutions."

Hanno ran a hand through his thick blond hair, making me sigh a little. "What's the equivalent to throwing a cup of dirt into the recipe?"

I could have said the one that flew into my mind, which was

being a girl that's taller than most of the guys out there, but it was too personal, so I said something else. "Uh, let's say, being overweight."

"Like your friend." Hanno blew up his cheeks, mimicking Gina's full face. "The good news is if she was anorexic, she's cured."

Yes, he was gorgeous, but that was a low blow. "Hey," I said, "that's not very nice."

Hanno leaned forward, propping his chin with his hand. "You're the one buying into a theory that marginalizes everyone but the anatomically perfect."

"It's my mom's theory, not mine!" Wasn't it? I didn't tell Hanno, but he had me wondering. How much had I come to agree with my mother's skewed way of seeing things?

"But clearly at some level you believe it. You're selling it like you work for commission."

I rolled my eyes. "You're crazy," I said, taking a bite and pointing my fork at him. "I am just explaining to you—"

Hanno waved a hand, signaling my time to defend myself was up. "So, according to your mom, what is an acceptable substitute for being a fatty?"

I chewed a little slower, considering if I should say it. "You're not going to like it."

"Try me."

I let out a breath. "Money," I said flatly. "Male or female, it's a pretty versatile substitute. It works for shortness, baldness, poor vision, thick foreign accents. If you've got money, you've got a chance at love."

Hanno whistled. "Your mom is one tough old bird, I'll give her that. But she's completely whacked."

"She's got a point. I mean, look at Hollywood." What was the matter with me? Just agree with him and get back to gazing into his Bahama-blue eyes!

"You can't be serious," he said, folding his arms. "The world is full of fat, unattractive married people."

"But they didn't start out that way, most of them anyway. I know it's not nice, but there is some truth to the way she sees things. And by the way, she's got a pretty good track record as a matchmaker." Which was true. My mother had a knack for bringing people together—gorgeous people, yes, but still people.

Hanno downed the last of the Marticello and wiped his mouth with the back of his hand. "The arrogance of it," he said. "As if you can distill why two people fall in love into something resembling a cake recipe."

My heart thudded hard in my chest. "Why do you think people fall in love then?" I asked, knowing that for me it had a lot to do with everything about him. Well, not everything. I could have lived without his knack for teasing me.

"Unlike your mother, I'm not going to pretend to know why two people fall in love," he said, spinning a butter knife on the table and then watching it slow to a stop in random directions. "But if you want me to guess, I'd have to say, among other things, a connection, electricity, secrets they alone share . . ."

If my mom's theory was severe, his was glossy. "You have to admit, though, that looking like a runway model doesn't hurt."

"Sophe."

"Be honest! Think about it. If a beautiful girl is with a short, bald guy, he's usually loaded—a doctor, successful actor, some kind of bigwig."

"You're jaded, Sophe," he said, grabbing my hand and making my arms explode with goose bumps. "Take off the lab coat and quit dissecting love. Just let love happen, and when it does, succumb to it."

I thought about telling him that just letting love happen didn't work for everyone. Like Sister Margolis, for example. She was pushing forty and so far hadn't had any marriage offers, which according to my mother, could change if she was willing to lose the mustache and go to vet school (potential dating pool). She was brilliant, but ambition wasn't her style. She liked taking care of the monkeys at the zoo, and every time my mother suggested applying boiling wax to her upper lip, she'd let out a little scream and cover her mouth. Not exactly a believer in the whole pain-is-beauty notion. But I didn't say this, didn't argue, because looking at Hanno, I was sure it was happening. Love was happening to me.

Hanno stumbled as we left the restaurant. With wine-driven enthusiasm, he took my face in his hands, smacked the top of my head with a toothy kiss, and put his arm around me. "Sofa! Sofa! Sofa!" he cried out as we walked down the street. "I can't believe I found you!"

Not only was this inaccurate (after all, I had found him), but if I was also being honest (which I wasn't), his outburst made me feel sort of like a rabbit's foot or a two-dollar bill, some misplaced trinket he was amused to have back.

"Sofa! Let's go back to my place!" he said, not noticing the many faces painted red, white, and green (what was going on?) or the sideward glances we were getting from passersby.

I knew I shouldn't go. It was late and I didn't need a Breathalyzer kit to know Hanno was tipsy, but I didn't care. Maybe the businessman on the train was right—the air here was like wine. I didn't need a glass of Marticello; just being in Florence I was under the influence, even with him shouting "Sofa!" at the starless sky like a complete dork. Taking a deep breath, I put my arm around Hanno's waist (partially to steady him) and told myself to relax.

Relax! As if that were possible! All my souvenirs slid back and forth on the backseat of Hanno's two-door Fiat (smallest car ever) as we winded along the kind of hillside roads movie directors are fond of when they need to shoot a car tumbling off a cliff and exploding. Hanno sped past other cars like our one ambition in life was to be organ donors. And, of course, me saying "Hanno, seriously, slow down!" was useless. If anything, the more scared I seemed, the faster he drove.

So as rain started to ping against the windshield, I closed my eyes to pray, but the truth is, it's hard to pray when you feel like a fool. I tried. I told myself Heavenly Father loves all His children, even the boneheads who get into cars they shouldn't, but every attempt at divine communication seemed to fizzle into me beating myself up. I should have known better! I should have made better choices!

I should have never agreed to . . . Nothing can bring an end to self-reproach faster than a good parallel parking job. I opened my eyes as Hanno slipped the tiny car into what didn't really look like an available spot. The street, a blurry scene of meager light from streetlamps and rain that now thudded hard against the car, reminded me of the Impressionist paintings I had seen in the museums in Paris, an observation that made me quickly forget how scared I'd been.

"Come on!" cried Hanno, flipping his hoodie over his head and opening his door. "Let's make a run for it!" And he took off, without opening my door or offering me part of his hoodie, which I know was impossible to share, but still, it would have been a nice gesture. Halfway down the block, Hanno pushed open a large wooden door and we entered a courtyard where outdoor furniture, potted plants, and children's toys were scattered about, all soaked by the downpour. An overhang along the perimeter kept us out of the rain as we headed for the stairs. Mixed in with the sound of the rain, I could hear children in nearby apartments wailing, the sounds from more than one television tuned into what sounded like a soccer match, and a few sharp-tongued mothers barking out commands. Clotheslines were strung outside windows, and strands of fairy lights crisscrossed the courtyard, dark now, but ready for the courtyard's next night of hoopla. More than anything I had seen during the day, this looked authentic, like the real Italy, especially once we arrived at the second floor and there sitting in an open doorway on a wooden chair was an old woman all dressed in black. Stooped from age, her silver hair was swept back into a bun and laced between her bony fingers was a rosary. Hanno leaned forward and kissed her on both her heavily lined cheeks, making her eyes light up with happiness. They spoke to each other in Italian, and I noticed that when she said something she covered her mouth with a dainty hand to subtly hide her toothlessness. But even with her mouth covered, her smile was still shining in her eyes, until Hanno introduced her to me.

"*Buona sera*," she said curtly, then pressed her lips together as if to keep from saying something snide.

"*Buona sera*," I said with a smile. Not because I enjoy getting the cold shoulder, but because even with all the rain, one thought had me feeling particularly sunny: if this lady was my competition with Hanno, I had it made in the shade. She looked old enough to have endured both World Wars.

We said good-bye and walked past a few doors to Hanno's apartment. Without turning on the lights, Hanno took me by the hand and walked me across his apartment to a pair of glass-paned doors. Though it was raining harder than ever, he flung them open, revealing a Juliet balcony made of scrolled rod iron. An overhang above kept all but a fine mist from entering the apartment. I leaned on the balcony and looked out at the surrounding countryside. Lightning flashed and for a moment I could see the outline of distant rolling hills in the storm. *What are you doing here?* I asked myself. *That's what I'd like to know*, said Gram's voice while my mom just rolled her eyes.

Hanno hooked his chin on my shoulder and wrapped his arms around me. "It's beautiful," I said, my heart pounding like it was trying to break free from my chest.

"You're beautiful," he said, his wine-tainted breath (ick) warm on my ear. Hanno moved my hair over to one side and outlined the curve of my neck down to my shoulder with his finger.

The air was chilly, but that wasn't why I shivered. "Hanno," I said, trying to mask how nervous I felt by sounding irritated, "what are you doing?"

Now his finger traced the curve of my ear. "Just enjoying the view."

I should have been melting, but I wasn't, because melting is hard to pull off when your mother and grandmother won't put a sock in it. *Do you realize how late it is?* chided Gram. *Sweetheart*, sighed Mom. *He's not right for you. And not just because he's too handsome for you . . .* To drown out my interfering family, I closed my eyes and focused on the sound of the rain pelting the roof. It sort of worked. The drumming was hypnotic, and soon the voices of Mom and Gram were muffled. The trouble was, *I* wasn't muffled. How was I supposed to just let love happen if I couldn't turn my brain off? Did he love me or like me? And if he liked me, was it an intense like that bordered on love? And how did that love and/or like compare to what he first felt for Jen . . .

Hanno kissed me just below my ear, quieting the questions in my head right when I should have been asking more, like where was this leading, and what exactly was he expecting to do, bringing me to his apartment this late? My mind wasn't blissfully blank, but I'm not going to lie, that kiss was potent, and my thoughts, though coherent, were slower, like I was coming to after dental surgery. Hanno cupped my chin in his hand and turned my face to his. *I . . . re-a-l-l-y hate the smell of Marti-cell-o-o-o*, I thought, but there wasn't time for me to say it, insist he brush his teeth or at least have an after-dinner mint. He was kissing me again, this time on the lips, urgently, with his hands tangled in my hair, and though I was thinking, *Ew, he tastes like ala-bas-ter mo-o-nk feet*, I didn't pull away, to my everlasting shame. I didn't pull away . . . not until someone turned on the light.

chapter **4**

"I SUPPOSE YOU'LL WANT me to find another place to sleep *again*," grumbled someone, and his words—especially that last one—were like a pitcher of ice water thrown in my face. I blinked, the stark light momentarily blinding me, and then I saw him, this boy. Okay, guy. He had to be at least my age, standing in the doorway, and so angry he refused to look at me.

"You know how it is," said Hanno, kissing me on the side of my head. I pulled away a little as he did, making the moment awkward, but I didn't care. With the light turned on, I could see a floral scarf and sun hat hanging near the door on a hook, and I knew, without asking, they belonged to someone Hanno had brought there. Maybe a week ago, or maybe last month, but it was a pitcher of ice water all the same: I wasn't special to Hanno. He was just doing what I had been telling myself to do all day—he was enjoying the moment. But the truth was, I didn't want to be someone's moment, not even if that someone was Hanno.

"No, you don't need to leave," I said, peeling Hanno's hand off my shoulder, just as a thought occurred to me that made another pitcher of ice water hit me in the face. The old woman sitting in the doorway. No wonder she had looked at me like that. How many other girls had she seen climb those stairs with Hanno? To her, I wasn't the competition, vying for Hanno's attention. I was just

37

another one of his silly conquests. Though good and sober now, the ice water kept coming.

Hanno plunked down on the ratty vinyl couch in the center of the front room. He patted the spot next to him. "Sofa, come sit on my sofa," he said. Then he laughed the way people do when they're made stupid by overpriced wine. "Peter doesn't mind leaving, do ya, Pete?"

The guy in the doorway, who apparently was named Peter, looked at the ceiling and grumbled something under his breath. This wasn't the time to notice it, but I liked the way his short dark hair, wet from the rain, curled a little at the base of his neck.

I shook my head to clear my thoughts. "First of all, I am not a piece of furniture."

Hanno hit himself lightly in the head, as if this bit of info kept slipping his mind.

"Secondly," I said, my throat tight now with emotion, "I'm going." And I headed for the door just as lightning flashed, illuminating the stormy night.

Hanno tilted his head back and closed his eyes, like it was time to sleep this one off. "Sophe," he said, groaning, "don't be like that."

"Like what?" I asked, my voice shrill. I wanted to kick myself for sounding like that, because I knew Hanno wouldn't like it, which was quickly followed by me wanting to kick myself for caring about what Hanno did or did not like in a girl. My brain had apparently missed the memo: This crush was over! "Don't be like what?" I cried as he started to softly snore.

He jerked awake. "Like *that*," he said, pointing at me and then raking a hand through his hair. "Sophe, we were having such a good time. Come here." Again he patted the ratty couch. "Curl up with me."

"You're drunk," I said flatly.

"Now you notice," mumbled Peter.

Hanno pouted, like this was all a joke. "It's your fault, you know," he said, extending his arms out to me to come to him, and when I didn't, letting them flop on the couch with a thud. "But I'm not too drunk to wrap my arms around you."

I rolled my eyes. "I'd have to be drunk too to let that happen."

"Ouch," he said and then grabbed a throw pillow to cuddle with and started snoring again. Talk about ouch. I was already replaced, and by thrift-store reject décor.

Bartender, that'll be another pitcher of ice water, heavy on the ice.

I let out a deep breath. So this was how it was going to end, Hanno not saying good-bye or "I'm sorry" or "I wish things could have worked out differently." Nothing. No concern about me or how I was going to get back to Florence in this storm. Hanno was out cold.

The last thing I wanted to do was turn to Mr. High and Mighty, a.k.a Peter, for help, but it didn't seem like I had any choice. I needed a ride, and as far as I could tell, he was my only option. Swallowing my pride has never been easy for me. I know it's the mark of the bigger person, but to be honest, it's always felt like I've been challenged to down a jumbo marshmallow whole. But this . . . this was worse. An entire bag of marshmallows (bag included) seemed lodged in my throat, and all I wanted to do was walk out the door. But to what? An empty, rainy street late at night in a place where I didn't speak the language? Did I look like one of those dumb girls in slasher movies? No way was I going out there alone. It was time, no matter how difficult, to swallow my pride and ask for his help. I took a deep breath and turned to Peter, but before I could say anything, he spoke.

"Where are you staying?" he asked.

"The youth hostel near Piazza Duomo," I said as Hanno mumbled in his sleep.

We both looked at him, slouched on the couch, a steady line of drool falling from his stupid lips, and then, for the first time, we looked at each other, and just as we did, lightning struck.

The boom was earsplitting. The light in the front room flickered, threatening to go off, and the curtains, caught by the wind, flew wildly about. Peter walked over and shut the glass doors, then grabbed Hanno's keys off a hook on the wall. And then he looked at me again. The first time, I chalked it up for nature's spectacle, this rush of emotion I felt when I looked at him, but the sky was silent now, yet there it was again, a zing that went through me.

"Are you ready? Is there anything you need?" he asked, the measured stiffness in his voice reminding me of my dad on family trips, making sure we were packed and potted before getting in the car.

Nope. Other than a moment to deliver a roundhouse kick to Hanno's face, I'm good. That's what I wanted to say, and actually be tough enough and over everything to mean it, but the truth was I wasn't. I felt fragile, and Peter's voice reminding me of my dad didn't help any. "No," I said, my voice brittle with emotion. "Let's go."

Seeing goose bumps on my arms, Peter frowned. "You're cold," he said, and before I could say anything he was walking over to the apartment's one bedroom.

"I'm fine," I insisted as he handed me a white sweatshirt emblazoned with ITALIA on the front in red and green. The sweatshirt was soft and holding it was comforting. I didn't want to give it back. Still, I tried, because I hated to look needy.

"Sophe—" he started

"Sophia," I snapped.

Peter nodded, accepting this correction. "Sophia," he said, "don't be childish. Take the sweatshirt," and he walked to the door.

I'll admit it, I'm a little sensitive, so normally someone accusing me of being childish might irritate me, but there was some sort of strange pleasure that I felt hearing him say my name, and it momentarily robbed me of the ability to dwell on anything else.

An umbrella, still dripping wet, was propped just outside the front door. Peter grabbed it, and side by side we headed into the storm. The rain pounded, the wind blew, but Peter managed to keep the umbrella directly over me, even when it meant taking a face full of rain himself. I should have been appreciative; after all, he was being a gentleman, but I hated appearing weak. I groaned imagining what he must have thought of me, and the storm didn't disguise the sound of my misery as much as I had hoped.

"Are you all right?" he asked, huddled close to me under the umbrella as he unlocked the passenger door. I grabbed the handle, but he was there first. Our hands, his warm, mine cold, stayed there for a moment longer than necessary, and yet not long enough. What was the matter with me? One second I'm nuts about Hanno, the next I'm falling for this guy? I pulled my hand back. "I'm not feeling myself," I said, getting into the car. "I just need to get back."

Peter shut the door then hurried to the other side of the car and climbed in. Once inside, he stared, keys in hand, at the windshield. The storm was beating against it like we were in the mother of all drive-through car washes. He closed his eyes for a second and sighed with relief, or was it frustration? Maybe a bit of both. I didn't know Peter, didn't even know his last name, but being in that little car with him, shielded from the storm that was raging all around us, one thing I did know—I felt safe.

Peter put the key in the ignition, then turned to me. "Do you have your seat belt on?"

"Yes, Dad," I said, trying to lighten the moment with sarcasm.

"I was just checking," he mumbled, sounding a little defensive.

I let out a deep breath. That didn't go as planned, but then again, nothing today had.

Peter turned on the headlights and slowly pulled the car onto the empty road. No one but a fool would be out in this weather, or someone forced to drive because they've got to get a stranded fool back to their youth hostel. What was the matter with me? He was going out of his way to help me and I have to say something to make him feel silly. I knew what it was; I felt judged, and it brought out my snarky side.

We drove at a pace that rivaled any upstanding senior citizen for attention to caution, crawling along the streets of Prato, out of town, and toward the winding wooded highway that led to Florence. I was glad for the slow pace, not just because my European plans didn't include hydroplaning, but because in the darkness with the storm taking center stage, it felt good to cry—to let the frustration and hurt and sadness of the day wash over me and allow the tears welling in my eyes to spill down my face. Not brushing them aside or trying to keep them bottled in, but just letting them fall, until they, like the rain, slowed. I thought I had kept Peter in the dark about the sob session happening in the seat next to him, until he dug into his pocket and brought out a handkerchief, the red kind cowboys wear around their necks. "I don't want to disturb you . . . but here," he said, handing it to me. It was a simple act of kindness and why I reacted to it the way I did I'm not sure, but some sort wall burst inside me, and the crying I'd already done was chump change compared to what happened next. I took the handkerchief and bawled. My boohooing was so loud and ugly that though the road was curvy and the rain had once again picked up, Peter took a hand off the steering wheel and patted my leg.

"I'm ruining your handkerchief," I sobbed, when I finally got myself together enough to choke some words out. "I can give it back, but it's super disgusting." For some reason saying this refueled my misery and I went back to bawling.

"It's all right," said Peter.

"No, it's not! Nothing's all right!" I blew my nose hard into Peter's hanky. "Ha-Hanno's a jerk and you think I'm te-terrible."

"I don't think you're terrible."

Another wave of sobbing and nose blowing hit me. I couldn't turn it off or dial it down, even when a passing car's lights revealed Peter looking worried and slightly grossed out. "Yes, you do," I blubbered. "You thought I was going to spend the night with Hanno."

"Well, I did think that," he admitted, and then learned firsthand that when dealing with a hysterical young woman, honesty is not always the best policy. Sobs and more sobs burst out of me, making my body shake and putting our conversation on hold.

I took a deep breath, trying to calm down. "Look," I said, blotting my face with Peter's hanky. "I wasn't going to *do* anything with Hanno." Rain was still pinging against the car, but in the distance, the city lights of Florence were now visible, and above them, surprisingly, fireworks. Not the awe-inspiring kind that fly over DC on the fourth, more like the gutless kind you buy on the side of the road. But there they were, popping and fizzing in the wet sky.

Peter glanced at me, then returned his full attention to the road.

"It's late, Sophia. I don't think we should talk about this," he said, sounding like a husband trying to skirt an argument.

"We need to talk about this, Peter," I said, like this wasn't the first time I'd said his name, but something I'd done countless times before in countless conversations with him. "You don't believe me," I said, like I was accusing him of a punishable crime.

Peter sighed, his eyes fixed on the slick and winding road ahead. "What am I supposed to believe?" he asked.

"Me," I said emphatically, my hand to my heart. "You're supposed to believe me!"

Peter laughed, but not in a cruel way. Even my hypersensitive nature couldn't mistake the kindness in his laugh. And as infectious as it was, I couldn't help but laugh too.

"What?" I asked, smiling now though tears still stained my face.

"First of all, I don't know you."

"Sophia Stark from Mesa, Arizona. And?"

"And second . . ." He made a circling motion with one hand, as if coaxing the words to come. "You let Hanno kiss you."

"AAAHHH!" I groaned. "I was just starting to feel better and then you say that! You really want me to destroy your hanky. What's the matter with you, Peter . . ." I made the same circling gesture he had made and waited for him to tell me his last name.

"De Boom."

"What's the matter with you, Peter De Boom? Wait, don't answer that, because if you say that you're an axe murderer this will officially be the worst day of my life. But, yes, I did let Hanno kiss me. I don't want to get into why, because it's a long story, but I admit it, I made a mistake."

"Like so many before you," Peter mumbled.

I swatted him lightly on the arm, surprising him (and me) with my playfulness. "There you go again! Was that supposed to feel like a brick to the chest? Because it did!"

"Sophia—" he began.

"Peter," I interrupted.

"Sophia—" he tried again.

"Peter De Boom," I said. "You wanna play? I can do this all night long."

"I'm sorry," he said, careful to omit my name. "I shouldn't have mentioned the string of girls—"

"There It Is again," I said, throwing my hands in the air. "A little turn of the knife, and without even trying." Traffic slowed to a crawl as we neared the old city gate. "Where are you from, Peter De Boom?" I asked as more fireworks shot into the sky, sending down a shower of cascading sparkles.

"Liechtenstein."

"Come on," I said, disbelieving.

"Why would I joke about being from Liechtenstein?"

"Since you've probably never told a joke in your life, I can see your point."

"What's that supposed to mean?"

"Nothing personal, you just seem stiff to me."

"Just because I don't go home with strangers."

"Knife, Peter."

"Knife? You're the one saying I'm stiff."

"Serious, then," I said as we passed by a group of teenage boys jumping up and down and cheering. "You come across as serious. Does that feel better?" Traffic was now at a standstill, a seemingly endless line of cars trying without success to wend its way through the city. "First of all, Hanno wasn't a stranger. I've known him since I was a kid. And secondly, if you're from Liechtenstein, why do you speak English like you're from Detroit?"

"I sound like I'm from Detroit?" he said, a challenge in his voice.

"Well, you don't sound like you're from Liechtenstein."

"People move to Liechtenstein all the time, Sophia," said Peter, with a hint of amusement. "It's a world leader in dental products. But answer me this, if you've known Hanno for so long, why then did you think it was a good idea to—"

"I'm not trying to avoid your question," I interjected, which was a total lie. That was exactly what I was doing. "But I was just wondering, what's going on? Why all the hoopla and traffic?"

"Italy has advanced to the World Cup finals," he said through gritted teeth. A policeman with a whistle was diverting us to the right, away from the city gate, and Peter had no choice but to comply.

"So you don't like soccer," I said, watching the rain get swished away by the windshield wipers.

"No, I don't like traffic," he said, looking both ways before taking a quick left on to a tiny street the celebration hadn't spread to and parking the little car on the sidewalk. "We're miles from your hostel, but there's no getting any closer. We're going to have to walk."

We're. It's amazing how comforting one word can make you feel. "Thank you," I said, tears welling in my eyes, but not the hysterical kind. These were sprung from gratitude. I blotted my eyes with that poor, overused hanky. "I realize this has all been a nightmare for you," I said and threw my hands in the air. "Why won't it stop raining?"

"Sophia," he said, sounding serious. "We have more important things to worry about right now."

"Like what?" I said, unable to read his face in the darkness.

"Like how you're going to answer the question you avoided earlier."

I gasped as if affronted, but I was smiling. Crazy as it was, I was smiling.

"Now stay there while I get your door," he said.

Huddled close under the umbrella, we made our way down the dark street, toward the celebration. We walked in silence, but it was a comfortable silence, not the kind that makes you start asking questions like *what's your major?* Still, after a while, and without further prodding, I answered his earlier question. "Hanno was my childhood crush," I said. "And today, running into him here . . . I don't know, it felt like fate was bringing us together . . . until it didn't."

"I see," said Peter. I tried to detect a note of judgment in his voice but couldn't find it.

"And you? How did a guy from Liechtenstein end up roommates with Hanno Olsen?" I asked as the sounds of cheering and singing grew louder.

"The Internet."

"Of course," I said. Our shoulders bumped under the umbrella, and I realized that had I been wearing heels he would have still been a little taller than me.

Peter put his hand on my back to guide me around a puddle. My shoes were already soaked, but I was glad to avoid it. "Hanno's a good friend," said Peter, "and a good enough roommate, except when . . . uh, never mind."

"I forgot your hanky in the car, so yeah, it's probably best we change the subject. By the way, you're going to want to wear rubber gloves when you pick that thing up."

"I'm not worried," he said as the sky pulsed with the light of fireworks.

"Ahh!" I groaned, turning around. "All my souvenirs! I left them in the car!"

Peter tugged my arm. "I'll get them to you."

"No, you've already done enough. Besides, now that I think of it, I don't want any mementos from today. But, thanks, I've been an emotional wreck and you've been so kind and now you have to walk in this rain when you could be home right now—"

"Sophia," he said, just stern enough to get my attention.

"What?" I asked.

"I think I liked it more when you were crying."

I stomped hard on a puddle, soaking us both, but him especially. "Very funny," I said.

"When I tell you not to worry, I mean it. I'll be home soon enough. It's no big deal."

"Yeah," I mumbled. "But you're not the one feeling indebted," I said, right as a scooter whipped around the corner and Peter pushed me onto the sidewalk, out of its path.

"The streets are going to get crazy tonight," he said, putting a hand on my shoulder. "Whatever you do, stay close."

The rain had thinned to a misty breeze, and the firework crew was taking full advantage. Boom after boom pulsed the night as the sky lit up in red, white, and green. We turned onto another street and saw the reason for the night's traffic jam: the streets were flooded with people. Some were waving Italian flags, others were singing, and still others were using karaoke machines to shout victory speeches (I assumed) to the crowd. There was no pathway. We weaved our way through the masses of people, stepping over discarded beer and wine bottles. Though this was a celebration, my gut was telling me that this gathering, like a match tossed on dry grass, had dangerous potential. Whether Peter sensed this too, I didn't know, but he took my hand in his and didn't let go.

Horns honked, music blared, and people, that massive sea of people, shouted and sang. Peter turned to me. "You're doing great," he said, and his dark, wet hair brushed against my temple, sending a chill through me.

This stupid town, I thought, *turning me into a spineless romantic. I'm falling for EVERY guy I meet.* This, of course, was an overstatement, a truth that became obvious when a group of drunk (seriously, does anyone in this town drink water?) Italian guys spotted me. We were far enough away from the touristy parts of Florence that seeing an American wasn't expected, and despite the Italia sweatshirt I was wearing and their inebriated state, they easily pegged me as a Yankee.

"American girl!" cried one after the other, and all five of them clambered off the low wall they were sitting on, and rushed toward me.

"Kiss, kiss!" shouted one, leaning in toward me as his friends cheered.

Peter hooked his arm around me and shoved the guy, pushing him back. They shouted at each other in Italian, and though the guy's friends were closing in, Peter didn't back down. A circle was forming around us, people willing to put their soccer celebrating on hold to watch a fight. The guy shoved Peter, or tried to. Peter caught his hand before he could do so. The guy, who looked to be in his late teens, smiled, revealing a missing front tooth, making it clear that a street fight was his idea of fun. A thick scar traced the contour of one of his cheekbones, and a skull was tattooed on his neck.

His cronies came in closer. "What time is it?" he snarled, not because he wanted an answer, but like so many Europeans, this phrase was the extent of his English, and he liked to say it. "What time is it?"

I knew what was coming next, or rather, what everyone expected to happen next: me cowering and Peter landing in the street after a few choice kicks to the stomach. But I couldn't accept that, not when I considered how he easily he could have bolted into the crowd, blended in, and made his way back to the car, burden free. Instead, here he was, trying to stand between me and five felons in training.

"What time is it?" he asked again, hitting his fist against his hand.

I didn't have a plan, and I didn't have time to make one, so I did the first thing that popped into my mind: I celebrated America. "I'll tell you what time it is!" I cried. "It's time to for 'Camptown Races!'"

Mr. Neck Tattoo looked confused, but not as confused as he did when I broke into song.

"CAMPTOWN LADIES SING THEIR SONG, DOO-DA, DOO-DA!" Every dance move my mother ever forced me to learn came bursting out of me. I twirled and jumped and slid all over the place, and as I did, the bad boys moved back to give me space. I didn't know all the words, but the crowd didn't mind. They clapped and sang along to the doo-das, and when I switched it up to "Yankee Doodle," they let out a cheer of recognition. "YANKEE DOODLE KEEP IT UP, YANKEE DOODLE DANDY!" I pulled out all my best revolutionary war dance moves, which involved a lot galloping and pretend flute playing, and I sang louder and louder as the crowd surprised me by cheering.

I finished the song and shouted, "New York City! Hollywood! La Brea Tar Pits! America loves Italy! Go, Italy!"

"Italia!" roared the crowd, and I waved as Peter grabbed my hand, and we slipped into the crush of people.

We didn't recap what had just happened. It wasn't necessary. Without it, we were comfortable. "La Brea Tar Pits?" he asked with a smile, once the crowd had thinned a bit and we could walk side by side.

"What do you mean? La Brea Tar Pits screams America," I said.

"You should have gone with Mount Rushmore."

"No one goes there," I said, my hand still clasped to his. "It's in the middle of nowhere."

"No one but thousands of people every year."

"I'm not the one who pledges allegiance to Liechtenstein, so I think I know what I'm talking about."

The rain picked up again. Peter pulled out the umbrella, and I was glad for the excuse to be closer to him. We talked as we dodged puddles and soccer fans. Peter, as I found out, was born in Denver, but his father, a civil engineer, had kept the family abroad for most of Peter's life, working as a contract employee for international firms. "It has its perks, the loneliness of boarding schools," he said.

"Like what?"

"Imaginary friends."

The miles should have been drudgery. Wet and tired, my only thought should have been of a hot shower and climbing into bed, but even with the rain coming and going, and a blister forming on my heel, I liked this tour of Italy. I liked walking past famous architecture at night while thousands celebrated in the streets, waving their country's flag and singing songs I didn't recognize. I liked the wimpy fireworks, and the local couples, arm in arm, speaking rapid-fire Italian as they walked past us. And I liked Peter. I liked him a lot.

We crossed a bridge, and the buildings started to look familiar to me. I could tell we were nearing the youth hostel. How close we were I wasn't sure, but it wouldn't be long before it was going to be time for good-bye, and for me to slip past the hostel's iron gate, head upstairs, and finally fall asleep. And then, without explanation, and way ahead of schedule, Peter did the thing I was dreading—he let go of my hand.

chapter 5

THERE WAS SO much soccer commotion, but it was impossible not to see the woman Peter had rushed toward. She was on her hands and knees in the street, sobbing uncontrollably, and from the looks of it, searching for something.

Yes, I was the person who had just belted out American hits of yesteryear in front of a large (and in the end, adoring) crowd, but this, Peter dropping everything (my hand!) to help a stranger, felt uncomfortable. *What if she's nuts?* I thought. Gram tutted in my head. *What if you were walking to Florence all the way from Prato because he assumed that about you?* she asked. She was right. She was always right, even when just a voice inside me. Shame, like a scratchy old coat, prickled my skin, so I did the one thing I could to cast it off. I went over to see what I could do to help.

"No!" she cried, on her knees, her fingers searching the cobble-stone street around her. "This cannot be happening! Dear God, this cannot be happening! I have to find it!"

Peter knelt beside her. "What are you looking for?" he asked.

"My ring!" she gasped, still searching. "My engagement ring! My fiancé gave it to me right before I left for Italy. There wasn't time to size it, and I think, I think . . ." She was starting to hyperventilate. "It slipped o-off my f-f-finger when . . ."

"It's going to be okay," he said, putting a reassuring hand on her shoulder. "When do you think it came off?"

She calmed down enough to speak, but she refused to stop searching. "When I pulled my hand out of my pocket."

"Where were you?" asked Peter, raising his voice to get her attention.

"Here, I think. I don't know! I thought I heard a sound like a small coin hitting the ground, but I don't know! There's so much noise, I'm not sure. I can't remember. But I have to find it! It belonged to his great-grandmother. I have to find it, but I can't see." She wiped her eyes with her dirty hands. "I'm crying so hard I can't see."

"We'll help you look," I said, trying to sound optimistic when inside my head a funeral dirge was playing for her fiance's great-grandmother's ring. That sucker was most likely a goner.

"My girlfriends have tried," she said, moaning, sounding about as optimistic as I felt. "They left to go find a flashlight or some help. Others have tried too, but we can't find it, and why won't it stop raining?"

"Do you have a flashlight?" I asked.

"Just the one on my key chain, but it's growing dim."

Peter dug into his pocket and pulled out a flashlight. "Let me look for a while and Sophia will sit with you."

The woman, clearly worn out, nodded, and I helped her find her way to the curb where we sat down, the umbrella shielding us both from the steady rain. The woman buried her face in her knees and sobbed. I'm awkward at comforting people, but when someone is sitting beside you crying their eyes out, you gotta try something. So I patted her back. "It's going to be okay," I said, and as I did I watched Peter.

Without asking, I was pretty sure Peter wasn't Mormon. Some things just give it away, like him telling me there was an open bar at his sister's wedding, compliments of his uncle Sheldon, and that the margaritas were fantastic. So, I don't know why, but I also assumed that meant he didn't believe in God. Not completely like we came from slugs and too bad if you die because this is all there is. But more like, there's something out there and as long as we're good, that's all that matters. So it wasn't what I expected, but as I patted this woman's heaving back, Peter, before starting to search, before even turning on his flashlight, lowered his head and prayed. I smiled, because him just doing that made the situation seem less hopeless. And so did his flashlight. For such a small light, it was really powerful.

The woman let out a groan of agony. It was time for me to do more than thwack her wet shirt. "What's your name?"

"Ellie," she said, her breathing quick and shallow.

"And where are you from, Ellie?" I asked, her breathing even more rapid now. "Tell me where you're from."

"Seattle," she said. "I came with my sorority sisters. They went to find help. We've looked for so long." She was beginning to peak into hysteria again.

"How did Sheldon propose?" I asked.

She looked up and stopped crying. Instantly. No lie, the tears were done. "My fiance's name isn't Sheldon," she said, sounding like me thinking she'd agreed to marry a guy named Sheldon was the ultimate insult. I detected snobbery, like this was a girl whose life was filled with designer handbags and weekly mani/pedis.

"Sorry," I said, bonking my hand to my forehead. "Peter's got an uncle named Sheldon," I said, pointing to Peter. "I'm getting my stories confused. So what's your fiance's name?"

"William," she said with satisfaction.

"And how did he propose?"

"In a hot air balloon," she sniffled. "It was noisy and hot and the strawberries were mushy, the champagne flat, but it was so romantic." She sobbed again and with new fervor. "He got down beside me. I was already on my knees because I'm afraid of heights, but he knelt beside me, told me he loved me, and put the ring on my fin—"

She couldn't finish that word, not with Peter's hand in front of her with a large pear-shaped diamond black with dirt pinched between his fingers.

"Is this your ring?" he asked.

It took a moment for her to realize what she was seeing. Her mouth fell open and then she started to cry again. Peter slipped the diamond ring on her finger, making an inexplicable twinge of jealousy rise up inside me.

Next, the clatter of sandals running on cobblestone came rushing toward us. "Ellie, we looked everywhere, but we couldn't find help."

Ellie raised her hand, showing her friends the ring on her finger. Screams of joy filled the night, catching the attention of many passersby. "He found my ring!" she cried, standing up. "This guy found my ring!" She hugged Peter, and wouldn't you know it, there was another twinge. But I didn't have time to dwell on it, because it was hugs, hugs, all the way around. Ellie's girlfriends hugged me, strangers passing by inquiring about what had happened hugged me, Ellie hugged me, and then it was Peter who stood before me.

With all the excitement caused by Peter finding the ring, I had dropped the umbrella. It wasn't far off, but neither of us bothered to get it. Instead, we stood in the rain facing each other, and as we did, it seemed to me as if the noises around us faded, and the buckets of water (it had picked up) now falling on our heads became vaguely imperceptible. All I could feel was the warmth of Peter's hand as he reached for mine, and the pounding of my heart. It was curious how much like a homecoming it felt, standing there, like we'd been apart for years, a soldier and his young bride, and now were at long last reunited. Needless to say, this wasn't an occasion for handshakes.

Peter drew me into a hug, not a quick, I'm-so-glad-you-came-to-my-party hug, but slowly putting his arms around me, he seemed to want to cherish the moment. We stood there embracing as the celebrating swirled around us. Italy had advanced, and what was lost was found. We pulled back and looked at each other for what felt like a long time. Above, fireworks fought against the rain, determined to fizz and crackle. But in my heart no battle waged. I knew Peter was going to kiss me and nothing had ever seemed more logical. So when he leaned toward me I didn't resist. His kiss was soft, sweet, and the sensation of being that close to Peter felt both new and familiar.

It was barely a kiss, the beginning of a kiss, and the magic it created had just begun to surround us when, like a pin pricking a balloon, Skeen Skarvegard spoke. "You have been busy, busy today, Sophie," said my tour director. My eyes shot open and I turned to see that he was standing creepily close to us. Skeen was wearing a raincoat and fedora, and as he spoke, rain dripped off the rim of his hat and landed on my shoulder. "First I see you canoodling with one boy and now I see you kissing another. Just one question for you: If there's a line, can I get in it?" Then he flared his lips and bit down, as if it was an attractive thing to do, and not something that made me want to vomit. On him, if possible.

But his words, they burned. They made my soul feel like it could curl in on itself and disintegrate like paper thrown into a fire. *Busy . . . canoodling . . . was there a line?* I pushed my hands against Peter's chest and broke free. "I need to go," I said, too embarrassed to look at him.

"Sophia," said Peter, grabbing me by the wrist.

Skeen shrugged. "I will take that as a no, for now," he said.

Peter wasn't letting go. Finding the strength, I turned around and looked at him. His hand slid from my wrist to my hand, and all I wanted to do was tumble back in to his arms, and let my head find refuge on his shoulder. But, no, I couldn't do that. I thought of Ellie and her fiancé, William. Though I had just met her, I got the feeling that what they shared was something real, something lasting. Skeen couldn't have been more wrong. There was no line, and there never would be. I wasn't available for just a good time, and if Peter thought he could pick up where Hanno left off, he was mistaken.

I pulled away. "This stupid town," I grumbled, rubbing my face with my hands as if trying to wake up. "A day like today wouldn't have happened in Mesa! People do their taxes in Mesa! They wash their cars and clip coupons! Why? Because there, the air, though tainted with a fair amount of pollution, is just that—air! Not some sort of potion that clouds your head with—"

"With what?" pressed Peter, grabbing hold of my hand again.

"Nothing," I said.

"With love," he said, taking my other hand in his. "It's not the city, Sophia. There's nothing in the air. It's just you and me."

"And the other boy from this morning," said Skeen. "Don't forget him."

We both jumped, neither of us realizing Skeen was still standing close by. It was annoying, but in a way I was glad for it. I needed a reminder, especially with Peter's hands in mine, that I was under the influence of Florence and shouldn't operate heavy equipment, let alone decide who I loved.

"I've got to go!" I said, trying to break free. The hostel was just a few blocks away. Normal was just a few blocks away.

"I think I love you," said Peter.

"A bold statement," observed Skeen. We both turned to glare at him, which he shrugged off easily enough.

The rain pelted us. In the street light, Peter's hair glinted black-ish blue, making me forget my creepy travel director. "Sophia," he started.

"No!" I shouted. I was crying now. "You can't think you love me! This is crazy! This town is crazy!"

A passerby confusing my outburst for soccer euphoria shouted back, "*Viva Italia!*"

I threw my hands in the air. "See?"

Peter reached out and brushed my wet cheek with his finger. "In a perfect world, we would have days and weeks, months even, to come to such a conclusion, but you leave tomorrow, Sophia, and I know it's fast—too fast—but I have to tell you how I feel, because I don't want tonight to be over, I don't want *us* to end, before we've had a chance to begin."

"In Prague, our next city, we could go out for goulash," countered Skeen.

It was, hands down, the most romantic thing any guy had ever said to me, and I'm not talking about the goulash invitation. I stopped pulling away, stopped resisting this undeniable force that made me feel as unsteady as a passenger aboard a ship in rough water, and I kissed Peter again. The rain, getting bumped by people walking by, scooters honking, nothing, not even Skeen, interrupted this kiss. Not until my mother's voice whispered to me inside my head, *Sweetheart, one day he'll see your faults, all your many imperfections, and he'll leave you . . . broken-hearted.* Then, without an explanation, without even good-bye, I turned and ran.

I didn't look back to see if Peter was following me. I ran toward the hostel, through its iron gate, raced up the stairs, and didn't stop until I got to the second floor. Breathless, I leaned against the banister, determined to resist the urge to walk over to the large casement window that faced the street and look for Peter. I was so close, just down the hall was my bed, a shower, a change of clothes. Just down the hall was the real Sophie Stark, and life making sense again. Shivering, I turned to go, even though I knew it was lie. I couldn't leave without looking, and so I did. I walked over to the window, looked down, and there below, standing in the rain, was Peter. The street light was dim, but I could still see the hurt in his face, and it caused a wave of misery to crash over me. I put my hand against the window to steady myself. "You can't possibly love me," I told him, though he couldn't see or hear me. "I'm such a mess. Clearly. Who but a mess kisses a boy and then runs away? Good-bye, Peter. One day you'll thank me."

That night, after the shortest, coldest shower of my life (hostel living for you), I fell into bed, and though others in the dorm snored contentedly, my sleep was fitful, constantly interrupted by the sound of a baby—one very loud baby—wailing away.

chapter 6

I COULD HAVE BEEN anywhere. Paris, London, Tokyo. I could have found a reason to not make it home for Christmas, a perfectly valid, wonderful reason. As an advertising agent with Percy Dilwooten Foster, I was constantly on the move, a definite job perk for a girl who was interested in seeing the world and dodging her mother's never-ending questions about her love life. I sighed as I parked my Mercedes rental in my parents' driveway. Why hadn't I begged off, claiming some sort of ad emergency? A new assignment, last minute deadline, obligatory skiing with a client in Switzerland. It would have been easy enough to do, which was precisely why I hadn't made it home for two years. Maybe it wasn't too late to pull out of the driveway, grab a flight back to New York, and concoct some sort of Christmas-trip-killing catastrophe. I gripped the key, considering making an escape, when through the sheer curtain hanging in the front window, I saw Gram watching me. She pulled the curtain aside and held my gaze, as if daring me to go.

"Great," I grumbled, and slid the key out of the ignition. I could disappoint my mom, even my dad, but I couldn't disappoint Gram.

She was waiting with the front door open as I walked up, a scarf from a recent trip to India wrapped stylishly around her shoulders. "My darling," she said, her arms opened wide. We embraced and worry flitted through me as I felt how much thinner and smaller she'd become since the last time I saw her. She was still my grand-mother—the same thick, white hair swept into a low bun, and the same brown eyes shining with intelligence and kindness—but like the plastic art I used to create as a child in her oven, she'd shrunken. "How was your flight?" she asked, patting my hand as we stepped into the entry.

"Excruciating."

"Did I hear someone?" asked my mother, approaching.

"But not as excruciating as that," I mumbled.

Gram leveled her "be nice" look on me and moved aside to make room for Mom.

"Well, look what the cat dragged in!" said Mom, pressing her cheek to mine, careful not to smudge her lipstick.

"Good to know I look like a dead rat," I said.

Mom dismissed my comment with a wave of her hand. "You know it's just an expression," she said. "But you're here!" She gave my arm a squeeze. "So good to have you home, my love, especially since you're hardly ever here."

I smiled, trying to be humored instead of annoyed that less than five minutes after my arrival my mother was bringing up one of her two chief complaints about me—that I seldom visit.

"She is a busy young woman," said Gram, defending me.

"*Woman*," corrected Mom. "Let's not forget that Sophia, though unmarried, is pushing forty."

And there it was, her second pet peeve about me: I was still single.

"Pushing forty? Mom, I just turned thirty last month."

"The clock is ticking, Sophia," she said. "Not that I think you need a reminder. That's why God invented wrinkles." My hand shot inadvertently to my face. "They're a little push to let us know it's time, past time, to tie the knot." Of course, all of this was said, as usual, in the sweetest of tones.

Gram hooked her arm through mine. "Sophie wants to make sure all her ducks are in a row, and there's nothing wrong with that."

"Except that by the time she's finished, all her ducks will be long dead from natural causes." Mom smiled like she was complimenting my handbag. "But, Sophia, I suppose the good news is you do seem to like your latest young man."

"Man," I corrected. "Let's not get carried away, Mom. He's just a few months younger than me." Mom, not catching my sarcasm, nodded in agreement. "But, yes, I do like him. I like him very much." A smile edged into the corners of my mouth. Ah, Griffin. Every time I thought of him, a list came to mind—*my* list of what I wanted in a future husband, and Griffin, as wonderful as he was, ticked every box: Eagle Scout, return missionary, smart, successful, handsome . . .

"Ploof," said Mom with a frown. "His last name is Ploof."

Okay, not every box. The must-have-a-cool-last-name box . . . yeah, he didn't tick that. "Ploof," I said, trying to sound upbeat. "Yes, his last name is Ploof."

"Well, that is unfortunate." She sighed, as if all Ploofs were known to disappoint. "But too bad he couldn't join us for Christmas, especially with the wedding. It would have been lovely to have you on someone's arm."

"You make her sound like she has vertigo," scoffed Gram. "Sophie doesn't need to be on anyone's arm to attend the wedding."

"What wedding?" I asked. "Who's getting married?"

"Hanno," said Mom. "I'm sure I told you."

My stomach flipped, tumbling like a world-class gymnast at the mention of his name, which was so stupid. I hadn't thought of Hanno in years. "Well, that's great," I said, brightly. Too brightly. "So where's the wedding taking place?"

Mom looked in the mirror that hung near the entry. "His parents' backyard," she said, placing two fingers near her jaw, pulling back, and mulling over the difference it made. She wanted a facelift, but she also liked having the moral high ground to criticize her friends who, for vanity's sake, had gone under the knife. It was quite the dilemma.

"His parents' backyard," I said. "How original."

"I agree. A change of venue would have been in good taste," said Mom.

Huh? My mother and I were on the same page? It was small, but a seed of hope took root inside me that maybe this trip we'd experience a breakthrough.

"But it's been fifteen years since the first wedding, and she's such a cosmopolitan lady. I'm sure having the wedding in the Olsens' backyard is a novelty."

"Even though it's been done before."

"Be kind," said Gram, nudging me, "especially when I tell you she's pregnant."

"Is he sure?" I asked, raising an eyebrow.

"Yes, quite," said Gram.

"So this really will be round two," I said, marveling.

"Except without you pining for him in the wings," said Mom.

That tiny seed of hope that had just been planted was essentially uprooted, but I smiled like her words didn't feel like a kick in the stomach.

"I'm sure you're well past that silly childhood crush," she said, with a toss of her hand.

I smiled, again too brightly. "I'm sure I am," I said as Gram patted my back reassuringly, trying to smooth out, as usual, what she could tell my mother had ruffled inside me. "So when is the wedding?"

"Tonight!" said Mom, clasping her hands together. "I do love a wedding! The invitation says the ceremony begins at six with a cocktail hour and dinner to follow." Mom frowned. "Croatian big wigs from the bride's family on the guest list or not, were it me, I would have held my ground and not allowed liquor to be served in my backyard. Very unprincipled of Chester and Norma," she said.

"Sophia," said Dad, his walk almost a trot as he came toward me, car keys jingling in his pocket. "So good to have you home." Dad wrapped me in a hug and kissed my head. Ah, it was good to be home.

"Especially after such a long absence," said Mom, and I felt my back stiffen.

Dad laughed, crinkling his brown eyes. "We just saw her

three months ago, darling," he said, smoothing a hand across his comb-over.

"That shouldn't count," said Mom, flicking her wrist, a little gesture meant to dismiss his words. "We were on our way to Amsterdam, *and* we didn't get to meet her boyfriend."

Dad smiled, choosing, as usual, to not contradict her. He stood back, his hands on my shoulders, taking in the sight of me. "So many people are going to be happy to see you tonight, Sophie. Did your mother tell you that Hanno's getting married?"

"Just now."

"I'm sure I told you weeks ago," said Mom.

Unlike my dad, I didn't just let my mom have the last word. I made her fight for it. "I'm sure you didn't," I countered.

"You just don't remember."

"Mom, I would have remembered it."

"It's that subway air. Dulls the synapses, makes you forget. I read an article on it."

"In what magazine?"

"It might have been on *Sixty Minutes*."

"There's nothing wrong with the air in the subway"

"If you don't mind forgetting whole conversations."

"Ladies, ladies," said Dad, trying to keep the tension from rising between us. "It's Christmas. Let's be nice."

"Or let's move the furniture out of the way and really let them go at it," said Gram, a twinkle of mischief in her eye.

"I don't know what you're talking about," said Mom, fingering the diamond pendant around her neck. "We were just talking."

"We were arguing, Mom."

"No, we weren't."

"Yes, we were."

"No, we weren't."

"Yes, we were."

Gram laughed. "Back and forth, back and forth. This isn't an argument. This is tennis!"

Mom's eyes glinted with anger, but her voice stayed sweet. "I don't know why we're all standing around. I've got to buy a wedding gift, and, Sophie, you should rest. Try and see if you can't get rid of those dark circles."

She was gone, dragging Dad along with her, before I could argue further. Gram leaned on my arm, and we made our way into the kitchen. "Well, that went well," she said.

"And she wonders why I don't visit more often," I said. "All we do is argue."

After taking a second to get her hips to cooperate, Gram sat down next to me. "I'm old enough now that I should be spouting pearls of wisdom at times like these, so how about this: people can be like cactuses."

"What's that supposed to mean?" I asked.

"That despite their many fine attributes, they can still be difficult to hug."

"That's pretty profound, Gram."

"It ought to be. I just heard De Niro say it in a movie," she said with a wink.

"Well, it's still true. Mom can be a lot like a prickly pear."

"And you like the mighty saguaro."

"I'm not difficult to hug."

Gram patted my arm. "Except when you are."

I was going to ask her what she meant by that but got distracted by the sight of Hanno's wedding invitation on the fridge. The paper was thick, with a torn edge, and embossed in a gold, flourishing script that read:

At Dusk, Everything Changes.
Hanno becomes a husband
Ingrid becomes a wife
And together a family.
Please join us for an intimate celebration
Shared with family and close friends
At the Chester and Norma Olsen residence

406 Hickory Lane
Mesa, Arizona
December 23
Six o'clock
Formal attire preferred

"Hmm," I said, disappointed. "No picture."

"She probably has a regrettable overbite."

"Gram."

"Or underbite. Either way, when we meet the new Mrs. Olsen, we'll be nothing but smiles," she said as my brother, George, walked in through the kitchen door with little Imogene in his arms.

"Hello, hello!" he said, dropping the diaper bag on the floor and giving us both a hug. "So good to see you."

"When did you get in?" I asked, taking Imogene from him and kissing her head.

"This morning," he said, yawning. "We're staying with Margaret's parents. She's there now trying to get Albert to take a nap. Meanwhile," he said, gesturing to Imogene, "I'm in charge of this one, who somehow happened to sleep all the way from London."

George and Margaret moved to London a few years ago when he was offered a position with a software company. Of course, I saw them less than when they lived in Jersey, but my work took me to London enough that Albert knew his Aunt Sophie. Imogene was another story. Just five months old, she still had her doubts about me, and as she studied my face, her little mouth tugged into a frown until, crying, she reached for her daddy. I bounced and cooed—tried everything I could to keep her in my arms—and to my surprise, she calmed a little. "So," I said as I swung her gently from side to side, "did you know Hanno is getting married tonight?"

"Of course," he said smugly as he adjusted the knot of an imaginary tie. "I would have been in the wedding party, if there were one."

"So they want it to be low key," I said.

"No groomsmen or bridesmaids, but I wouldn't say low key. I just drove past the Olsens' house." He flared his fingers and made the sound of a quiet explosion. "Looks like they're pulling out all the stops."

"So have you met her?" I asked as Imogene snatched the cracker Gram was offering her.

"Who?" asked George, rubbing the blonde stubble on his chin.

"Ingrid, Hanno's fiancé."

"Oh, sure."

"Does she by chance need braces?" asked Gram, grinning wide, trying to coax a smile from Imogene.

"Let me put it to you this way," he said. "She's a celebrity in Croatia."

I let out a puff of air and rolled my eyes. "Who isn't?" I said. "It's a country practically the size of Costco."

"Pooh-pooh a lesser known European country all you want, but you'll see. She's a looker." George pointed at his daughter, who was contentedly covering me in crumbs. "Hey, sis," he said, "do you mind watching Imi? I've got to go pick up a wedding guest at the airport."

"Sure," I said. "Anyone I know?"

"Doubt it, unless you've been to the South Pole lately."

"Not lately. What about you, Gram? Ever been to the South Pole?" I asked.

"Surprisingly not on my bucket list," she said, offering Imi another cracker.

"Just as well, Gram," said George, "It's five days by dog sled to the nearest Walmart."

Gram smiled. "Couldn't do it. I've too many prescriptions that need filling."

Imogene was studying her mush-covered fist. Unwilling to risk giving her a good-bye kiss, George blew one instead as he quietly headed for the door. "Thanks, sis, and sorry about the mess," he said, pointing to my shirt.

"No worries," I said, though it'd have to be dry-cleaned.

"Just remember," he said, poking his head back in the kitchen, "if she cries"—he lowered his voice to a whisper—"it's your problem."

"Thanks for the helpful hint."

"Anytime."

George was right. The new Mrs. Olsen was not in need of orth-odontia. Perfect as she was, she wasn't in need of any improvement, which had me eating pot stickers at an alarming rate. Not that I wasn't happy for them. Who couldn't be happy for two beautiful people tying the knot in a garden wonderland? While Chester and Norma had always been avid gardeners, it was obvious that deep pockets from Croatia had assisted in turning their backyard into a veritable Eden aglow with candlelight and innumerable tiny lights which at times, here and there, mimicked the random, easy blinking of fireflies.

Even Bishop Obray's sobering words at the end of the wedding ceremony about death and the finite nature of their union did little to dull the evening's sparkle. And rather than appearing awkward, Ingrid's baby bump, enveloped in antique lace and lovingly caressed by Hanno, made it seem like this was the pinnacle. This was what every girl should shoot for—getting pregnant and marrying in your in-laws' backyard. Of course, I knew this wasn't true, but the only way to deal with what appeared to be solid evidence to the contrary was to feed my face.

Chewing greedily on a mini egg roll, I watched as, during cocktail hour, the happy couple posed for pictures near an array of white tulips. The new Mr. and Mrs. Olsen appeared positively bliss-ful, their heads tilted together, his hand resting on her bump, and both bestowing on the other sweet, spontaneous kisses. "Waiter!" I called out to a random tux walking past. "I'm in need of some serious garlic shrimp, and while you're at it, a few of those pastry thingies."

Random tux turned around and the piece of egg roll I'd just bitten off shot out of my mouth, arched impressively in the air and hit him in the chest. He wasn't a waiter, and though I hadn't seen him in ten years, I recognized him instantly.

"Peter De Boom," I said, my voice soft with wonder.

"Sophia Stark," he said, not sounding particularly surprised.

I paused, not knowing what to do next. Shake hands? Hug?

Wipe the grease off his suit? He didn't wait for me to figure it out. Placing a hand on my arm, he kissed my cheek, and the sturdy part of me that had learned to live alone in New York and succeed in the cutthroat business of advertising, that part of me seemed to buckle. And taking in the sight of him didn't help any. He was taller than I remembered. His hair, cut shorter now, was still thick and bluish-black with just a few distinguished-looking gray hairs at his temple. His eyes were the color of melted chocolate, and he looked trim and impossibly handsome in his tux.

I gulped, trying to stem the nervousness rising inside me. "How have you been?" I asked.

"Cold," he said, then smiled at my look of confusion. "I've been on ice the past several years, literally, working at the Amundsen-Scott South Pole Station. How about you?"

I played with my necklace, zipping the pendant back and forth on its chain. "Hot, uh, in the summer, cold in the winter, fairly comfortable in the fall. October's lovely, because I like to wear sweaters. Just sweaters. Well, not *just* sweaters, but not the whole overcoat, gloves, scarf, hat thing. I live in New York City. In Midtown . . . near a world-famous Korean restaurant," I said, rambling in the frantic way people generally do when held at gunpoint.

"I meant, how are you?"

I squinted and blinked like my vision was clouded by hallucinations of floating purple elephants. "I'm well, fine, great," I said, my voice high and fluttery. "I guess I'm just surprised to see you." I held out a finger and paused as my brain connected the dots. "Wait, my brother, George, picked you up at the airport today."

"That's right," he said, like there wasn't anything unusual about this. "It was a long flight, but I had to come. Hanno's an old friend, and he introduced me to the gospel."

"Do not bring that up!" moaned my brother, George, good-naturedly as he walked toward us with baby Imogene in his arms. "I busted my chop knocking on doors in Germany for two years without any success, only to find out Hanno, while schlepping his way across Europe, converted his roomie."

"Hanno accepted a Book of Mormon from a pair of missionaries," explained Peter. "He left it on the kitchen table, and I read it."

My mouth would have hit the floor, but I was too shocked to open it.

George bounced Imogene in his arms, trying to keep her from squawking. "I'm not bitter," he said, "but I would like to point out that I beat Hanno in Words with Friends last week, so the latest victory is mine." Tucking Imogene in one arm, he shook hands with Peter. "Hey, Pete. How's it goin', bro?" he said like they were old friends.

"Not bad, not bad," said Peter, before puffing out his cheeks and crossing his eyes to make Imogene squeal with delight. "Imi's getting so big." Imi? He knew my niece's nickname?

"Dude, I swear it's like holding a horse," said George. Imogene, though not offended by her father's silly exaggeration, still thwacked him in the face.

The Olsens' backyard seemed to spin like a carnival ride. "Hang on, how long have you guys known each other?" I said, pointing from one to the other.

George squinted as he thought. "What is it, like two years now?"

Peter nodded in agreement.

"But how did you meet?" I asked.

"Hanno," they said in unison.

George raised an eyebrow. "How did you meet?" he asked, pointing to Peter and then to me.

"Hanno," we said in unison, though my voice was more of a mumble.

"More commonly known today as one of the luckiest men in the world. If you're gonna marry, you might as well marry a Croatian pimento princess. I hear her parents are loaded," George said, singing the last word like a member of heavy metal band.

"I'm not a Croatian pimento princess," said George's wife, Margaret, walking up and poking him in the side.

George kissed his wife and handed her Imogene. "But you are to me, sweetheart," he said, lovingly, "even though your parents work at the post office."

Smiling, Margaret rolled her green eyes. "I'll take that as a compliment," she said, then turned to Peter and me, and gave us each an Imogene-filled hug. "Sophie," she said. "I didn't know you knew our Peter!"

Our Peter. An absurd twinge of jealousy passed over me, hearing Margaret claim Peter as theirs. "Yes, we've met before," I said, and looked at him briefly. Or I tried to anyway, but he held my gaze, and I found it impossible to look away.

Margaret and George didn't seem to notice this, which may have had something to do with Imogene blowing out her diaper. "Oh no!" cried Margaret, horrified at the brown streak that now smeared the back of Imogene's white dress.

"Darling," George said, moving one of her unruly brown curls out her eyes, "I think it's important to tell you right now that I love you and that you're holding her, so . . . possession being nine tenths of the law . . . this one is yours."

Margaret grabbed her husband by the tie. "This one is ours. You know it's a two-man job."

"Not with your skill set, my love. Shouldn't I at least go find Albert?" he tried as she dragged him toward the house.

"Not to worry. He's with Gram," said Margaret.

Looking back, George said to Peter, "By the way, Margaret says you can't stay at a hotel."

"I did," she said, pulling her husband behind her.

"You'll stay at my parents'," he said, over the heads of several guests.

"No, I couldn't possibly," Peter said.

"Are you kidding me?" cried George. "It's Christmas!"

They were too far now for Peter to say anything in return. He looked at me and smiled. "They're a great family," he said.

"They are," I said.

"Are you?" he asked.

"What?"

"A family yet."

I cleared my throat. "Well, no, not yet. I mean, there is someone.

I have a boyfriend, a super serious boyfriend." Peter's expression seemed faraway, vacant almost, like watching me speak was mesmerizing. "And what about you? Are you a family?"

Peter shook his head and smiled. "No, but your sister-in-law is working on it," he said. "Any time I'm in London, she lines me up with someone."

"Do you mind?"

"Only when they bring their ferret on the date."

"That's never happened."

"Twice."

A bell chimed letting us know that cocktail hour was now over and it was time to enter the party tent for dinner. Peter, as naturally as anything, took my hand. "Do you think your super serious boyfriend would mind if I danced with you later?"

I was lost in his eyes so it took me a moment to respond. "Peter."

"Sophia."

"Peter."

"Sophia," he said. "You wanna play? I can do this all night."

I knew what he was doing, what part of our tiny history he was referencing, and it made me laugh. "Fine," I said. "Find me later."

He wrapped my arm around his to escort me into the tent. "I will," he said as we walked. "I'll keep looking until I find you."

$\mathcal{A}$ S IF MONEY could buy anything, the weather was in perfect compliance with the night's festivities, allowing all sides of the tent to be rolled up, and the gorgeous outside décor to blend seamlessly with the opulence inside the tent. Blue and purple lighting washed the scene in a wintry glow, and everywhere you looked candles flickered—long stem candles in silver baroque candelabras, clusters of votives, floating candles, and candles in antique jars of every size. All were grouped beautifully together on mirrored tables, shimmering and blurring next to tall vases overflowing with white hydrangeas, silver bowls filled with white roses, and, as if that weren't enough, white woodland creatures, made especially for the occasion (according to a placard) at her uncle's porcelain factory in Dubrovnik.

Peter escorted me across the glowing dance floor to my assigned table where George, Margaret, their kids, and my gawking parents already sat. The wedding couple was about to make their grand entrance, so Peter quickly introduced himself to my parents and went to find his own table.

"Where's Gram?" I asked, pointing to her seat.

"Gone home," said Dad. "Her hips were giving her trouble."

Tapping her index finger to her chin, Mom studied Peter as he walked away. "He seems nice," said Mom as we all stood to welcome the bride and groom.

Once the applause died down and the newlyweds were sharing their first dance, Margaret spoke, her voice far louder than appropriate, but with a hand cupped to her mouth to appear discreet. "Peter is better than nice—he's a catch! Not only is he handsome, but he's also a convert, *and* he's great with kids. Albert and Imogene absolutely love him!"

"Is he spoken for?" asked Mom, not shouting but close to it.

Margaret shook her head, and Mom, blessed with a new wellspring of patience or possibly just noticing the shushing coming from the table next to us, decided to wait until after Hanno and Ingrid were finished dancing before delving further.

"So he's single," she said, tapping her chin.

Margaret buttered a roll for Albert, who had slid off his chair and was now lying on the ground. "Well, not for lack of *me* trying," said Margaret. "I'm constantly setting him up when he's in town, but he works at the South Pole."

"The South Pole? That's ridiculous. No one works there," she said.

"Except Peter, and a few hundred other people," said George. He snapped his fingers to tell his son to get back in his chair, but he did so without oomph, jet lag having drained his parental drive, and Albert stayed put.

"Always wanted to visit the South Pole," said Dad.

"You have not," said Mom, waving a hand in the air to hurry away his words. Mom leaned toward Margaret. "What does he do at the South Pole?" she asked warily.

"He's a physician—"

"Oh!" squealed Mom, bouncing in her seat and clapping her hands.

"Assistant," Margaret finished. "Physician assistant."

The clapping stopped. "Oh," she said, not flat, but no longer giddy.

Rocking Imogene's car seat with his foot, George reached across Margaret, grabbed the roll she'd buttered, and tossed it to Albert. "You sound like you're deducting points, Mom. Sophie's not interested in him. She's nuts about Gryffindor."

"Very funny," I said.

"Thanks," he said sweetly, putting his hand over mine. "I take my big brother responsibilities very seriously. But Peter is great, Mom. A real nice guy, which works out well, since I invited him to stay with you for Christmas." George winced, waiting for her response.

"I think that would be lovely," she said, making Dad's mouth fall open.

The waiter stepped over Albert and served us our salads. "But you took down the guest bed to make room for your Christmas village," said Dad, sounding confused.

Mom shrugged. "We can scooch."

Dad's eyes were wide with wonder. "Okay then. We'll scooch."

"Sophie, you can make up the couch for Peter," she said, sounding smug, "and see to it that he's comfortable."

George tossed Albert a cherry tomato from his salad. "So Sophie's gonna fluff his pillow and Peter's going to fall in love with her. Is that what you're planning?" he asked.

"I don't know what he didn't see in Elinor," said Margaret to no one in particular. "She owns her own pet store."

"He's away from home at Christmas," said Mom, sounding magnanimous.

"Which you plan to use to your meddling advantage," said George, pointing his spoon at his mother.

Dad rubbed the top of his head and sat back in his chair. "We haven't had company at Christmas for years," he said.

Mom speared a tomato with her fork. "I'm not meddling, but if he falls in love with Sophie, I won't stop him. They looked right together."

"Mother," I groaned.

"Oh, I forgot," she said, cutting into her salad with unnecessary vigor, "your precious ducks. You must have everything just so. Well, sometimes when it comes to love you have to make it so, you have to fight for it, arrange it, push it into being, not stand back and wait and wait and wait for it to materialize, all perfect, all ducky."

"But you're not meddling," said George, "though I think the Griffster would disagree."

"George, dear," said Mom, "pass the salt."

Margaret snapped her fingers. "Celestina!" she cried. "She's such a nice girl. I just met her —"

"At the morgue," said George, lowering his voice an octave.

"At the bakery," corrected Margaret. "But she is an undertaker, which I think is great, very plucky. Not gross at all."

She stood alone in this assessment. The rest of us looked like we'd just caught wind of one of Imogene's soiled diapers.

"I think they'd be perfect together," Margaret continued. "She's not a member, but that doesn't mean she couldn't be. George, remind me to call her when I get back."

"Of course," he said, then looked at me and mouthed the word *not*.

While their guests dined on their choice of roast duck, filet mignon, or Chilean sea bass, a jazz band played mellow renderings of old standards and Christmas songs. Peter sat at a table across the dance floor from us, eating his dinner and chatting pleasantly. I tried to sneak glances at him when I was sure he wasn't looking, but apparently I'm a terrible judge of when to sneak glances because again and again our eyes met, making me blush and quickly look away. Still, I couldn't stop trying. Waiters rushed, bringing us course after delicious course, Ingrid danced with her father, Hanno danced with Norma, Chinese acrobats contorted and tumbled, elephants formed a pyramid. Okay, I'm joking about that last one, but seriously, there was so much happening that was vying for my attention and yet my eyes searched for Peter.

After all the traditional American and Croatian wedding hoopla was out of the way, the jazz band called it a night and a cover band got the party started. Margaret and George, though compatible in practically every way, parted company when it came to dancing. Margaret loved to dance and George found it agonizing, so as soon as the band started playing, Margaret grabbed me by the wrist and dragged me to the dance floor where Albert, clearly his mother's child, was already unleashing his entire arsenal of preschool dance moves. A disco ball descended from inside the tent's peak, speckling the packed dance floor with bits of light that seemed to signal to everyone that it was now time to let loose, and no one more so than Albert. His previous sluggishness that had made sitting in a chair impossible was gone, replaced with joy-filled jumping and spinning so entertaining I didn't notice Peter beside me until he tapped me on the shoulder.

He danced alongside Margaret and me, enjoying the Albert spectacle, and twirling Margaret when she insisted. I was lost in the moment, just having fun dancing, not thinking about what was going to happen next, until it was already happening—the first slow song. Peter mopped his forehead with his handkerchief, returned it to his pocket, and took me by the hand. My heart skipped a beat, but not because I was slow dancing with Peter. Doing so, I felt perfectly at ease, and besides, this wasn't high school. But I could have sworn, though it seemed unlikely, ridiculous even, that I had glimpsed . . . I had to ask him.

"I have a question for you," I started, as we moved in a slow circle.

"Republican," he answered.

"That's not it."

"Fine, I'll switch to Democrat. You're one tough lady."

I smiled. "Just listen. This is kind of silly, but that hanky you just used, is it the same one you loaned me ten years ago?"

"It is."

I groaned. "Super gross, Peter! Why didn't you pick it up with tongs and burn it in your backyard?"

"Well, there can only be two reasons," he said, and then spun me around. "Since it was covered with your DNA, either I wanted to frame you for a crime, or I liked having it to remember you by."

"Please tell me you've washed it."

"Only with my tears," he said, trying not to smile.

I gave him a soft thwack on his arm. "So other than crying into your hanky, what have you been doing?"

"Mostly just been on ice, working."

"Do you like working there, at the South Pole?"

"Yes, except for the dating scene. When you ask someone to go for a walk and it's seventy-five degrees below zero, all you end up talking about is the weather."

I laughed. "That does sound like a problem. But on a night like tonight you can end up talking about the weather too; it's so lovely."

Peter looked at me rather than the cloudless indigo sky. "I guess it's all right," he said, "but I prefer rain."

I blushed, no doubt making my cheeks, even in the tent's subdued light, appear aflame. Rain! I hadn't forgotten the details of our crazy night together in Italy, but still, I was surprised that he had remembered so much. Guys just didn't care about stuff like that, right? Peter spun me around, making my long brown curls take flight. While I turned, I caught a glimpse of my mother. She was watching us, looking rather pleased with herself, which irritated me, but not enough to leave Peter stranded on the dance floor. I was having a good time, and besides, a large Croatian couple was now blocking her from my view.

The twirling was over and I was back in his arms. "You've got a good memory, Peter De Boom," I said close to his ear.

"Thanks," he said.

"So let me just say this, if you request the band play 'Camptown Races'—"

"You mean, 'Oh My Darlin', Clementine.' "

" 'Camptown Races,' " I corrected.

"We'll agree to disagree."

"Fine, if the band plays either one, I swear I will see to it that my mom shows you her entire Christmas village."

"Duly noted," he said, and I nodded with satisfaction. "But," he continued, "I gotta tell you, my mom has a Precious Moments collection that could fill the Sistine Chapel, so, as far as threats go . . ."

It was time to pull out the big guns. "I'll suggest she bring down from the attic (with your help, of course) all the villages, every major holiday, so you can see the subtle and not-so-subtle differences."

"Not cool."

"And the Hummels in the china cabinet. All three hundred bubble-wrapped pieces."

"Very uncool, Miss Stark. Fine, no 'Clementine.'"

I gave him a don't-push-It look, and he twirled me again.

As we swayed in time to the music, I found myself wishing the song wouldn't end. I liked dancing with Peter, and there was more I wanted to say to him, *needed* to say to him. Time was slipping past, the song winding down, so I took a deep breath and went for it. "Um, did you know I would be here tonight?" I asked, suddenly more aware of his strong, warm hand pressed against my back.

"I hoped," he said.

"Peter," I said, hesitating a little, "I'm sorry for the way I left that night. I didn't mean to—"

"Shhh," he soothed, tucking a rebellious curl behind my ear. "Your apology is making it hard to focus on the lyrics, and this is my favorite song."

I gave him a skeptical look. "Really, 'Muskrat Love' is your favorite song?" It had been requested by Chester and Norma, possibly the only two people on the planet who wanted to hear it.

"Well, now it is," he said as the band's synthesizer made lovey-dovey rodent sounds.

"Oh, please," I said.

"Shh." He touched his finger to my lips. "You're interrupting a terrible hit from the seventies."

I didn't try to say more. Apparently it was time for music appreciation, which was fine since I needed a moment to wrap my head around what was happening. Peter and I had met once ten years ago. Once! Yet, being in his arms, a tenseness I carried with me nearly always, like a frantic secretary reminding me to work harder, be smarter, look cuter, and not neglect my abs, that busy bee of industry finally seemed to be taking a break, and I could feel myself relax. It had been a long day, filled with travel and celebrating, and it was starting to catch up with me. I stifled a yawn. The urge to rest my head on Peter's shoulder was nearly overwhelming. But no, I told myself, it would make my mother too happy. Still, maybe just for a moment. My jet-lagged brain was certain it would feel like falling slowly through a cloud in a dream.

My head had just begun to drift toward Peter's broad shoulder when from behind, someone covered my eyes and said, sounding like a creepy Yoda, "Who it is, guess you!"

Fatigue must have robbed me of the most basic deductive reasoning skills, because until I turned around I didn't know the person surprising me was my boyfriend, Griffin Ploof. It should have been obvious since Griffin tends to imitate Star Wars characters when he's trying to be lovey-dovey. Sort of like girls who lapse into baby talk. It's a Griffin thing. Anyway, what I did know was that I should look happy to see him. Even happier than I felt. I jumped into his arms and he spun me around. "Oh my gosh!" I cried. "Griffin, I thought you couldn't make it!"

He gave me a smacking wallop of a kiss and placed me back on the ground. "I did some shuffling," he said, then good-naturedly extended a hand to Peter. "Griffin Ploof, Sophie's boyfriend," he said.

They shook hands, both seeming to want to get in the last vigorous shake, which made the whole thing take a little longer than usual. "Peter De Boom," said Peter, "Sophie's old friend," which was true, so why did it seem like an understatement?

Griffin hooked an arm over my shoulders. "That's fantastic!" he cried, as if instead of stating his name, Peter had just saved a puppy. I smiled. Griffin could be overzealous in social situations, and it was so cute, or at least that's what I told myself. "Wow, what a party. So, Sophie, are you friends with the bride?"

"No, the groom," I said.

"Too bad," said Griffin, loosening his tie. "The bride's where the money is at."

Mortified, I felt my back tighten. "Griffin, that doesn't matter. This is a wedding, not a business opportunity."

Griffin snapped, pointed his fingers like guns, and waggled them at me. "You know I never clock out!"

It was time to change the subject. Either that or grab the nearest napkin and stuff it in his mouth. "When did you get here?" I asked, noticing for some reason that though a bit taller than Peter, his shoulders were narrower.

"Just," he said, running a hand through his thick, rust-colored hair. "The flight from Waikiki was a nightmare,"

"Did an engine catch on fire?" asked Peter, clearly joking.

"No, the chicken in business class was rubbery," said Griffin, not getting it.

Peter almost succeeded in concealing a smile. "Unbelievable," he said.

The food in business class may have been lacking, but the air conditioning must have been working overtime. When I grabbed Griffin's hand, it felt cold. "Griffin," I said as the song ended, "Peter works at the South Pole."

"Great Scott!" he cried. "Or I should say, Amunsden-Scott South Pole Station!" Griffin chuckled at his own joke, and Peter, amused by this, tried to share with me a knowing glance, but I was careful to keep my eyes fixed on my mother's sour expression. (The song had ended, the dance floor cleared some, and she was in full view.) We all have challenges in life, and Griffin, perfect as he was, happened to still be working on his sense of humor. I thought it was sweet when he cracked himself up, sort of like a baby clapping with glee after a few wobbly steps.

"But seriously," said Griffin, "how fascinating! The South Pole! I've always wanted to talk to someone who works there. Let's go grab a table, I'll flag down a waiter for something to eat, and you can tell me all about it!"

For some reason I didn't want this to happen. "Darling," I said, nudging Griffin in the ribs, "Peter doesn't want to do that."

"Oh yes, Peter does," said Peter, with a hint of my sugary sweetness.

"Fantastic!" cried Griffin.

"Yeah, fantastic," I said.

As the band picked up the pace, we made our way over to where my mother sat, looking stiff.

"Mom, guess who made it after all!" I said, sounding extra chipper, hoping she'd follow my lead.

She didn't.

Mom shook hands with Griffin. "Mr. Ploof," said Mom, managing to sound polite and cold at the same time.

"Sister Stark," he said, unwittingly getting things off to bad start. According to my mom, any adult who calls her Sister Stark outside of church is probably a con artist. "Such a pleasure to finally meet you!"

"Likewise," she said, her lack of enthusiasm in stark contrast to his overabundance.

"Thank you so much for inviting me into your home at Christmas!" Mom's eyes widened with shock, but then again so did mine. "Very generous of you!" Mom shifted uncomfortably in her seat. "Wish I could stay longer, but I've got a 5:00 a.m. flight to Cleveland Christmas morning. Mother can't abide latecomers to Christmas brunch," he said, his expression momentarily grave after saying this. "But, not to worry, I'm sure you'll find someone to take me!"

"I'll take you," said Peter.

"I thought you'd already be snowshoeing it back to your igloo," said Griffin, which he followed with an undeserved chuckle.

"No, I'll also be staying at the Starks for Christmas," said Peter, making me wonder what happened to *No, I couldn't possibly.*

"Fantastic!" cried Griffin.

"I don't know about fantastic," said Mom, reminding me of a doctor about to share grim news. "You see, I only offered to have Peter stay after you told us you weren't coming, so I am very sorry, but there's really no room in the inn."

"There's always room in the inn at Christmas for out-of-town guests," I said, more forceful than friendly.

Mom smoothed her skirt. "Mary and Joseph were out-of-town guests and they slept in a barn."

"Barn's out for me," said Griffin. "I've got a touch of sciatica."

Dad returned to the table with two frothy pink drinks. "Hello, hello," he said brightly.

"Dad, you've met my friend, Peter, and this is my boyfriend, Griffin Ploof."

Dad put down the drinks and shook their hands. "What a pleasure. Are you both staying with us? I hope so. If you haven't heard, this Christmas we're scooching!"

"That's right! We're scooching!" I said, my eyes focused on my mother.

Mom folded her arms in defeat. "Sophie, you'll sort this out."

"I will, Mom."

"Let's go, Howard," she said. "I have a headache." Dad tried to get her to first enjoy her drink, but she refused, and the two of them left. She did this, of course, to make me feel guilty. It was her little message: *You're forcing me to have one more guest for Christmas, and that has given me a headache and robbed me of my previous thirst! I hope you're proud of yourself.* She could be so dramatic when she didn't get her way. Fortunately, though, I hadn't robbed her of her ability to enjoy herself at a lavish wedding. She led my dad over to a table with a pair of empty chairs by their friends, the Curtises, and soon they were chatting and ordering more dessert and, you guessed it, frothy drinks. Whew.

If Griffin had wanted to learn all about life at the South Pole, he had a strange way of showing it. Digging into all three entrees (I guess when you survive a flight like his, you don't hold back), he told Peter all about Hawaii, and the new passion (his word) in his life that led him there.

"Recently I've embraced the didgeridoo, and I've got to tell you it's been beyond fantastic," he said, chewing and chewing and chewing part of a roll, the mush in his mouth getting tossed around like laundry in a front loader. Griffin regularly entertained clients at five star restaurants, but sometimes, when excited, it was easy for him to forget to do simple things, like swallow.

"You embraced the what?" asked Peter.

"The didgeridoo," said Griffin. "That long instrument played by the Aborigines."

"So you served your mission in Australia?"

Griffin paused to shovel braised asparagus and another chunk of roll into his mouth. "No, Delaware, but since hearing it for the first time two months ago, I've been overwhelmed by the simplicity and genius of it."

"Doesn't it sound like a whale?" asked Peter.

"To the untrained ear, sure. But to the careful listener, it bursts with variety."

Whale variety, I wanted to say, but I didn't. I just sat there, listening to Griffin chew.

"And it's a completely different animal when you hear it in concert," said Griffin. "Just ask Sophie."

Peter looked at me, knowing without asking that I enjoyed the didgeridoo about as much as fingers on a chalkboard. "You've taken Sophie to a didgeridoo concert?"

"We live in New York City, Peter, the heartbeat of the world!" said Griffin, cutting off a hunk of filet mignon and stuffing it in his mouth. "Everything is at our fingertips." Bits of partially chewed meat protruded from his mouth, making me think of cavemen and dating rituals that involved dragging the one you liked by the hair. "So, yes, I've taken Sophie to a concert." Griffin tilted his head back and laughed. "In fact, we try to hit one a week." This was true. For the past several months we had attended weekly didgeridoo concerts together, and without him clubbing me over the head first.

"Wow," said Peter, shaking his head.

Griffin swallowed, proof positive even hasty prayers are answered. "We've seen all the big names in the business," he went on, "and even gotten connected with some of the powers that be, which is how I found out about the conference in Waikiki this past week. And, of course, once I knew about it, you know I had to go!"

"Of course," said Peter.

"It required moving some things around, and unfortunately, I had to miss Sophie's company party, but it all worked out in the end!"

It was probably not a good idea for Griffin to mention my company party, since thinking about it made me want to kick him. Who knew telling your boss your boyfriend's a no-show because he's at a didgeridoo conference would bring forth howls of laughter. HOWLS! I grabbed a frothy drink off a passing tray and drank deeply.

By the time Griffin was finished with his conference recap, the party was winding down. Stifling a yawn, I waved good-bye to George as he left, a flowery diaper bag slung over one shoulder and a sleeping Albert in his arms. Watching my brother, my heart pinged, aching, but for what I wasn't sure. All I knew was that it left me feeling empty, which was ludicrous. The one thing my life wasn't was empty! I had a great job, a small but well-situated apartment in New York City, lots of friends, and a super serious boyfriend. Sure, he liked an instrument that—I'm not going to sugarcoat it—I hated, but every couple had their differences, didn't they? And besides, giving Griffin the space to pursue something of his own made me feel like a good girlfriend. As we got up to leave, Peter reached for my chair and Griffin for his phone. "Oh! There's one last photo from Waikiki I've got to show you!" he said.

I looked at a picture of my boyfriend arm in arm with yet another international didgeridoo superstar and whatever hollowness I'd previously felt was filled, regrettably, with annoyance. Seriously, how many didgeridoo aficionados did the world need? Griffin raced after a waiter to see if he could get a frothy drink in a to-go cup, and Peter and I started to exit the tent, but before we had made much progress, Hanno stumbled toward us. "Hey, hey, my man," he said, giving Peter a hug. "Means the world to us that you came. And Sofa!" He gave me a sloppy kiss on my cheek. "It's been forever! So good to see you." He hooked an arm around both of us. "So have you two met yet?"

My mouth fell open. He didn't remember?

"Actually," said Peter, "we're just getting to know each other."

Hanno motioned to a waiter carrying a tray of champagne-filled flutes. "Cool," he said, taking one of the bubbling, thin glasses and handing another to Peter. "Let's drink to that."

Peter put the drink down on a table. "Hanno, you're forgetting I joined your Church."

Hanno smacked his forehead, making his drink slop a little over the edge. "That's right! My one convert. Oh, how I love rubbing that in George's face. Where is he?"

"He had to take the kids home," I said.

Hanno gulped down his champagne. "What have I gotten myself into?" he asked, trying to mask his fear with a smile.

"What have you gotten yourself into?" said Peter. "If this baby gets your nose, Ingrid will never forgive you."

Hanno touched his flawless nose. "Very funny, man."

"Come on," said Peter. "It will be a pleasure—a sleep-deprived pleasure."

Wincing, Hanno grabbed Peter's discarded glass of champagne and raised it high. "To nannies and boarding schools," he said, slurring his words a little.

"To your baby melting your heart and throwing your world happily out of whack," said Peter.

"You just want my snowboard."

"Don't be ridiculous. What I want is your condo in St. Moritz."

"My friend, any time, any time at all," said Hanno, giving Peter another hug. "And, Sophe." He put his arms around me and rocked back and forth, extending the hug, making it seem like he didn't want to let go. And to be honest, I didn't mind. We were friends, childhood friends, and it felt good to rekindle that. Besides, if Hanno had forgotten about Peter and me meeting in Italy, maybe he'd forgotten other things. Hope flickered inside me . . . until it didn't. "Try to keep the shampoo out of your eyes, sweetheart," he said as we rocked back and forth one last time, and I reminded myself that it's never good form to strangle the groom at a wedding. "And get to know this guy." He released me and pointed at Peter. "I'm telling you, he's one of the good ones."

Peter, his eyebrows raised in a hopeful look, moved his hands in slow circles, as if trying to coax more compliments out of his friend.

Hanno shoved him in the shoulder.

"I'll keep that in mind," I said, spotting Griffin, to-go cup tucked in one arm, handing Hanno's bride his business card. "I'll keep that in mind."

chapter 8

HAVING DEEMED THE daybed in my mother's sewing room (a.k.a George's childhood room) squishy but serviceable, Griffin climbed into bed and was snoring before I could return to give him the second pillow he'd requested, not to mention a kiss good night. "Sleep tight, Griffin," I whispered and shut his door. Arms full of bedding, I headed downstairs and found Peter sitting at the bar in the kitchen, looking at his phone.

"Texting someone?" I asked.

Peter kept his eyes on the screen. I liked the way they narrowed when he was concentrating. "No, just comparing prices."

"On what?"

"Didgeridoos. I swear your super serious boyfriend has lit a fire."

I knew what he was trying to do, and it wasn't going to work. I wasn't going to open up and tell him that the only fire I wanted lit was one made with stacks and stacks of a certain aboriginal musical instrument. That's not the sort of thing a loyal girlfriend admits to, so I did the only thing I could—I smiled and changed the subject. "Where are we going to put you?" I asked, placing the bedding on my mother's gleaming countertop.

"I'm going to guess that the white couch in the living room with a sign on it saying "DO NOT SLEEP HERE!" is off limits."

I sighed. "Yeah, that's a safe bet." I closed my eyes, trying to focus, and felt sleepiness bump me like a gentle wave. "Let me think, let me think," I said. "The family room? No, it's right by the kitchen."

"I don't mind," said Peter.

I looked at him. "My parents make waffles Christmas Eve morning. Trust me, you'll mind. What about the study?"

"Sure," said Peter.

"No, I forgot. My mom switched out the couch in there for a love seat."

Peter rubbed his hands together like we'd found the answer. "I love love seats." I gave him a disapproving look. "On second thought, I hate love seats," he said.

I leaned against the counter. "There is no way you're cramming yourself into a love seat. And you're not sleeping on the floor, not at Christmas. I'm not going to be like, 'Welcome to my house for the holidays. Now let me show you where you and the dog will be sleeping.'"

Peter put his hands on my shoulders. "Sophia, you don't have a dog."

"Yes, I do! Well, buried in the backyard," I said, gesturing to the patio door.

"What about out there?" asked Peter, pointing to the patio.

"So now you want to sleep with the parakeet."

"You don't have a parakeet."

"Did. It's buried next to the dog."

I slid open the glass door that led out to the porch. Illuminated by the soft glow of a bug zapper was a double hammock, acquired sometime since my last visit. "Won't you feel like you're on a boat?"

Peter stretched out on the hammock, giving it a try. "No, this will be perfect. I've got the moon and the stars, fresh air, and moldering pets nearby."

In the half light of the porch, I could see him again, the Peter I met ten years ago, standing in the rain outside my hostel, wearing a pained expression, and I had to resist the urge to reach out and touch his hand. I cleared my throat. "But don't you think it's a little chilly out here?" I said, the mound of bedding still in my arms.

Peter stood up and took the bedding from me, his hand brushing against mine. "I promise, it's not even close to a little chilly."

"Oh, right," I said, folding my arms. "I forget that you live in a freezer."

"Or as we at the research center like to call it, the Big Popsicle." Peter handed me one end of the sheet and together we spread it out over the hammock. "Sort of like the Big Apple, only without expensive real estate, and the penguins don't live at the zoo." We unfolded the blanket. It was thick and Downy fresh. (According to my mother, a woman's devotion to her family was measured by her use of top-brand fabric softener.) We draped the blanket over one end of the hammock. "Plus the subway system's not the best," he added.

I grabbed his pillow and fluffed it. "But you can see the stars," I said, placing the pillow on the hammock.

"Yes, but you can't hold them," he said, looking at me. "Even though they feel so close, within reach, and you're practically convinced it's what you're meant to do, born to do. Yet they stay, as always, beyond your grasp."

The zapper buzzed, signaling that a bug's life had come to a hasty end.

My heart banged against my chest like it was trying to break free. "Well, uh." I paused to gulp. "I guess every place has its pros and cons." He was talking about stars, right?

Not knowing what else to do, I gave the pillow one last fluff and turned to go. "The guest bathroom is just down the hall. Is there anything else you need?"

"Actually, would it be okay if I made myself some warm milk?" asked Peter. "It's sort of a bedtime ritual."

"Of course," I said, "help yourself," and I bent down to take off my shoes. My feet were killing me.

Peter reached to open the sliding glass door and brushed against my shoulder. It wasn't deliberate, just a random touch, the sort of thing that happened all the time in life, so why was I hyperaware of it with him? "Great," he said, "and if you see your super serious boyfriend, tell him I'm planning to run at seven. He wanted to join me."

"*Griffin* is asleep, but I'll leave him a note," I said, stressing his name to send the message that's what I'd prefer he call him.

Peter ignored this. "Good night, Sophia," he said and gave me a hug, the quick, friendly kind, but it triggered memories all the same, memories of Italy, celebrating in the streets, and kissing in the rain. Kissing Peter.

I shook my head a little to clear it. "Good night, Peter," I said and started for the stairs.

After sticking a Post-It Note to Griffin's door, I got ready for bed and waited for my heart to stop hammering. What was it? Why did I feel so unsettled? I prayed, read a chapter from the Book of Mormon (without paying attention to a single word), checked my phone for texts (there was one from my boss, Dale Dilwooten, telling me to call him ASAP) and then crawled into bed, certain that sleep would come quickly, and it did . . . until it didn't.

"Hey! Hey! Wake up!" someone shouted. That's what I remember happened first. Well, that and getting shoved repeatedly in the shoulder. It was a valiant effort, but I was in a deep sleep, and my eyelids refused to open.

"Wake up!" came another cry.

I tried to say, *Just give me a minute*, but sleepy as I was, it came out more like, "Juh-guh-min-uh," with a whole lot of lip smacking after.

There was another shove to my shoulder, this one hard enough to make my eyelids budge, but not for long. I turned on my side, hugging my pillow. "Can't this wait?" I asked, already drifting asleep again.

"No, it can't wait! That's the whole point! You've had long enough! I'm sick of waiting!" said a shrill and desperate voice. I was awake enough to make out that whoever was speaking to me was around ten, a girl, and possibly wearing braces. But I was groggy, deeply groggy, so a preteen yelling at me in my parents' home in the middle of the night didn't really seem that odd to me. And I succumbed again to deep, hard, near-comatose sleep.

"WAKE UP!" came another shout, this time right in my ear.

My eyes blinked open. What was going on? Who was waking me up at this hour, not to mention everyone else in the house? I was surprised my mother hadn't already burst into my bedroom, tying her robe, ready to get to the bottom of the situation. I rubbed my eyes and then, looking around, said, "Okay, okay, I'm up!"

My closet light was on and moonlight was pouring through the open window, plenty of light to see the young girl sitting at the foot of my bed. She had ropey, honey-colored hair that fell to the middle of her back, almond-shaped eyes that even in the subdued light I could tell were a deep dark brown, and spindly legs that seemed to reach to her armpits. She sat cross-legged on my bed, her bony elbows and knees jutting, sharp as arrows. Her smile was tinny (I knew I heard braces!) and reached from ear to ear, and she wore silky pajamas covered with hearts, peace signs, and a boy band I couldn't place.

"Finally! Finally! Finally! You're awake!" she said, bouncing a little as she spoke, making the frame of my bed squeak.

I propped myself up on my elbows. "Excuse me, do I know you?"

She bit her lip. "Not exactly, but sort of, kind of, more like you should, or you will, you hopefully will, but you don't, not yet, and that's why I'm here. Does that make sense?" she asked, bouncing still (someone get this kid a trampoline) and twisting a bit of hair around her finger.

"Uh, not really. Do you live down the street?"

"Nope."

"Where's your mother?"

"Here."

I lay back down. "Then go talk to her."

"I am talking to her."

"Sweetie, I'm tired. I don't have time for this."

"It's always about you! I'm the one who doesn't have time for this! I'm the one who doesn't have time!" she cried, switching from peppy to dramatic.

I rubbed my face, hoping that when I was finished she'd have vanished, like a bad, loud, obnoxious dream. But she didn't. She was there. I propped up to my elbows again, determined to stay calm. "Sweetheart, what's your name?"

She jutted her chin and folded her arms tight against her. "How am I supposed to know?"

I sat up. "What do you mean how are you supposed to know?"

"That's your job."

"Why would that be my job?"

"Because that's what moms do, geez!" she said, swapping pouty for impatient. This girl's emotions were all over the map.

"Mom? You think I'm your mom?" I asked, confused.

"Duh," she said, laying on the attitude.

The situation reminded me of the time I landed in Tokyo and a driver at the airport patted his cardboard sign and grabbed my bag. And though I tried to tell him "Sorry, pal, I'm not Nell Wilcox from Waco, Texas," he just wouldn't accept it.

"Sweetheart," I said, determined to stay calm, "I have never had a baby."

"Tell me about it," she grumbled.

My resolve was short lived. "Oh my gosh!" I cried. "You're driving me crazy!"

"No, you're driving me crazy!" she shouted, peaking her knees and hiding her face behind them.

I took a deep breath. "Look, what do you want from me?"

"To be born, Mom. I want to be born." Her attitude melted, and all that was left was sadness.

At this point I wouldn't have been surprised to see Alice sprinting across my bedroom after the Mad Hatter. I touched the hem of her pajamas (making her jump back like I was a cobra), caught a whiff of her peach-flavored lip gloss, noticed her fingernail polish— splotchy electric blue dots on a white background that appeared to me to be the ambitious attempt of a best friend on a boring day. She wasn't real, and yet, somehow I understood that in a sliver of space between waking and sleeping, she was very real, she was here, and she was mine.

chapter **9**

I LOOKED AT MY alarm clock. It was three in the morning, the perfect time to have a conversation with a tweener. I took a deep breath. "Hey," I said, my voice deliberately soft, "I'm sorry I snapped," which, for some reason, made her pout harder. "I should have handled *this*"—I drew a circle in the air between us—"better." Of course, this wasn't the truth. I thought I'd handled the situation pretty well considering I hadn't fainted, but when it came to pacifying a prepubescent, you had to do what you had to do—even if it meant saying sorry when you were absolutely, positively, 100 percent free of blame.

She wiped her nose on her forearm (ick). "It's all right," she said, her voice quavering. "I guess it's not every day you meet your future daughter, and that it's sorta weird and creepy." She burst into sobs, woe-is-me-the-world-is-ending sobs, and then used the back of her hand as her Kleenex of choice (double ick).

I grabbed a tissue off my nightstand and handed it to her. "Okay, first let's get your nose under control." She blew hard, wadded up the gooey tissue, and left it on my bedspread. "Probably not the best place for that," I said, using the end of a pencil to pick it up and toss it in the trash.

"You hate me!" she cried.

"No, I don't."

"Yes, you do! You can't even handle my boogers. How are you going to handle what I'll do to a diaper as a baby? This is hopeless. HOPELESS!" She tilted her head back, sobbing, reminding me of Charlie Brown and Snoopy when hysterical—their big mouths open wide, exposing their dangling uvulas.

I touched her arm. It felt so small, so thin. "No, I don't hate you. Really, I don't. But you're right about one thing. This is weird. Not bad weird, just weird. And I'm still trying to wrap my head around what's happening." I handed her another tissue. "Maybe you could help me do that, better understand what's going on here. What do you say?" She blew her nose and then put the used tissue on the end of the pencil I was extending toward her. "You see, we're starting to get the hang of this already!"

She dried her eyes with the palms of her hands. "Fine," she said. "What do you not get?"

Prickles of irritation rippled over me. What did I not get? How about everything! I took a breath and forced myself to sound pleasant. "Well, for starters," I said, pulling out a bottle of hand sanitizer from my drawer and handing it to her, "why are you here now?"

She squirted a too-tiny dot into her hands and rubbed them together.

"Maybe just a smidge more," I suggested.

She huffed. "Quit telling me what to do!"

Ugh. Being the bigger person was exhausting. "Sorry, my mistake. I was just trying to help," I said, sounding so composed that I wondered if I had missed my calling in life and instead of an advertising agent I should have become someone who talks people off ledges. "How about we get back to my question?" She nodded. "What brings you to my bedroom tonight?"

Without shutting the lid, she tossed the hand sanitizer onto the bed, but I didn't say a word. If I had learned anything since waking up (was I awake?) it was that in preteen land, well-meaning suggestions were often mistaken for personal attacks.

"Well," she said, brightening a little, "I already told you that you're taking forever to get married."

"Or stepping cautiously toward a decision of profound importance."

She knit her brow, her face clouding. "Did you just agree with me?"

"Sure," I said. Whatever it took to avoid a meltdown.

"So, it's time, Mom, and I—"

"I agree. You're right," I said, cutting in. "And I have good news. I think he's going to ask me to marry him!" Her eyes lit up and she clapped her hands. "We click on so many levels, as you perhaps know, and he came all the way here." She was nodding, agreeing with everything I said, her head moving up and down like a jostled bobble head. "It's not official yet, but I really think that once we've found the right apartment and we're a little farther along in our careers, Griffin will—"

She blew a raspberry.

"What's that supposed to mean?" I asked.

"I don't want Griffin to be my dad," she said, her voice whiny. "He's a doofus."

"No," I said, trying to tap into my supply of get-off-the-ledge calm, but it was nowhere to be found. "He's not a doofus; he's a hedge fund manager," I said, noticeably edgy.

"Same thing!" she said

I pressed my palms to my eyes, tired and tired of trying to be reasonable with someone who wasn't. "Look, I don't want to be rude, but this is my decision, not yours."

Her eyes glistened with fresh tears. "Why should it just be your decision when whoever you marry is going to be my dad!"

She had a point, but I wasn't going to admit it. "Well, you can trust that as your future mom, I will pick a good guy for your dad."

Tears were now spilling down her cheeks. "But you're going to get it wrong and this isn't a decision that comes with a do-over! I want a dad, not a hedge fund manager!"

I was losing my cool. "This is silly. All dads have to work, and I would think you'd want one who could provide well! When the time comes and you're clamoring for horseback riding lessons or tennis lessons or a week at sleepaway camp, you'll be glad your dad is a hedge fund manager!"

I had raised my voice a little, but she took it as license to scream. "I WANT A DAD WHO LOVES ME MORE THAN HIS JOB! AND IS FUN AND DOESN'T PLAY A STUPID INSTRUMENT—"

"Well, I'll give you that," I mumbled

"WHO WILL DROP EVERYTHING FOR MY PRE-SCHOOL GRADUATION AND BALLET RECITALS AND WILL WRITE ME NOTES AND LEAVE THEM IN MY LUNCH BOX AND GET UP IN THE MIDDLE OF THE NIGHT WHEN I'M AFRAID AND BE PATIENT WHEN I'M LEARNING HOW TO DRIVE AND CALL ME JUST TO SAY HELLO AND NEVER EVER BE AWKWARD AND HAVE TO SOUND LIKE SOMEONE FROM STAR WARS WHEN HE'S TRYING TO SAY HE LOVES ME. AND I KNOW GRIFFIN WOULD LOVE ME, IN HIS OWN WAY, BUT DON'T MAKE ME HAVE TO LOVE HIM, MOM! I DON'T WANT HIM! AND DON'T TAKE SO LONG TO FIGURE OUT WHO THE RIGHT GUY IS THAT I SLIP AWAY!"

I'm not going to lie, she had my attention. "Okay, okay," I said, placing my hands on her shaking shoulders. "Let's assume for a moment Griffin isn't the right guy for me, which I'm not saying is the case. Who do you think I'm supposed to marry then?"

She sniffed and gave me a puzzled look, like I was asking her what was the color of grass. "Peter De Boom, of course," she said.

Stunned, my arms fell slack at my sides. "Peter?" I said, disbelieving, "I hardly know him," but as I said it, I could feel again his hand clasped in mine, and his gentle tug as he navigated our way through the soccer-crazed streets of Florence. And I could feel his cheek, slightly scruffy brushing against mine as he leaned in to kiss me. I shook my head like I had water in my ears. *That was ten years ago!* I told myself. *We were practically kids! So much has happened since then.*

My future daughter was bouncing on my bed again (lucky me).

"Don't worry, Mom," she said, gathering her hair to the side and beginning to braid it, "all you need to do is get to know Peter, fall in love with him, have him fall in love with you, say yes when he proposes, and get married fast." She lowered her eyes on me. "A long engagement is out."

"So should we shoot for getting engaged by New Year's?" I asked, sounding calm though close to blowing my stack.

She stopped braiding her hair and gave me a concerned look. "New Year's is in nine days. Don't you think that's rushing it?"

"You're the one in a rush!" I cried. "In fact, you're in such a rush that you're here, even though you're not supposed to show up until the delivery room at a hospital or an upscale holistic birthing center. I haven't decided. But my point is, you're supposed to come later—after I've decided who I'm going to marry, and not chiming in with an opinion before!"

As soon as I saw her chin quiver I regretted all of it. I should have known that losing my cool would get us nowhere, but she was so frustrating, making outlandish demands, telling me who to marry. I loved Griffin! He was sweet and sometimes funny and so good-looking that all my girlfriends were jealous. And wealthy! He was just thirty and already owned a third of a house in the Hamptons. Yet none of that mattered to my future daughter. In her opinion he was a doofus. Sure, Peter was handsome and easy to talk to, not to mention rugged (I guess living at the South Pole does that to you), but that didn't mean he was the one for me. To be honest, I didn't believe in "the one"—the idea that somewhere in the world there was a person meant just for you. It was fairy-tale garbage. Marriage, when you got right down to it, was a lot like a business merger and Griffin was a great future partner.

I pressed my hands to my face and groaned. "I think as a future mother and daughter, we need to establish a rule that we don't yell at each other anymore."

"You're the one who just yelled at me!" she cried. Outside, darkness was lifting, making it easier to see how adorable she looked when she tucked her chin in anger.

"I know, and I shouldn't have done that. Even though you were insisting I marry a guy I barely know, I should have kept my cool."

She wiped her nose on her sleeve (heaven help me). "Fine, I won't yell at you either, unless you make me really angry."

"Well, that's a start," I said and put my hand out to shake. Slowly, she did the same.

"But you're not sticking me with Griffin for life," she said, sounding determined.

"That's for me to decide," I said, equally determined.

"Then we need to establish another rule," she said, her hands curled tight into fists. "Until you're engaged to Peter, I'm not going to rest . . . and neither will you." Just then, the sun poured through the window and my future daughter vanished. I rubbed my tired eyes and looked at the clock. It was eight in the morning.

chapter 10

"OH MY HEAVENS, you look terrible!" said my mother as I sat at the bar in the kitchen.

"Well, I don't know about terrible," said Dad. "A little pooped maybe."

Mom untied her apron and draped it over a nearby chair. "Howard, if she had bags like those under her eyes yesterday, the airline would have charged her extra. Take over. I'm getting my Princess Marguerite concealer. It's amazing; nurses who work the graveyard shift love it."

I didn't have the strength to stop her.

"Rough night?" asked Dad.

I leaned on the counter, propping my head up with my hand. "You could say that," I said. "Where are Griffin and Peter?"

"Out on a run," said Dad. "Griffin said he peeked in to see if you wanted to come, but you were sleeping like a baby."

"I suppose looks can be deceiving," I muttered, but it was drowned out by my mother rushing in to save my appearance. She stood in front of me, frowning. "You're not twenty anymore," she said, applying the concealer under my eyes with a skilled hand. "You need your beauty rest and a little help from Princess Marguerite." She handed me a little mirror to inspect her work, and I had to admit I looked better.

"Thanks, Mom."

She tutted. "My guess is guilt wouldn't let you rest last night."

"I don't know what her name is yet, but that definitely won't be it," I mumbled, but my parents didn't hear me. My dad had started whipping heavy cream in the mixer, and Mom, undeterred by the whirring, had continued to speak.

"I can't believe you let Griffin stay upstairs! Just two doors down from you. What must the neighbors think?"

"Probably that your Christmas village has engulfed the guest bedroom," I said, accepting a cup of cocoa from my father. It was hot and sweet and helped lift my fatigue.

My mother dismissed this comment by cranking up the mixer. "I walked out of my bedroom this morning, and there he was, heading to the bathroom in his robe!" she practically shouted.

"Scandalous," I mumbled into my cocoa.

"When you're single, all male guests should be kept downstairs, and not just for appearance's sake. You never know when you could be swept away by a moment of weakness."

This was a perfect example why I hadn't been home to visit in two years. My mother said things that drove me crazy. Dad turned off the mixer and the two of them got busy chopping strawberries. "Mom," I said, "if we were interested in messing around, Griffin being downstairs wouldn't have stopped us."

Mom kept chopping, her eyes darting from me to the cutting board and back again. "It's like the story about the stage coach and the cliff's edge. Howard, you remember that story."

"I do not remember that story," he said, cutting much slower.

"Yes, you do. And the moral of it is caution." She pointed her paring knife at me, as if doing so reinforced the point. "You cannot be too careful."

"So you want me to booby-trap my room?"

"Sophia, don't say that word."

What I wouldn't have given for a ticket on the next plane out of Phoenix, but even if I had one, there was no way. I was too tired. I had hoped to sleep through breakfast, assuming that while the sun was up my future daughter wouldn't bother me. But the minute I closed my eyes and started to drift to sleep, there she was, dressed in a green-and-blue plaid school uniform and playing a very squeaky clarinet. So I took a freezing shower to jolt myself awake, dressed in the denim capris and striped boatneck shirt I had just bought at J. Crew, and headed downstairs for waffles and what I knew would be stimulating conversation with my mother.

I was just about to say something (snide) to my mother when the kitchen door swung open and Griffin strutted in, followed by a somewhat beleaguered-looking Peter. "Good morning to all!" said Griffin. He planted a sweaty kiss on my cheek, and then breathed/growled/whispered in my ear, "Sophie, I am your boyfriend," trying to sound like an affectionate Darth Vader, but resembling more a heavy smoker.

"How was the run?" I asked, rubbing my ear.

"Fantastic!" said Griffin, stealing a strawberry despite my mother's disapproving glare.

Bent over with his hands on his knees, Peter was still catching his breath. "It was good," he said. "Griffin gave me a run for my money." He looked at me and his face clouded with worry—just the reaction every girl dreams of. "Are you all right?" he asked.

I smiled. "Yes, I just didn't sleep well."

Griffin looked at me and frowned with concern. "You know," he said, "the lower tones of the didgeridoo are said to have medicinal properties. I bought one at the conference. If you like, I could race upstairs—"

"No!" I shouted, like someone was about to get hit by a bus, then coughed, trying to peg my outburst on a scratchy throat. "Thank you, but no."

Peter washed his hands and dried them on a paper towel. "Are you feeling sick?" he asked, pressing his hand to my forehead, his gentle touch making me feel even sleepier.

"No rest for the wicked," said Mom. No one asked her to explain this.

"No," I said, "I'm fine. But until George and Margaret get here, I think I'll just put my feet up and watch the boob tube."

Mother shot me a look.

"I'll sit with you," Peter said. "Griffin called dibs on the shower anyway."

Griffin took a long whiff of the stack of fresh waffles, his nose closer to them than my mother preferred. "I'll be back soon to gobble these up."

Mom waited until Griffin was darting up the stairs before saying, "We do not gobble in this house, even at Christmas."

"It's just a figure of speech, Evelyn," said my dad as he slid the last of the strawberries into the large glass bowl.

"I don't like it," she said flatly. "It makes me think of cavemen, turkeys, and Pac-Men with their never-ending appetites."

"It makes me think of peach cobbler," said Dad.

"Don't be absurd," she said, as usual, refusing to let him have an opinion. "Come on, Howard, George and Margaret will be here soon and we haven't started the eggs and bacon."

I walked casually, but the truth was I couldn't get away from her fast enough. Peter, not wanting to sit on the couch (especially after my mother suggested he not), brought up a wooden bench to where I sat and then took my wrist between his fingers. "You let her get under your skin too easily," he said, his eyes fixed on his watch.

Though the family room was connected to the kitchen, it was spacious enough that I didn't fear being overheard. Plus my parents were at it again with the mixer. "You can tell that by taking my pulse?"

"No, your clenched jaw gave it away."

"Hmm."

Peter took my face in his hands and gently pulled on my lower eyelids with his thumbs. "Learn to embrace her quirkiness. It will lower your risk of heart disease. Of course, listening to Griffin play a few low notes will most likely do the same."

"You give me options like that and you call yourself a doctor!" I said, my voice rising enough that my mother chimed in.

"So Peter," she said, "what made you decide not to go on and become a doctor? Did it seem too hard?"

I gave Peter a knowing look.

"Just the path I chose," he said, which didn't interest her as much as the bacon she was frying, and she left us alone.

"You see," I said as he pressed his fingers to either side of my neck.

"Shh, Sophia. Don't let it get to you," he whispered.

I thought about telling him why that was impossible, but the truth was I was drowning in his touch; it felt almost like sleeping.

"Why couldn't you sleep last night?" he asked.

His exam was finished and my neck felt cold. "I can't explain it," I said, which was true. How could I tell him that I'd spent the night arguing with my future daughter about him? No, I wasn't going there, unless, maybe, he too had received a visit. I decided to check. "And you, did you sleep well?"

"I was out cold," he said.

"So unfair," I said, because it was unfair. Weren't both parents supposed to be up all night? Not that we were parents. We weren't anything, but still!

George and Margaret opened the kitchen door, and Albert, spotting Peter, came running over and jumped in his lap. "You're stinky," said Albert.

"And you're . . . ticklish," said Peter, jabbing Albert in the ribs. Albert protested until unable to stop himself, he erupted in giggles.

This went on until Griffin, appearing out of nowhere, poked Albert in the side and said, "Hey there, sport!"

Albert ran to his parents. The party was over.

"Don't take it personally, Griffin. He's just shy," I said. Griffin wasn't taking it personally. He was texting.

"Breakfast will be ready soon. You better get cleaned up," I said.

"Okay, boss," Peter said.

"Boss!" I cried. "Oh no! I was supposed to call my boss first thing this morning!" I raced up the stairs to get my phone, not bothering to answer my mother's questions about why I was suddenly bright-eyed and bushy-tailed. Flying into my room, I snatched my phone from its cord, and, as my heart jumped into my throat, noticed I'd missed two calls, both from my boss, Dale Dilwooten. Mr. Dilwooten was *the* Dilwooten of Percy Dilwooten Foster, the advertising firm where I worked. He was a no frills, get-to-the-point kind of guy who liked to make money—no, loved to make money—but hated to talk on the phone, which meant he spoke in choppy, rushed sentences that reminded me of telegraph messages in old movies and made me jittery, because if there was one thing Dale Dilwooten didn't like it was a long answer to a short question.

Rehearsing my concise apology, I sat down on my unmade bed and pressed "call back" on my phone screen. Mr. Dilwooten picked up after the first ring. "Miss Stark, finally you call."

"Sor—"

"Not to worry. Good news. Got a chance at the Luxe Air account. Handing you the creative reins for the pitch. Your thoughts?"

This was huge, spectacular news, and I was speechless, which, considering who I was talking to, was probably a good thing. I gulped back rising self-doubt. "Great," I finally said.

"Strict deadline attached to deal. Must get working ASAP. Need presentation by Dec. 30. Can you do it?"

"Yes," I said, because that's what you say when your boss is handing you the opportunity of a lifetime.

"Good. Call if needed. Best of luck."

"Best of luck to you too, er, uh, enjoying Christmas." I squinted in agony. What a stupid thing to say.

"Will need it. At the in-laws. Merry Christmas."

"Merry—" I started, but there was no point in finishing; Mr. Dilwooten had hung up. I lay back on my bed, phone in hand, and let excitement and fear settle over me. I was going to head up the Luxe Air pitch! Or was I going to be sick? Clammy and covered in goose bumps, I rolled on my side, clutching my stomach, and tried to think of what I knew about Luxe Air. They were a new player in the airline industry and wanted to become *the* name in luxury business travel from New York to London. Presentation emphasis would be on perks, not price. Not an airline for the budget traveler. And certainly not an airline for schoolchildren practicing the clarinet, so why was there one in front of me?

My future daughter played the last few notes of "The Eye of the Tiger," then she waved at me, clarinet in hand. "Hey, Mom," she said, leaning back in her chair and propping up her feet, tennis shoes and all, on my bed.

I sat up. "Hello again," I said, giving her a disapproving look and pointing to the floor.

She huffed but put her feet on the ground.

"Young lady, those are the same shoes you wear inside the bathroom at school. They should come off before you walk in the door."

"Actually, Mom, I've never stepped inside a school bathroom. You gotta be born to do that. It's one of those quirky rules," she said, not holding back on the sarcasm.

My body tensed. Her mouthiness bugged me, but not as much as my bossiness. What was it about having a daughter—even a future one—that turned you into a control freak? So far, motherhood wasn't much like the happy vignettes I'd created for diaper commercials. I took a breath, trying to stay calm. "I realize you want to be born,"

"Super bad, Mom. I wish I was born yesterday," she said, wanting to be taken seriously, but the combination of her unintended meaning and her lower lip jutting struck me as hilarious.

I tried not to laugh. My instincts were telling me that doing so would offend, but though I pressed my lips together, laughter broke through. And unfortunately, once my giggle switch is flipped, it takes time to turn off. "Sorry, sorry," I said, gaining composure, only to dissolve into another fit of laughter.

"It's not funny!" she cried, dropping her clarinet, diving onto my bed, and burying her face in my pillow.

I touched her leg. "You're right, it's not funny." I exhaled loudly. "I don't know what came over me."

"You hate me!" she sobbed.

"I do not hate you," I said, stroking her hair, expecting at any moment for her to bat my hand away, but she didn't.

She turned her head to me, pressing her wet cheek against my pillow and letting a thin line of drool dangle from her mouth. "Yes, you do!" she said. "You think it's funny I'm sad. If I broke my arm, you'd probably fall over laughing!"

I continued to stroke her hair, tucking it behind her ear. "That's not true," I said.

"You don't want me. You haven't even bothered to name me," she said, tears and drool now falling freely.

I swear once she was born I was going to have to get a job at Pottery Barn just for the employee discount. This girl was tough on bedding.

"Of course I want you," I said. And I did want her. Crazy as she made things, just touching her hair sent an ache of longing through me. "But naming you is no small decision. You'll have that name for life."

"Duh!" she said, anger making her eyebrows almost bump into each other.

I smiled like I didn't mind being interrupted. "Naming you is not something I want to be hasty about," I said. "Trust me, I'm mulling it over, but it's not just my decision to make. I'm sure your dad will want to have a say in the matter." This slowed her tears, but she still looked wounded. "I'm sorry about laughing. Really, I am. Is there anything I can do to make it up to you?"

She sat up, her eyes suddenly wide with hope. "Yes, break up with Griffin," she said.

I sighed. "Can't do that."

"Why not?" she asked, her eyebrows colliding again.

"Because I love him," I said.

"You *think* you're in love with him, just like you *think* your chunky black glasses make you look smart."

"They do make me look smart," I said, uncertainty making my voice uncharacteristically high.

"They look like you swiped them off a patient in a nursing home."

Yikes. Maybe she was right. "Let's try and stay focused," I said, wanting to change the subject. "What is something, *within reason*, that I can do to make it up to you?"

She sat on her knees, bouncing a little and leaning toward me with excitement. "Kiss Peter," she said, and when I rolled my eyes, she just spoke louder. "Which should totally be considered within reason since you've done it before."

"How perfect that you know that," I said through gritted teeth, wondering if it was possible to file a complaint with heaven. "Yes, I admit it. We kissed once before."

My future daughter snorted. "Once," she said, "you kissed him more than that. It was so romantic . . . and gross."

I covered my eyes with my hands for a moment, trying to stay calm. "Sweetie," I said, "I have a boyfriend now."

She was still bouncing. "Right, a super serious boyfriend, but that doesn't make you married."

"What would I be teaching you if I kissed someone other than Griffin?" I asked.

"That prayers are answered."

I pressed my hands to my head. "I don't have time for this," I said, exasperated. "Thanks to our little conversation last night, I'm running on zero sleep, right when I'm supposed to be entertaining house guests and brainstorming ad ideas."

"Come on," she said, nudging me. "Kiss Peter."

"I can't kiss Peter," I said, ignoring a faint twinge of disappointment.

My future daughter wasn't giving up. "Kiss him and I promise I'll let you sleep for three hours. No clarinet, no cymbals."

"I haven't heard any cymbals."

She nudged me again. "They're coming."

I groaned at the thought.

"All I'm asking for is one solid kiss on the lips," she said, shaking me now by the shoulders and sounding strangely like my mother. "Just one kiss! Sophia, do you hear me? Oh, for heaven's sake!" The shaking stopped, replaced by a light patting beneath my eyes. "Sophia!"

I blinked awake and just that fast my daughter left, replaced by my mother. She stood over me, looking perturbed, Princess Marguerite concealer in hand. "Honestly, Sophia," she said, smoothing a touch more concealer over my dark circles, "this isn't the time to conk out. Breakfast is ready. Everyone's downstairs waiting."

I sat up and started to rub my eyes, but my mother grabbed my hand to stop me. Her hand was soft, just like I remembered, but what I couldn't remember was the last time she had held my hand. It had been so long. There had been a time, of course, when doing so felt natural, but as I grew up she let go. Or I let go. And that was what was supposed to happen, wasn't it? After meeting my future daughter, I didn't know anymore. Did her growing up have to mean that we'd grow apart? I hadn't held her hand yet, but I knew I didn't want the day to come when I couldn't. Didn't want doing so to ever feel awkward.

My mother pulled me to my feet and then let go. "There isn't time, but you really should have done something more with your hair, and when did you last wear a skirt? You have pretty legs, Sophia. I have no idea how that Dobson girl got married with legs as squatty as hers. She is sweet, though; I'll give her that. But at any rate, a skirt would do you a world of good. Wear one tonight for Gram's Christmas Eve party. If you didn't bring one, we can dash over to the mall. But, for heaven's sake, look alive. I swear, my dear, you look like you've seen a ghost."

Don't let her get to you, I thought, remembering Peter's advice. "Sure, that'd be fun to go shopping with you, Mom."

"You're always glad to spend my money, I suppose," she said, which simultaneously bugged me and comforted me—bugged for obvious reasons, and comforted because it was proof that the distance between us wasn't just my fault. My mother could be a tough lady to love. "And you should know," she continued as we headed toward the stairs, "that if you marry Griffin—and heaven knows you're running out of time to make such a decision—not only do your children run the risk of inheriting his calves, they're much too small, but on the rare occasion you make the effort to be present at Christmas Eve breakfast, we'll be regaled with stories about how he won yet another trophy. He hasn't let anyone get a word in since you slinked off upstairs for some alone time." Make that a really tough lady to love.

As the day wore on, it felt like I had swapped out my head for a cast iron kettle bubbling over with thick, lumpy chowder made from stress, fatigue, excitement, ad ideas, girl names, really nasty things to say to my mother, guys, and how much I hated pretending to enjoy it when Griffin played the didgeridoo. Though the brew had become a blurry, bubbling mess, one thought, like heavy steam, kept rising to the top: *What was I willing to do for three hours of uninterrupted sleep?*

chapter 11

GRAM DIDN'T SKIMP when it came to Christmas lights, or anything else for that matter. She did everything big, even intimate Christmas parties for family and a few close friends. This meant every detail—decorations, food, entertainment—was lavishly done, something my mother, without fail, criticized.

"I'm sure we all appreciate the effort, Gram, but there's no need to go all out on our account," said my mother as we sat (all ten of us) around the long dining room table in Gram's mid-century home. When Sullivan Whitefield designed their home, Gramps told him he wanted to feel outside in every room, and so thick glass, protected from the scorching Arizona sun by sweeping porches, surrounded the home. It definitely made for a lack of privacy, but Gram said she didn't mind waving, and I could see her point. Set on a hill, the view was stunning, especially at night when moonlight outlined the desert landscaping and the city lights sparkled in the distance.

Mom bit into her butternut squash tortellini, nodding and mmm-ing as she chewed, eliminating any doubt about whether she was enjoying her meal. Still, Mom being Mom, she looked for reasons to complain. "This sauce is delectable," she said, savoring another bite, "but don't you think at Christmas we should feed the starving children in Africa?"

Gram, who sat at one end of the table, smiled, unflappable as always. "I tried, but Chef Boris is on the no-fly list at the moment. He got in a little, shall we say, tiff with a flight attendant over a wheel of cheese. It wasn't pretty."

Just then, the door separating the kitchen from the dining room swung open, and a glowering Chef Boris appeared and placed (dropped) a plate in front of Albert with a peanut butter and jelly sandwich on it. Gram thanked him, waited until he was clanging pots around in the kitchen again, and said, "And besides, feeding starving children isn't really his forte."

Mom cut into her braised beef. "And I'm sure that poor man in the living room playing the Spanish guitar would rather be home tonight enjoying Christmas Eve with his family," she said as strains of an elaborate version of "Good King Wenceslas" drifted into the dining room.

I ripped a roll in half. "Mom, he's wearing a yarmulke," I said, clearly agitated.

Mom held up a finger, indicating she needed a moment to swallow. "I'm pretty certain that what I saw was a cheap toupee."

Peter was sitting across the table and down a bit from me. *Don't let her get to you*, he told me with a glance, and I shot one back to him that said, *Easier said than done!*

"Mother can spot a toupee," said Griffin, using his knife to corral peas onto his fork.

"It's nice to know she's not legally blind. Anyone can do that, my dear," said Mom, in the pleasant, sing-songy tone she was partial to when leveling insults.

Griffin dabbed his mouth with his napkin. "Mother is a keen life observer. There is little that slips past her."

"So what does she think of our Sophie?" asked George, giving me the kind of big-brother smirk that in years past would have caused me to bolt from my chair and chase him all over Gram's house.

"An interesting question," said Griffin, leaning his elbows on the table. "They've only met via Skype, but she considers Sophia a serious contender." He gave special emphasis to the last word, making my stomach clang like an empty tin can, but I cleared my throat and smiled like this was good news.

"A contender!" said George, amused. "You make falling in love sound like a competition—an event involving brackets and commentators."

Griffin, his mouth full of tortellini, was about to speak, but Mom got there first.

"Oh, George, don't sound so naive," said Mom, taking Imogene from Margaret. "When you're searching for your one true love, there is always competition—contenders to speed past or run off the road."

George took a moment to look grave. "Dad, was there by chance a string of unsolved hit and runs around the time you proposed to Mom?"

Dad stopped to think. "No," he said, his knife and fork forming an x in front of him, "but I do recall a jewelry heist around that time."

My mother rolled her eyes. "Oh, please," she said.

Chef Boris pushed open the kitchen door, his face set in a scowl, and a tray of sorbets to cleanse the palate in his hands.

"Ice cream!" shouted Albert as Chef Boris served us, grumbling in French.

"There's truth in what your mother is saying, George," said Margaret, nodding in thanks as her sorbet was placed in front of her. "Love has its competitive side. I haven't worn false eyelashes since our wedding day."

"I should have gotten a pre-nup," said George, shaking his head.

"To protect your twelve-speed bicycle and impose mandatory false eyelash wearing on my part?" asked Margaret.

"This is why I married you, babe. You can read my mind," he said and then kissed his wife on the cheek, making her lips edge up into a smile of satisfaction even as she chewed her dinner.

"I agree," said Heddy, one of three widowed friends of Gram's who had joined us for Christmas Eve. "Once I snagged Morris, the girdle came off." She pointed a tremulous finger at us to emphasize her point.

Ada and Ernestine sat on either side of their friend, Heddy, each white-haired and tiny, but only Ernestine nodded in agreement. "It's putting your best foot forward, that's all," she said, "even if it means scraping off a few warts."

"Edgar used to like to say that the day we met I was the only woman in the room," said Ada, her voice quavering, "because it was true. I was working at my uncle's fish packing plant that summer in Fairbanks, and was indeed the only woman. There I stood, sur-rounded by fish heads, my hair in braids, and a smudge of fish blood on my cheek, and he said never before had he seen anything more beautiful."

My mother snorted. "Well, it's easy enough to stand out when you're in the backwoods of Alaska," she said, bouncing Imogene on her knee, which was probably good. It kept me from throwing my spoon at her. So rude, so typical of her.

Ada looked thoughtful. "I suppose that's so," she said, "and at the time he was just a lowly wildlife photographer, but when he became a fashion photographer—"

Gram put up a hand to stop her. "Don't be modest, Ada," she said. "What he became was a world-renowned fashion photographer."

"When he became *Edgar Addison*," Ada said, her thin voice attempting to sound stuffy as she said her late husband's name, "I was still the only woman in the room—always the only woman in the room for him."

She dabbed her eyes with her napkin and for a moment the only sound was the playing of "We Three Kings" floating in from the living room.

"That was beautiful," said Peter, raising his goblet of sparkling apple cider. "To Edgar."

We raised our goblets as well. "To Edgar," we all said, with the exception of Albert who thrust his sippy cup into the air and shouted, "To Santa!"

Laughter scattered the lingering melancholy and conversation around the dinner table resumed—my mother picking apart the party to anyone (mostly my father) who would listen; Margaret coaxing Albert to eat his vegetables, telling him that little boys who refused to do so would only be getting office supplies from Santa; Griffin pitting his knowledge of US capitals and presidents against Peter's; Gram and her friends reminiscing about their late husbands; and Albert crying with his mouth full of steamed broccoli about how he hated office supplies. Everyone was talking. Everyone, that is, but me. Yawning, I poked at my dinner and watched Griffin as I mulled over what he'd said about me. A week ago, hearing that he considered me a serious contender would have sent me skyrocketing into happiness, so why did it leave me feeling flat now? Maybe it was sleep deprivation. Tired as I was, it was surprising I wasn't seeing tap dancing hippos, let alone feeling a little emotionally off kilter. But maybe it was something more, maybe it was me wanting more—wanting not just to be a serious contender in the eyes of my husband, but to be the only woman in the room. I closed my eyes, just for a moment, and there she was, my future daughter, puckering her lips together. "Come on, Mom," she said. "One kiss and you sleep for three hours. But, who knows, maybe you prefer listening to fine music," and she smashed a pair of cymbals together an inch from my nose.

I jolted awake. "The minute she's born, she's grounded," I grumbled as conversations flowed uninterrupted around me, most of them anyway.

"Is everything okay?" asked Peter, looking ready to reach across the table and check my pulse.

Griffin snorted. "You're stalling, De Boom," he said. "The capital of Vermont has eluded you and now you're hoping Sophie needs the Heimlich maneuver so you can have a little more time to think!"

Peter looked at me, letting me know in a glance he was annoyed I wasn't home lying down with a cold compress on my forehead. "You win, Ploof. A medical emergency and I might have had time to figure it out, but you win . . . again."

Griffin took a bite of chocolate torte. "What can I say, De Boom," he said as he chewed, "I'm on a roll today."

Peter took the paper by his side that outlined the night's menu and began folding it. "Yes, I figured that out after our chess game lasted five minutes."

Griffin smiled like schoolyard bully with a kid in a headlock. "Too bad Sophie's parents don't have a Ping-Pong table or I could have really humiliated you," he said.

"Yes, too bad," said Peter. He made a few more tucks and folds with the paper until it wasn't a menu anymore, but a rose. And then he handed it to me, which Gram's friends noticed.

"Isn't that special?" said Heddy, her eyes misty.

"Just like my Walter used to do, only he'd make me frogs, sometimes crickets," said Ernestine.

"So sweet," said Ada.

Griffin's nostril's flared and his eyes widened in shock, reminding me of Albert when someone snatches a toy out of his hands. He tapped the side of his goblet with his fork. "Can I have your attention, please?" Satisfied we were all listening, he continued. "I was going to do this later, but it seems fitting that right now while we're all gathered here on Christmas Eve that I give Sophie her gift." He reached in his pocket, pulled out a small box, shoved aside a few dirty dishes, and slid it toward me.

I gulped, trying to tamp down the emotion rising inside me, but it was useless. This was the moment I had waited for, hoped for, worked for—Griffin Ploof was about to ask me to marry him. My heart pounded and my eyes filled with tears as I looked at the little box's Scooby Doo gift wrap.

"It was all I could find in the hotel gift shop," he said, explaining his adorable choice of gift wrap. And it was adorable, just like everything about him.

"That's okay," I said, slowly tearing the paper, trying to savor the moment and preserve it in my mind—my fingers trembling, the strains of "Oh Holy Night" in the air, Gram's widowed friends oohing and awing in anticipation, Imogene banging car keys on the table. I wanted to bottle it all up and keep it with me forever, this perfect moment. Okay, sure, it would have been nice if instead of drumming his fingers on the table Griffin was beside me on one knee, but it didn't matter. His asking Peter if he knew what the capital of Ohio was didn't matter. All that mattered was he loved me and wanted to give me what was inside the box.

I opened it and with eyes still watery stared blankly at Griffin. "It's a rock."

"She says it's a rock!" said Ernestine. "It must be enormous!"

"Like Greta's no doubt," said Heddy. "So heavy it bruises her finger, but of course her skin is paper thin."

"Let us see your rock, my dear," said Gram, a hint of knowing in her voice.

"Yes," cried Margaret. "We're all dying to see!"

I took my gift out of its box and showed it to everyone as Griffin beamed.

"Oh," said Margaret.

"Thank the heavens above," said Mom, her eyes flitting upward.

"It's just a dumb rock," said Albert.

"It's not just a dumb rock," said Griffin, taking the golf ball–sized hunk from my hand. "It's a gratitude rock. Unoo, a didgeridoo craftsman, was selling them at the conference. You're supposed to put one in your pocket and when you touch it, think of something you're grateful for."

"It looks like you picked it up off my driveway. Shouldn't it at least be pretty?" asked Heddy.

"He had some flashy ones, but gratitude is something that makes us beautiful on the inside, and I wanted to choose a rock that reflected that."

"Honey, I don't think that's the kind of rock she was expecting," said Ada to Griffin.

"No," I said as Griffin handed me the rock. "It's fine, really. I love it. Thank you, Griffin."

"You're welcome," said Griffin, then he turned to Ada and gave her a look that said *Ha!*

It was strange becoming the object of pity at the dinner table, and even stranger that Griffin was oblivious to it. How could he be so out of touch with my feelings? And Peter, who I barely knew, how was it possible that one look from him could say all at once, *I'm so sorry, you're doing great, keep your chin up, and you have to admit, a paper rose beats a gratitude rock any day of the week.*

New York Sophie, the Sophie Griffin knew, would have waited until after the dinner party, after Christmas, maybe would have given it a good month before she said anything about tonight. She would have slapped on a smile and been a good sport about it, but for whatever reason, New York Sophie was beginning to annoy me. Always patient, always put together, always up for another didgeridoo concert. Who was that girl? One thing was for certain, she wasn't me, not the real me, and now I was too tired to pretend otherwise.

"Um, Griffin," I said, rising and placing my cloth napkin on my chair, "could I have a word with you in the living room?"

Griffin reluctantly agreed. He was quizzing Peter on US presidents and was on a roll. The score was Griffin 9, Peter 3, and only after Peter promised to not study on his phone in Griffin's absence did he agree to come with me and talk.

"So, how can I help you?" asked Griffin, rubbing his hands together like we were about to move a piece of furniture and he wanted to do so quickly.

Having just returned from a short break, the guitarist sat in the corner of the living room near the fireplace, playing again. I should have asked him to leave, but agitated as I was, it didn't occur to me. Instead, I barreled forward with what I wanted to say, unconcerned by the lack of privacy. "Griffin," I said, "we've been together eight months now, and I don't want to rush you, but I need to know where you see this relationship going."

Griffin gave me a patronizing smile and put his hands on my shoulders. "Tick tock, tick tock," he said.

"What's that supposed to mean?" I asked, stepping far enough back that his hands fell from me.

"Your biological clock has begun to tick and it's making you antsy," Griffin said, reaching out to hold my hand.

Annoyed, I folded my arms. "I'm not antsy," I said.

"Darling," he said, wrapping his arms around me from behind

and hooking his chin on my shoulder, "it's nothing to be ashamed of, sensing your fertility narrowing like elevator doors slowly but surely sealing shut." He paused, probably to give me a moment to mull over what he'd just said, but all I could think about was whether or not to elbow him in the ribs. "The truth is," he continued, "you don't have as much time, especially considering the ideal age for a woman to conceive is about a decade younger than you. Tick tock, tick tock. It's unavoidable."

I wriggled out of his hug and turned to face him. "Seriously, Griffin, my biological clock is fine. *I'm* fine, but for reasons I'd rather not get into, I need some things clarified. You said I'm a serious contender, so does that mean you see us getting married, and if so how soon?"

Griffin smiled again. "Tick tock, tick tock."

"Enough with the tick tock!"

Griffin raised an eyebrow. "Sophie, did you just raise your voice at me?"

I pressed my fingers to my temples and took a deep breath, trying to calm down. "Yes, Griffin, yes, I did."

"Are we fighting? We've never fought before. Mother says—"

Maybe I didn't press hard enough or breathe deep enough, but the calming down thing didn't work. "You know, I don't really care what your mother says right now," I snapped. "What I want to know is how soon after getting married do you see us trying for a baby." I had a sense that the situation was unraveling, a well-ordered relationship tangling and toppling into something messy.

Griffin laughed. "A baby! I don't know what's gotten into you, Sophie, but it's adorable. You're so earnest and testy! I love it." Apparently Griffin liked messy. "Scrumptiousness, you know I don't have time to think about marriage and babies. I'm booked! I've got the Milwaukee half-marathon in a few months, zip lining in Costa Rica with a few clients, not to mention planning the mid-year conference for the Greater New York Didgeridoo Society. But, Num Nums, that doesn't mean we can't make a little snuggle time." He tried to gather me into a hug, but I shoved him, which, to my surprise, he found endearing.

"You're like a mama bear protecting her young!"

"Oh my gosh, I want to punch you so hard right now," I said, noticing the guitarist watching us like we were a daytime soap.

"Or a tiger looking out for her cub!"

I threw my hands in the air. "Could you just cut it with the comparisons and focus for one minute. Do you love me?"

"Love you, I do," said Griffin, his voice hoarse and sing-songy like a certain Jedi master. Then dropping the imitation, he added, "Especially when you're angry," rolling the *r* in angry like an overzealous Spanish teacher.

I poked him in the chest. "I need to be able to rest, Griffin. If you see us getting married, you have to give me a time frame."

Tick tock, tick tock, he mouthed, his lips curling into a smile.

"Griffin, this isn't a joke."

"I know it's not a joke, and one day, most likely, the odds are definitely in your favor—we will get married and soon enough have a little Sylvania toddling around."

"Sylvania?"

"I know. I shouldn't get my hopes up for a girl."

"You're telling me you want to name our daughter Sylvania."

"After my first TV."

"A tiny newborn that I've just spent hours pushing into the world, you're going to name her after an electronic device."

"That's right," he said, like this was a perfectly reasonable thing to say.

"So where is it now?"

"Where's what?"

"Your old television."

"I sold it on Craigslist, but that's not the point. The point is it's a happy childhood memory."

I walked away from him, my hair flipping behind me in what I'm sure the guitarist found a dramatic fashion. "She will hate that name."

"She'll love it," he said, staying put, but reaching his arms out toward me. "It will make her stand out in a crowd. I've looked and there were no Sylvanias born last year. Three in 1979, but that's it."

I thought of my future daughter, all arms and legs with a tendency to break into sobs over the slightest thing. I thought of her adorable metal mouth smile and her long, lovely hair. I thought of the way she bounced a little and her eyes widened when she was happy, and then without thinking, I shoved my hand in my pocket, curled my fingers around Griffin's present, and threw it at him.

It missed him (my mom should have put me in softball) and went driving into Gram's glass wall, lodging there and creating web-like cracks around it.

The music came to a stop. Leaning on his instrument, the guitarist watched us like we were a summer blockbuster, and all he needed was a box of popcorn.

"You just threw your gratitude rock at me!" cried Griffin. It was hard to tell if he was incensed or impressed.

My eyes stung with tears. "Even if you had given me an engagement ring tonight, I would have thrown it at you. You fill your life with races and trips and stupid hobbies, not thinking about what you're putting off, *who* you're putting off." Griffin opened his mouth to say something, but I got there first. "And you want to name an indescribably precious albeit mouthy girl after something you can pick up at Radio Shack. I thought you were the one, was convinced you were the one, but maybe she's right. Maybe you are a doofus."

My words had wounded Griffin. I could see the pain in his eyes, and I felt terrible. Yes, I had just tried to hit him with a gratitude rock, but still, a girl can feel bad about what she's done. And I did feel bad, horrible even. I had ruined everything: Christmas Eve, our relationship, Gram's glass wall.

"What's going on in here!" said Mom, standing in the doorway, her hands on her hips, surveying the scene.

Tears had begun to spill down my cheeks, "Tell Gram I'm sorry, but I hate Sylvania," I said, and then knowing all eyes were on me, I grabbed my keys and left.

chapter 12

$\mathcal{I}$F IT HAD been possible to kick myself I would have been black and blue. Why, why had I made a scene! I hadn't done something that mortifying in years. My life since graduating from college and moving to New York had been a mostly calm, well-calibrated affair. I had become New York Sophie—a polished, well-spoken ad executive who shined at dinner parties and wouldn't dream of throwing a rock at her boyfriend. Tonight, all that sophistication had come to an end, like it wasn't really me at all, just a lucky streak. New York Sophie knew it was childish to stay holed up in her bedroom for the rest of Christmas Eve, but Arizona Sophie didn't care. In the morning George and Margaret would come by with their kids, and Aunt Sophie would be expected to emerge, but until then I wanted to hide.

I stared at the ceiling, thinking of what Griffin had said to me, and feeling regret. Not for throwing that rock, but throwing and missing. Of course I felt terrible (beyond terrible) about breaking Gram's window, but how dare he think I was experiencing a biological clock crisis! Before coming home for Christmas and getting hounded in my sleep by my future daughter, I hadn't even thought about having kids! I took a deep breath, felt tears leak into my eyes, and admitted to myself this wasn't entirely true. Sometimes when I jogged past a playground, I would stop and watch—the toddlers sitting on the ground swatting at the sand with their shovels, the little girls swinging, their long hair flying in the wind behind them, and the boys running around, arms open wide, pretending to fly. It was a scene that never failed to make my heart ache, but I had convinced myself this wasn't out of longing, but because they were so sweet. Now, however, wishing sleep would come so that I could touch her again, my future daughter, I didn't know what to think.

Embarrassment worked on me like a double espresso. Not that I'd had a double espresso before, but I assumed it was hard to sleep after knocking one back. It was well past midnight, all attempts to cajole me out of my room had ceased, and from the sounds of it, everyone was now asleep, except me. Bored after a while with the entertainment my phone had to offer, I got off my bed and opened my closet door. Inside, my childhood had been packed away in plastic bins, each one labeled and sealed tight. One bin in particular caught my eye. On it, in Sharpie, my mother had written *Odds and Ends and Her Silly Book*. I pulled it from the shelf and pried off the lid, wondering what book my mother was referring to. And then I saw it, wedged between my first grade spelling bee trophy and a lopsided pot I'd made in middle school—the book my father had given me for writing letters to my future husband, the one she had ruined by cutting its leather strap.

Irritation crawled over me as I fingered the severed strap. Of course, she had said she was acting as a concerned parent, breaking in and peeking at my book. But even then I knew the truth: she was just being snoopy. "So typical of her," I mumbled, opening the book. I read for a while, flipping here and there, smiling at my early handwriting. It was sloppier and bigger, but still bore the hallmarks of my signature: rigid, very up and down, and with what my friends called an unforgiving S. I felt more awake than ever as I read some of the letters I'd written to Hanno, and my embarrassment soared to new heights. There was no denying it, I had been love struck by that boy for a good long time. "Thank heavens you don't always get what you pray for," I said. Our time together in Italy had dealt a deathblow to that infatuation. I had zero interest in Hanno, which was what I preferred to dwell on, rather than that he had never had any real interest in me.

I read some more, laughing at the lists I'd written that were mixed in with the letters. They itemized the various things I wanted in a future husband. During first and second grade I must have been worried about my personal safety because at the top of the list was that he be either a policeman or a fireman. Professional joke teller was right up there, but a guy with a siren—that was the ultimate. I wanted someone who didn't skip in line or say bad words or have a snake for a pet. I wanted a husband who could do flips on the trampoline. By the fourth grade, I was demanding more out of my future husband. I wanted him to be a tall millionaire with an Australian accent. I wanted him to like dogs, know how to fly a plane, play the piano and guitar, have a black belt in Karate, speak four or five languages, water ski, snow ski, jet ski, and be nice. I wanted him to be nice.

Sometime during the fifth grade, I stopped writing in the book, but that hadn't stopped me from making the same kinds of lists, in my head anyway. I had been so certain that Griffin epitomized everything I was looking for: tall, handsome, successful, spiritual. And he was all of those things. But being away from New York, having him here, it was easier for me to see that Griffin Overland Oscar Ploof III was also obnoxious. New York Sophie wanted to be the best girlfriend ever—fun, smart, smiling, never demanding, and always willing to give the guy in her life the freedom to pursue his dreams. It was exhausting. And sometimes when my smile felt forced, like while listening to *A Didgeridoo Christmas* in Griffin's car, I had to wonder, what did being the best girlfriend have to do with one day being a wife? Wives, at least the ones I knew, were not perpetually smiling, compliant creatures. They had opinions.

I grabbed a pen off my nightstand, turned to the next available page, and began to write:

> *Hey,*
> *It's me, your future wife, Sophie, wondering where you are.*
> *I hope you're well and you're happy, but I hope you're missing*

*me, because I miss you. I miss you making me laugh and fall-
ing asleep on your shoulder. I miss telling you my worries, and
you surprising me with a kiss on the back of my neck while I'm
fixing dinner. Of course, none of this has happened yet, but I
miss it. I miss it, and more, every day. If you read this book of
letters, assuming I don't burn it first (it's embarrassingly gushy),
you'll see that more than once I thought I knew who you were
or what I wanted you to be, but that's not what I care about
anymore. Don't get me wrong, I'd still like it if you were handsome and smart and scuba certified. But what's more important
to me now is who I am when I'm around you.*

*I want to be happy, not because all my girlfriends are jeal-
ous I'm the one you're with, but because that's how I feel when
you're near me. And I want to burp. Not really, but I don't
want to feel like I have to be perfect all the time. I want to know
that you know my faults, and you still love me. But here's the
tricky part: I want to be better around you—not because I fear
you'll reject me if I'm not fabulous, but because being with you
inspires me to be a better person. Blond, black hair, it doesn't
matter. These are the things I want, and I want you, however
you are, whoever you are. But please be taller than me, and at
least slightly coordinated. Sleep well, my love, wherever you are,
and I'll try to do the same.*

*All my love,
Sophie*

Book and pen still in hand, I lay back, rested my head on my
pillow, and wondered if I should have mentioned something about
our future daughter pestering me in my sleep? *No,* I thought as I
closed my eyes, *that isn't the sort of thing you say in a letter.* And
besides, what she thought didn't matter. She was a kid! And like most
kids, probably changed her mind every five seconds. I want popcorn;
no, make that cotton candy; no, make that a puppy. I wasn't going
to hand over the most important decision of my life to anyone, let
alone someone who smelled like fruity lip gloss. "She's just a kid," I

mumbled, turning on my side and letting the book and pen slip from my fingers. "A sweet but fickle kid."

Sleep, stone-cold and dreamless, enveloped me, and like an astronaut in space, I floated in dark, quiet nothingness, until as jarring as an alien encounter, terrible violin music began to play. Opening one eye, I saw my future daughter. She sat at the foot of my bed, her instrument tucked under her chin, stumbling her way through a "Mary Had a Little Lamb" that was so screechy it made my teeth hurt.

"She doesn't know anything," she parroted, sounding bitter. "Oh yeah, I know how to wake you up!" Then she stuck out her tongue at me, put bow to strings, and started hacking to pieces "Twinkle, Twinkle, Little Star."

Reminding myself to be patient, I rubbed my eyes then propped up to my elbows. "I thought you played the clarinet," I said, sounding groggy but friendly.

She tossed the violin and bow onto my bed. "It's hard to know what to throw myself into since I'm not alive yet!" she cried, her eyes narrowed to angry slits.

I sat up. "How long was I asleep?"

"Two hours," she said, her anger shifting to pouting. "You didn't kiss Peter, but you did throw a rock at your boyfriend, so I thought you deserved something."

I touched her arm; she didn't pull away, but she kept her eyebrows scrunched together and her lower lip jutting. "Thank you," I said. "I really needed that."

Her hands were balled into fists and she shook a little as she spoke. "What you needed was to reach across the table and plant one on Peter! You'd still be sleeping right now if you did!"

My goodness she was adorable. Unreasonable and exasperating, but so adorable. "Sweetie," I said, "you have to understand how things work. I know you think Peter's the one for me, but if I had done what you just said, he would have thought I was crazy."

"He loves you, Mom." My heart melted at those words, not that I let her see it. "He's not going to think you're crazy. But I'll tell you crazy, wanting to name your daughter SYLVANIA!"

I don't know why I did it, but I defended Griffin. "It's connected to a happy childhood memory," I said.

"If he wanted to name me Summer Camp, you'd probably go for it."

"Hey, I threw a rock at him!"

"But you didn't break up with him! And you didn't kiss Peter! You're supposed to kiss Peter and fall in love with him and marry him and have me, so I can be in my middle school orchestra and play the violin. Or the clarinet. I'm not sure yet. But you're taking forever, Mom. And you don't have forever. *We* don't have forever!"

Her facial expressions were over the top, ridiculously melodramatic, sort of like the girl in silent movies who winds up tied to the railroad tracks. Still, the back of my neck tensed and somewhere inside me I heard the faint ticking of a clock. "Exactly how much time do I have?" I asked.

"For what?"

Was she kidding? "To become your mom," I said, sounding a little irked, which is never a good idea when dealing with a smoldering volcano.

She didn't blow her stack. She just shrugged. "How am I supposed to know?"

"Oh," I said. "I don't know how this works, but I thought maybe you knew something."

"I do know something: you should kiss Peter."

"Here we go again," I said, my eyes shooting upward in frustration. "Why do you think kissing Peter will make a difference! To be honest, after tonight I don't know how I feel about Griffin. If nothing else, I think I'm going to need to step back from the relationship, take a breather."

"Breathers take forever!"

"They do not take forever."

"Yes, they do, Mom. You need to dump Griffin, marry Peter. No breathers," she said, making a motion like a baseball ref when a player is safe.

"You want me to rush the most important decision of my life!" I said. "Let me tell you something. Even if I decided that I didn't love Griffin, that wouldn't mean I was going to fall in love with Peter. It doesn't work that way. There are a lot of guys out there."

"You ought to know. You've dated most of them," she grumbled.

I ignored this. "I would have to get to know Peter, date him for a while, and see if we were compatible."

"But that's what I'm trying to tell you. You are compatible! Why don't you trust me? You'll never trust me with anything!" she cried, jutting her chin and turning away in a huff.

"When the time comes, I'll trust you with all sorts of things: folding the laundry, taking out the garbage."

"So you'll trust me to be your slave!" she cried, her eyes burning with intensity.

I pinched the bridge of my nose and took a deep breath. "Look, you need to trust me," I said, a strange new joy darting through me as I reached for her hand and curled my fingers around hers. "Trust that I know what I'm doing when it comes to picking your father."

Like a shooting star, the joy was gone as quickly as it came. My future daughter threw her hands in the air. "How am I supposed to trust you when you just blew the last eight months of your life on a guy who wants to name me Sylvania Summer Camp?"

My jaw clenched, and I heard Peter in my mind saying, *Shh, Sophia, don't let her get to you.* But it was no use. "Enough!" I said. "Who I marry is my choice! When I marry is my choice!"

"Quit shouting at me!" she cried, tears spilling down her face.

"I'm not shouting. I'm just speaking sternly." It was a fine line, but I was convinced I'd walked it.

She wiped her nose on one of the cartoony monkeys that covered her pajamas. (Yuck.) "That's not true! You shouted at me! You always shout at me!"

"I do not always shout at you!" Now I was shouting.

"See!" she cried. "And you never listen to me! Why don't you believe me when I tell you to marry Peter?"

"Because I barely know him!" I shouted, but to my credit, not as loud as before.

"So?" she cried, jumping up and standing like Peter Pan, legs apart, fists on hips.

I knew I was supposed to be the bigger person in the situation, but how do you reason with someone who makes accusations about you *always* or *never* doing something, and counters in a disagreement with "So?" She was impossible. It was the truth, but I never should have said it.

"I'm impossible!" she cried. "You're the one who's impossible! Even Grandma Evelyn says so."

"Wonderful," I said. "My mother, the most impossible person on the planet, thinks I'm impossible,"

"And pigheaded," she said, stamping her foot.

I bristled. "Just because I don't let my life become *The Evelyn Show* I'm pigheaded."

"She's been telling you for years that you need to get married and start having children, but you won't listen to her."

"I listen to her."

"While checking the latest entertainment news."

I didn't bother asking how she knew that or trying to deny it. "She wants me to do what she wants."

"She wants you to be happy."

"Ha!" I cried. "Look, you don't know her. She's interfering, opinionated—"

"She's a good grandma!"

This I couldn't deny. I had seen her enough with Albert and Imogene to know it was true. Still, I relished the idea of living so far away when I got married that Grandma Evelyn couldn't swing by on her way home from the grocery store. "As long as your size ten feet don't crush her dreams of your becoming a ballerina, she's great."

"What's a rolodex?" she asked, out of the blue.

"It's a filing thingy. Why?"

"Grandma says you have one, of every mistake she's ever made," she said.

I opened my mouth to say something, but too many words

rushed forward wanting to be first, creating a bottleneck, and I was left speechless.

"She says you ignore her."

This was true. It was one of the pleasures of being an adult, keeping my mother at bay, hitting ignore when she called. "Because I don't want to hear it! 'Have you found a husband, Sophie? Time is running short, Sophie. Hurry, Sophie. Hurry, hurry, hurry!'"

"You do need to hurry!"

"So the two of you can gang up on me, I don't think so."

"You're so d-u-m-b, Mom!"

"Why'd you spell it?"

"Because you won't let me say it!"

"Oh," I said, surprised and emboldened by this little act of obedience. "Well, I think we've talked long enough about this."

"You're right!" she cried, grabbing her violin and bow. "It's time for me to practice my music!"

"Whatever floats your boat," I said, as if I had no problem hearing more.

Too frustrated for words, she screamed instead. It was screechy, piercing, and painful, but I acted unruffled.

"Good-bye, Sylvania Summer Camp!" I cried as she marched out of my room and slammed the door shut. I sighed. *It isn't fair, fighting with your future daughter*, I thought, *because when she storms away in anger, she takes your heart with her.*

chapter 13

$\mathcal{M}$Y EYES BLINKED open and searched the room for my future daughter; she wasn't there. I knew she wouldn't be. Still, a faint whiff of peach-flavored lip gloss seemed to hang in the air, and I longed to have her at the foot of my bed again, scowling and butchering the violin. I longed to touch her honey-colored hair, and see her eyes sparkle or blaze, depending on whether she was happy or mad. Without her, my room was quiet, the kind of quiet that made me think of snow falling on cabins, blanketing rooftops, and piling on the ground higher and higher until it has barricaded the front door, and everyone inside is forced to subsist on Spam until help arrives. Needless to say, for me, it was an uncomfortable quiet, and I grabbed my robe and left my bedroom, just because I could.

Heading downstairs, I turned on the kitchen light, remembered Peter on the hammock, and turned it off, only to turn it back on after seeing the time glowing on my mother's pristine oven. It was 4:00, which meant Peter wasn't asleep on the porch; he was taking Griffin to the airport. *Good,* I thought as I hunted for Nesquik to make myself hot chocolate, *our breather has officially begun.* My heart apparently hadn't tucked itself into Griffin's carry-on and left with him. His absence created no void within me or pang of regret that we hadn't ironed things out before he left. My mood was far more "see ya, sucker," and so I didn't think about Griffin again until I heard

Peter pull into the driveway, but mostly I thought about bed head, and whether or not I had it.

Glancing at my reflection in the microwave door, I combed my fingers through my hair, trying to make it look wind tousled from a day at the beach, but the truth was, it just looked messy, and combined with the dark circles under my eyes, I resembled a prisoner of war far more than a beach bunny. Ugh. I figured the best I could do was try for perky prisoner of war, so I pinched my cheeks, slapped on a smile, and waited at the kitchen table for Peter to walk through the door.

"Hey," I said as he stepped inside, his eyes fixed on his phone.

He glanced up and gave me a disapproving look. "You should be asleep," he said.

I yawned, perkiness already draining from me. "I did, for a while anyway, so hurray for that," I said, then shook my arms like an apathetic cheerleader.

"We need to get you to sleep," he said, looking back at his phone and shaking his head.

I sipped my hot chocolate. "What are you doing?" I asked, gesturing at his phone.

"Losing," he said with a hint of irritation.

"Losing?"

Peter turned off his phone and put it in his pocket. "At 2048 to your super serious boyfriend," he said. "He won the last game too. So, yeah, it felt good to dump him at the airport curb."

I put my elbow on the table and propped my head against my hand. "Thanks for getting him there."

"Not a problem," he said, then paused to take a good look at me. "You're exhausted, Sophia. What is keeping you up?"

I yawned. "Arguing, mostly," I said.

"If you're upset about throwing a rock at Griffin, don't be. That's all he could talk about on the way to the airport. Well, that and how if we were gladiators he'd win because I lack the killer instinct, but he liked that you hurled that rock at him; he said it took spunk. My guess is if you try to hit him in the head with a shovel, he'll most likely get down on one knee and propose."

The last thing I wanted was to reward his joke with a smile, but I couldn't seem to stop the corners of my mouth from turning upward. "Food for thought," I said, "but Griffin is not the one robbing me of sleep."

"Is there anything I can do to help?" asked Peter.

I searched his face for an indication, some sign that he knew. Had he met my future daughter? Was she pestering him too? No, it was clear to me he hadn't. His eyes held no secret, just sincerity. "I don't think so," I said, resting my cheek on the rim of my mug, but just for a second, since it was uncomfortable. "I mean, unless you know something about dealing with kids."

"I'll tell you everything I know," he said, pulling me to my feet, "but first let's move this conversation over to the couch."

"Why?" I asked, noticing the warmth of his hand as he guided me to the family room.

"No reason," he said, sitting beside me, "other than you just tried to use something ceramic as a pillow."

"Hmm," I said as Peter put his arm around me and I leaned my head against his shoulder. Fatigue had stripped away all pretense, making me unaware of personal bubbles.

HIs shoulder was definitely harder than a pillow, but softer, way softer, than the rim of a mug. And besides, I liked being there. He smelled like soap and musky antiperspirant, and if I paid attention, I could hear the thudding of his heart, but it was hard to pay attention. Maybe it was the hour or the lowness of his voice, but I was getting sleepy.

"So you want to know about kids," he said, stroking my head.

"Yes, the sassy, prepubescent kind," I said as I yawned.

"Boy or girl."

"Girl."

"Well, that changes everything," he said.

"How?"

"They're emotional."

"You have no idea."

"You have to be careful how you approach things."

I closed my eyes. "I've tried that and she still ends up in a tizzy."

"So are you ending up in a tizzy too?"

"Only a small one."

"That's the problem."

"So unfair."

"Sophia, you have to keep your cool when dealing with kids. The minute you raise your voice, you get their attention, but you lose credibility."

"You don't understand, Peter. She's so determined to get what she wants. There's no talking sense to her."

"You don't have to give in."

"But if I don't, she won't give me a moment's rest, and I need rest! I have work to do, and this huge client to impress. It's the opportunity of a lifetime, but I can't focus because she just keeps harping on and on and on."

"Shh," he soothed. "I'm sure she's a good kid. Are you her mentor?"

I nuzzled my cheek against his shoulder. "So to speak," I said. "And she is a good kid. So smart and pretty and eager; you'd love her."

"I'm sure I would. Just don't lose sight of the things you love about her when she's being demanding. Remain calm, and the good in her will rise to the surface."

"But if she doesn't get what she wants—"

"She has to learn that she can't always get what she wants, but you can say rather than scream that message."

I nodded off for a moment, and Peter continued to stroke my head, not bothered by the silence.

As soon as I was asleep, there was my future daughter, holding a sign that said, KISS HIM!! When she winked at me, I woke with a start.

My head jerked off Peter's shoulder. "Are you all right?" he asked.

I lay my head back down. "I'm fine, just twitchy," I said, which seemed to satisfy him. He didn't ask more.

"Peter," I said after a while, "if you had a little girl, what would you name her?"

"Well, it wouldn't be just my decision."

"That's what I said! Still, assuming it was just up to you, what would you want to name her?"

"Well, in that case it would be simple. I'd want to name her after my grandmother."

"What's her name? Please say Gertrude."

"Why?"

"No reason. I'd just like to see it make a comeback," I said, instead of the truth, which was I was being vindictive.

"Sorry to disappoint," he said, his fingers moving across the top of my head, "but her name isn't Gertrude; it's Sarah.

"Sarah," I said, turning the name over in my mind, like a jeweler judging the quality of a gem. "She'd love that."

"Who?"

I ignored that question. "Tell me about Sarah."

Peter's voice was soft and low and made me think of water gently lapping on rocks. As he spoke, his fingers continued to stroke my hair, and the knot of tension at the back of my neck began to soften. Closing my eyes, I listened to him talk about Sarah. As a young woman, her glossy, black hair had tumbled past her shoulders, but somewhere along the way she'd cut it, and for Peter it was always hard to believe that his grandmother, whose silver hair was some-times shorter than her husband's, had ever had such a long, beautiful mane. *No fuss, no muss*, she'd say with a smile when as a boy he'd ask why she'd cut it. It wasn't until he was older, catching snatches of conversations between his parents, that he heard words like *leuke-mia* and *chemotherapy*, and understood that though his grandmother didn't mention it, she was sick.

Sarah had been the one who comforted him when, at eleven, his parents first sent him to boarding school in Switzerland. Overwhelmed as his mother was to move from Denver to the Middle East, she could not see through his I'm-fine façade, but his grandmother could. *You're so brave*, she had told him, *going off to school so far away, and without even a tear. Still, though I suppose you won't need it, I'm going to write you every day.* And she did.

Each week a large envelope arrived with seven letters in it, a letter for every day of the week. She made him promise not to read ahead, but at night, when finally alone, he would read all seven letters, along with her letters from previous weeks. She could have emailed him like his parents, but he was glad she didn't. It was nice to have something arrive for him in the mail, and comforting to see her handwriting. Her letters sometimes chronicled her garden club meetings, or trips to visit friends up north, but he didn't care. He could hear her voice when he read them, and that, more than anything, staved off the horrible homesickness that threatened at times to overwhelm him.

When as a young man he joined the Church, she said a prayer for his soul, but accepted his choice and soon came to respect it. She liked the missionaries, liked stopping them in passing and telling them her grandson had joined the Church, and liked how earnestly they tried to get her to agree to a teaching appointment. She never would. Buy them groceries, mend their shirts, yes, but never sit down and let them teach her. Peter had just begun working at the South Pole when he got word that Sarah's cancer, which had been in remission, had returned. Testing showed that the cancer had spread to her brain and the doctors told her to prepare for the worst. Her family, church, and friends gathered to say good-bye.

The weather at the South Pole was too severe for Peter to be there to say good-bye to his grandmother. While she was in hospice, Peter contacted the missionaries and asked them to visit her. She hadn't been conscious for days, dividing her time between hallucinating and sleeping. When the missionaries walked into her room, she looked at the taller one, smiled, and said, "Peter." He didn't correct her, but held her hands as she gave her grandson her final advice, which the missionary later wrote him in a letter. "Don't give up, Peter. She loves you; she just doesn't know it yet."

It's possible she said other things too, but I drifted to sleep as my future daughter softly sang:

Sleep, Mom, sleep next to Dad
And when you wake
Make wedding plans
Kiss his face
Hold his hand
I'm stir crazy in heaven, but you'll be forgiven
If you marry Peter and I get my own room.
BTW, Sarah is TONS better than Sylvania.
Told you he was a kee-ee-ee-per.

It was bad enough that it should have kept me up, but I adored her voice, and between it and Peter lightly combing my hair, I fell asleep, and stayed that way until Albert shouted, "Did Santa come here too?"

"Of course he did, sweetheart," said Mom, "but shush, Sophie is sleeping."

"Why?"

"She couldn't earlier, dear, but she fell asleep on Peter's shoulder and we've all been as quiet as church mice trying not to wake her."

"I'm up," I said, lifting my head off Peter and blotting the patch of drool I'd left on his shirt with my sleeve. Mortifying.

"Well, thank heavens," said Mom. "George, go turn on the Christmas trees in the living room. One blinks in time to Christmas carols, and the other has little jalapeño lights."

"How many Christmas trees do you have?" asked George, looking at the gargantuan one in the family room.

"You can never have too many Christmas trees," said Mom

"Said the lady with too many Christmas trees," said George before lifting Mom off the ground in a huge hug. "Merry Christmas."

"For heaven's sake," she said, feigning impatience but clearly enjoying this show of affection. I squirmed a little, trying to remember when I had last shown her that kind of warmth. It had been a long time, not because I didn't love her, but every annoying thing she did always seemed to get in the way. I thought of my future daughter and my heart tugged as if attached to an invisible yet unbreakable cord that somehow connected to her. If she were to brush me off year after year it would, without question, turn that tugging into an unbearable ache.

"If anyone deserves to fall asleep on Peter's shoulder, it's me," said George, coming over to talk to us before turning on Christmas trees. "Imogene was up all night teething, and Santa *had* to drop by with a bunch of stuff that won't fit in our tiny flat and needed loads of late-hour assembling."

"It will fit!" said Margaret, chiming in. "You're forgetting the sunroom."

"Sweetheart, the sunroom already looks like Toys 'R' Us."

"We'll find room."

"Room," he moaned to us. "We're a family of four living in nine hundred square feet. Some free advice: if either of you intend to raise a family in London, become a rock star first. All that cash comes in handy when you're trying to afford something larger than your college dormitory."

"But I don't play guitar," said Peter.

"Learn, my friend. Learn," said George, patting Peter on the shoulder before moving on to the living room.

I looked at Peter and smiled. "Thanks for the use of your shoulder," I said.

"Glad you got some rest," he said, removing his arm from me and shaking it.

I sat up. "How are you doing?" I asked. "Did you sleep too?"

"No, but my arm did," he said, continuing the shaking, "so that ought to count for something."

I nudged him. "You should have moved me."

He picked up his arm and let it flop at his side for comic effect. "I didn't want to wake you," he said. "But it's a no for me for tennis today, or rowing. Fencing's pretty much out too."

"Looks like I'll have to revamp our schedule," I said.

"You two look cute together on the couch," said Margaret, jostling Imogene on her hip. "But don't get too cozy with him, Sophie. I've got just the girl for Peter when we get back home."

"The undertaker named Celestina. Can't wait," said Peter. "I think for a date we'll go on a walk on stilts since when we're done we can throw them in the back of her hearse."

"You laugh now," said Margaret, "but when you fall in love with her, you'll be thanking me. I have an eye for these things, you know."

"Everyone to the family room!" cried Mother. "It's time to open presents! Howard? Where are you?"

"Coming, coming," said Dad, trotting toward us with a small present in his hands. "Just tying up some loose ends, some Christmas loose ends." Happy anticipation shining in his eyes, Dad tucked the gift under the tree. And suddenly it felt like Christmas. Not because of the endless décor or the electronic, soulless carols playing in the living room. What made it feel like Christmas was seeing my dad's joy in giving.

Placing Imogene on the ground to play, George and Margaret sat with us on the couch. Dad sat in his chair, a beaten leather recliner my mom needled him constantly to give to Goodwill, and Mom and Albert sat on the carpet next to the Christmas tree, a busy twosome, Mom announcing who a present belonged to and Albert delivering it, but only after the prior present had been opened, because Mom liked to savor Christmas. There had never been an everyone-simultaneously-rips-open-their-presents free-for-all in the Stark home. Around here, Christmas was judicious.

"Are you missing your family?" I asked Peter as Mom and Albert tried to remember whose turn it was next.

"Yes," he said, "I'm missing *my* family," but there was something in the way he said it that made me wonder if we were talking about the same thing.

"Here, Aunt Sophie," said Albert, dropping a fairly heavy present in my lap. "Grandma says this one is for you."

Attached to the present, which was obviously, according to its shape and weight, a coffee table book, was a tag that said, *To Sophia from Peter: Something to look at on a rainy day.* "But I didn't get you anything," I whispered to Peter, my face hot with embarrassment.

Peter shrugged. "You can regift me the Almond Roca the Olsens gave you. I love that stuff."

"My dad's already eaten half of it."

"I'm a can-is-half-full kind of guy. It'll be fine," he whispered back.

"So nice of Peter to think of Sophie," said Mom, sounding syrupy sweet and bouncing Imogene on her knee.

I peeled back the wrapping paper, and as suspected, found a book, but it was what the book was about that made me blush: *Soccer and Italy—A Country in Love.* In it was picture after picture of Italians rejoicing over their team's victory. Some were of crowds cheering, others of couples embracing and kissing. A bright red siren had fired up in my brain. It was spinning and wailing and making it impossible not to lean in to Peter and whisper, "We're not in this, are we?"

"Unfortunately not," he whispered back.

"What is it, Sophie?" asked Mom. "Let us have a look." I turned the book around for all to see. Mom screwed up her face, clearly puzzled. "I didn't know you were a soccer fan," she said.

"Well, not as big as Peter," I said.

"Celestina adores soccer," said Margaret.

"No one adores soccer," corrected George. "You either like it or you don't. It's a game, not a doily."

Margaret ignored this. "I'm telling you, Peter. You two are going to fall in love," she said, her voice rising with giddiness as she spoke.

"I think I'm falling in love already," he said good-naturedly, and again I wondered if he meant what we assumed. As Imogene opened (licked) her present, I stole glances at Peter, studying him. What had he meant by giving me that book? Was he trying to embarrass me, bringing up the night we first met? No. I hardly knew Peter and yet I knew he wouldn't do that. He was kind. All I had to do was watch his enjoyment in Imogene's inefficient unwrapping skills to know that. But what did he think of me? Had he let me fall asleep on his shoulder because he wanted to be near me or was he just being kind?

Dad popped up from his recliner, jarring me from my thoughts. "Albert," he said, "I think I see a small gift hiding over there. Why don't you get it and have Nana see who it's for." Albert crawled under the tree and came out holding a small box.

"Here you go," he said, handing it to my mom.

Mom read the attached card. "Well, it looks like this one is for me," she said, her voice tinged with excitement.

"Open it, Grandma!" said Albert.

"Good things are rumored to come in small packages, so let's see what it is. Earrings perhaps, or a new ring." It didn't take long for Mom to tear past the paper, open the small box, and get to the gift, and even less time to show she was annoyed. She held up a small piece of paper. "Cooking classes!" she cried. "Why in the world did you get me classes?"

Agony like a brick to the chest hit me as I saw my dad's face fall. "Well, I thought you'd like it."

"Like it!" she scoffed. "I'm always in the kitchen as it is. What more do I need to know about cooking?"

"It's Italian cooking taught by a Claudio Bartoli, a chef from the Cuisine Channel, and it's a couples class, so I thought it would be fun for us to do together," Dad said, trying to get her to catch his vision of this gift.

Mom tutted. "A swindler, no doubt, who's going to teach us how to open a can of Ragu. You should have stuck to the list. I gave you a list."

Dad looked sheepish. "I wanted to surprise you."

Mom crumpled up the small piece of paper and tossed it in the trash. "Never mind. Albert, let's see who's next."

My fists clenched and my jaw tightened, and Peter sitting beside me made an almost imperceptible soothing sound. "Ssh."

With a glance I told him I wanted to strangle my mother, and with a glance he told me that would land me in jail. Not really, but he did somehow urge me with just a look to not blow up at her, to let it pass and enjoy Christmas. And that's what I did, or tried to do. Though I could shake off my annoyance with my mother well enough, now nearly fully rested, something else was beginning to weigh on my mind: the ad campaign I was supposed to put together for Luxe Air. If I failed, it would be a huge opportunity lost, and yet what of other opportunities? In the living room, the musical Christmas tree flashed in time to "I'll Be Home For Christmas," and on the couch, I let my hand fall against Peter's forearm and thought of opportunities.

chapter 14

WHEN I DID Trek as a teenager, I did not sneak a battery-operated curling iron into the handcart. I've never been *that* girl—you know, a girly girl who has to look pageant perfect 24/7. Still, there was no way I was going to spend Christmas Day schlepping around in my robe and jammies. My legs pricked with new growth and my mouth felt as fuzzy as the vegetables I'd left at home in the refrigerator, so as soon as I could, I ran upstairs and didn't return until my shoulder length hair was fresh again and sculpted into mellow curls, my face was dusted with a smattering of make-up, and I was dressed in skinny jeans and a vintage tee, a young, casual look which highlighted the results I'd achieved from hitting the gym, unless you talked to my mother. Then I just looked like a day laborer.

"Don't you have something nicer to wear?" she asked, putting the finishing touches on brunch as I walked down stairs. "You look like you're ready to paint the living room."

"I wish I looked ready to paint the living room." Margaret sighed, and patted her post-pregnancy paunch over her flouncy peasant shirt.

I rolled my eyes. "There's nothing wrong with what I'm wearing."

Mom sprinkled cheese on the omelet casserole she was making. "A pair of slacks perhaps, from one of your many shopping trips without me."

That little jab was meant to make me feel guilty for not inviting her on a recent shopping spree to Atlanta, but it wasn't going to work. I would have rather shopped with a pet monkey, off leash. "I look fine," I said.

"You look more than fine," said Peter, stepping into the kitchen from the garage. "I mean, if you ask me."

Mom brightened at this. "Well, Peter, if you say so!" she gushed.

Peter slid his hands in his jean pockets and something inside me fluttered as I watched the muscles in his forearm tense. *Oh, please,* I thought, chiding myself. *Do not lose your head over this boy. He has penguins for neighbors, and falling in love with him would make Mom, not to mention that bossy future daughter of mine, unbearably smug.* "Apparently, whatever you say goes. So do you have anything else to add, Peter?" I asked, like he wasn't making my heart race.

"Yes, brunch smells amazing," he said, making Mom beam, "and . . . well, maybe, Sophia, I should whisper the next bit in your ear."

"Something romantic, no doubt," cried Mom, raising the spatula in her hand for emphasis.

"It better not be. Celestina wouldn't like that one bit," said Margaret as she diced an onion.

Peter took a step toward me. "No, no," I said, "whatever you have to say, you can say to us all."

"All right then," he said, rocking back on his heels. "Your grandmother would like a private word with you in her car. She's parked in the driveway."

I glared at Peter, letting him know he should have told me that in private, and in return he bugged out his eyes as if to say, *Hey, I tried!*

"Busted!" said George from where he sat in the family room with Albert, flipping through my present from Peter.

"Dad," said Albert, "is Gram going to spank Aunt Sophie for cracking her window?"

"Definitely," said George. "Hey, Sophe, grab a wooden spoon on the way out, just in case Gram forgot hers."

"Ha-ha," I said.

"But you have to admit it was the dumbest gift ever," said

Margaret, sliding the onion into a bowl. "What girl wants a rock for Christmas? Well, *that* kind of rock."

"Hurry up, Sophie," said Mom, pulling cinnamon rolls out of the oven. "Go face the music. Brunch is almost ready."

I let out a deep breath. "Fine," I said and headed outside.

She was, as Peter had said, sitting in her spotless Buick, and when she saw me coming, she smiled.

I got in the car and shut the door. "Gram," I started, "I'm so sorry about breaking your window. I fully intend to—"

She put up a hand up to stop me, and a needle of worry pricked my heart as I noticed how her index finger was bent like a gnarled twig. "I'm not worried about the glass," she said. "I think when your grandfather built our home, he was anticipating a hailstorm more than a hotheaded granddaughter, but either way, he made sure to provide replacement glass for all the windows. They've been in the shed all these years, just waiting for some unsuspecting beau to hand you a rock."

"I honestly don't know how it happened."

"I know how it happened. You're a terrible aim," she said, and we both laughed.

"But I shouldn't have let myself get so mad."

"What you shouldn't have done was talk yourself into believing Griffin was the right person for you." Again I started to speak, and again she stopped me. "I'm not saying he's not impressive or handsome or temple worthy or any of those things. What I am saying is eternity is going to feel like an eternity if you're in it with someone you'd like to hit with a rock.

"The fifty-one years I had on this earth with your grandfather, they passed in a wink. 'Where did the time go?' I'd ask myself when another anniversary would roll around. Where did it go?" she asked again, her gaze distant and her voice trailing off.

"But what if I can't find that, Gram? What if that's not out there for me, and I've just got to make a decision, marry that decision, have kids with that decision," I said, sounding less and less enthusiastic.

"Light a candle, and sweep the house, and seek diligently until you find it."

I raised an eyebrow. "Gram, we may need to adjust your medicine," I said, teasing. "You're not making any sense."

"Very funny, missy," she said, patting my leg. "It's part of a parable."

"And?"

"When I met your grandfather, it felt like finding something that belonged to me, something that'd been lost. Never having been in love, I hadn't expected to feel that way. It reminded me of the parable in Luke of the woman and the lost piece of silver, how she searched for what was missing, and rejoiced once she'd found it. For some time, I've come to associate that scripture with meeting your grandfather, so naturally, it is one that I know by heart."

I slid down in the leather seat. "I don't know if anyone could ever make me feel that way, Gram. Like I'd found something that belonged to me."

"Then you need to keep sweeping, my dear, and while you're at it, take time to check out the dust bunny inside your house."

"You mean Peter," I said, rolling my eyes. What was the deal? Now Gram was nuts about him too.

"Yes, I mean Peter," she said. "Get to know him, Sophie. Find out if he's the one you're searching for."

I bit my lip. "I don't know, Gram. Margaret's pretty convinced she's got his love life all wrapped up in the UK."

Gram shook my arm. "Sweep!"

"Okay, okay, keep your shirt on," I said, like she was twisting my arm. "I'll sweep."

After brunch, exhausted and on Imogene duty, George lay on the carpet, where his daughter climbed over him, patted his head, and covered him with sloppy kisses. "I'm sure they teach this babysit-while-you-nap technique in all the latest parenting books," said Peter.

"I heard that," said George, eyes closed, face pressed against a throw pillow.

"Daddy, can you hear this?" asked Albert. "Pee-pee-poo-poo."

Eyes still closed, George reached out for his son, but moved no further as Imogene had done a face-plant on his ear. "Come here so I can tickle you!" he demanded.

"No!" cried Albert, all happiness. He kicked and protested some more, nearly knocking over the Lego fire truck he had been building on the floor with Peter. The excitement was too much for Imogene, who startled, looked up, and then began to cry.

"This is the best nap ever," groaned George, sitting up to comfort his baby girl.

Peter gestured toward the porch. "You realize your wife is asleep on the hammock," he said.

"Yes," he said, soothing Imogene by bouncing her on his knee, "and I believe her parting words to me were, 'It's your turn to watch the kids. I'm taking a nap, and if you let them come in and wake me, so help me I'll whip . . .' It was either 'my hide' or 'together a lasagna.' I was only half listening." Imogene was happy again. George sat her on the carpet and handed her some plastic keys, which she quickly stuck in her mouth.

Peter walked toward George. "She wouldn't mind being interrupted by *you*, would she? That hammock fits two."

"I'm willing to risk it," he said, his voice rising with enthusiasm.

"Then why don't you let me take Albert and Imogene for a—"

"Done!" he said, scooping up Imogene to hand her to Peter.

"George, you agreed before Peter could say where he was going to take them," I said, looking up from my tablet. Though I had promised myself I wouldn't think about the Luxe Air campaign until the next day, I was searching the Internet looking at airline ads, particularly those that promised luxury.

George handed Peter his baby and stood up. "Okay, so no horror houses or bounce houses," he said, like a coach trying to pump up his team. "Stay away from cement factories and areas that require a hard hat, and I think we're good to go."

"I want to go to a bounce house!" cried Albert. "And a factory!" There was a note of hysteria in his voice, an indicator that he was prepared to throw a fit to get what he wanted.

"Uh-oh," mumbled George. "Albert, I was kidding."

"A factory!" cried Albert. "A factory, a factory!"

I was certain a meltdown was coming, hurling toward us like a ball launched from a pitching machine, but then, to my surprise, Peter sidestepped it. "Let's go find a factory," he said.

"Yes!" shouted Albert, jumping up and doing a wild dance that made his sister giggle.

"Where's the stroller?" asked Peter.

"In the garage," said George, then he mouthed the words *thank you* and headed for the porch.

"Sophia, are you coming?" asked Peter.

I turned off my tablet and stood up. "I'd better," I said. "My brother just handed you his offspring without bothering to conduct a background check."

Peter handed Imogene to me, her little fingers seizing my hair and pulling. "First of all," he said, "your brother and his wife know me well, and second, you didn't bother with a background check before crashing on my shoulder."

Only because I know—even without knowing you well—that I can trust you. That's what I could have said, but instead I shrugged like what he'd said wasn't relevant, and said, "Then I think it's high time we conducted one."

Pushing Imogene in the stroller, I walked beside Albert, who was holding Peter's hand and scanning my parent's upscale neighborhood for a cement factory. "So," said Peter, "how do you think we should proceed with the investigation?"

"Good question," I said, slowing to give Imogene her bottle. "Why don't we stick with the essentials?"

"What do you mean?" he asked.

"I'll say something and you tell me if you think it's essential."

"All right," said Peter, putting his hand out briefly to stop us from stepping into the street while he checked for traffic. "Let's do it."

I lowered the stroller off the curb. "Okay," I said, "I'll begin with . . . professional sports."

"Essential or not essential. Hmm, I suppose that depends on the weather and the company I'm keeping," he said, smiling.

I nudged him as if annoyed by this reference to our little past, but the truth was I didn't mind. He was being playful, not mean. "So your official answer is . . ."

"Not essential," he said, "but fun all the same."

Spotting the neighborhood park, Albert tugged on Peter's arm. "Can we go play? Can we, can we?"

"But the factory, Albert," said Peter. "Once we find it, it's going to be so fun scaling the barbed wire fence, outrunning the watch dog, and disabling the security cameras."

Albert thought for a moment. "We can do it next time."

Peter let go of Albert's hand. "If you say so," he said as Albert ran for the slide. "Now, where were we?" he asked while pointing out a bench.

Imogene had fallen asleep. "You were breaking rule number one," I said, parking the stroller beside the bench and sitting down.

"I didn't know there were rules," he said, sitting next to me.

"There are always rules, Mr. De Boom."

"And rule number one is?" he asked while keeping his eyes fixed on Albert.

"No explaining your answer. Either it's essential to you or not, end of story."

"Just, bam, give your answer. Professional sports, not essential," he said, recapping.

"Exactly," I said. "Okay, my second pick is—"

"Hey, wait a minute," he said. "You're forgetting rule number two."

The sun had hidden behind dark clouds, making it cooler. "Which is?" I asked, tucking Imogene's blanket around her.

"That I get to conduct a background check also. You're not off the hook just because you have aunt status."

I let out a sigh of exasperation. "Fine," I said, waving at Albert, who was demanding we watch him go down the slide. "We'll take turns."

"Okay then," he said. "My first pick is the gospel."

I shook my head, disapproving. "Of course the gospel is essential. Pick something less obvious."

Amused, Peter's eyes opened wide and he laughed. "How is that obvious?" he asked.

"That whole 'let your light so shine, city that is set on a hill' thing. I'm thirty and live in Manhattan. Trust me, if it weren't essential to me, you'd be able to tell."

"I suppose so," he said, studying me for moment in a way that made me wonder if he were checking for a tattoo or some other sign of worldliness, but then I looked in his eyes. There was an intensity there, but not the kind that comes from finding fault. It looked like he was trying to decide whether to say something, whether doing so would be bold or reckless. "So how about me?" he asked. "Is it obvious the gospel is essential to me?"

"Of course," I said with a wave of my hand, trying to sound casual enough for the two of us. "You have a testimony, I have a testimony; let's move on to the less transparent essentials."

"But shouldn't knowing that be enough, especially if . . ." He paused, and again there it was, a look more suited to a base jumper standing on the edge of a cliff than a guy sitting on a park bench.

"Excuse me, Mr. De Boom," I said, ignoring what he'd said, and in particular what he hadn't, "but you're interrupting an official investigation."

The sun reappeared, glinting off Peter's black hair. "My apologies," he said, and just that quick, like a bird alighting from a branch, his courage left, and Peter was himself again. "Feel free to proceed with the inquest at anytime."

"Thank yo—"

"I won't interrupt."

"Thank—"

"Wouldn't dream of it."

I elbowed him. "Come on!" I cried.

He laughed. "All right, all right," he said. "Where were we?"

"It's my turn," I said as we both waved at Albert, who had climbed to the top of a little rock wall and was frantically waving at us.

"Fire away," he said.

"Chocolate."

"Not essential."

"You're dead to me."

"My turn," said Peter. "Mani/pedis."

I bit my lip. "If it's been a really stressful week and I—"

"You're breaking rule number one."

"Fine, essential, but does that make me sound spoiled?"

"Only outside of Beverly Hills," he said.

I nudged him again. "My turn," I said. "An enormous, disgusting reptile for a pet."

"Not essential."

"Good answer."

"Designer clothes," he said.

I threw my hands in the air. "What is your deal? I give you a softball question and you go for the jugular."

Peter wasn't wearing sunglasses, and I liked the way his eyes crinkled when he turned to look at me. "Cotton candy, then."

"Don't be ridiculous."

"All-inclusive trips to Siberia," he said, trying again.

"Peter," I groaned.

"Or stuffed animals so big they can't fit through the doorway," he said, his arms held out wide.

I grabbed hold of his arm, bringing it down. "Thanks for the options," I said, "but, on second thought, I'll answer your first question."

He took my hand in his like he was comforting the grief stricken. "You don't have to," he soothed. "Just tell me what you think of pork rinds; that will suffice."

"No, it's time to put on my big girl pants—"

"Big girl designer pants," he interjected.

"—and answer your question."

"You're so brave," he whispered, patting my hand.

Griffin likes to say with a chuckle that I have a personal bubble the size of the Hindenberg, and maybe sometimes I do keep him at a distance, particularly when he has onion breath or has been working out, but right then, my hands clasped in Peter's, I had no intention of pulling away to create a comfortable distance between us; I was already comfortable. "Okay, fine," I said. "It's true. Designer clothes are essential to me, but so are clearance sales and consignment stores. And I know I'm breaking rule number one by explaining that, but you have to understand, if I went into a meeting on Madison Avenue dressed in Walmart, I would lose credibility (unless I'm pitching to Walmart), and most likely break out in hives."

"Why hives?" asked Peter. "Are you allergic to polyester?"

"No," I said. "Don't laugh, but I find wearing it traumatic."

Peter leaned back and draped his arm on the bench behind me. "I would never laugh," he said, "at someone who suffers from polyester stress disorder."

"You realize you're mocking my honesty," I said, and though I wasn't truly annoyed, that part of me that takes offense quickly bubbled to the surface, just to see if it was needed; it wasn't.

"Sorry," he said, smoothing down a few of my wind-tossed locks. His fingers lightly grazed my temple, and my arms erupted in goose bumps.

"I expect the same soul-exposing candor from you."

Peter looked at me, courage flickering for a moment in his eyes.

"Hey! Don't watch Aunt Sophie. Watch this!" cried Albert, jumping off a fake boulder.

We cheered (softly for Imogene's sake), but Albert wasn't listening. A family with a little boy had entered the park, and Albert was ready to make a new friend. "I'm probably faster than you!" he yelled, and the two of them were off, climbing in the tunnels.

"Motorcycles?" I asked, getting the ball rolling again.

He shook his head.

"Good. Owning one puts you on the organ donor fast track."

"Expensive jewelry?"

"No," I said. "I like accessorizing too much to throw a wad into one necklace or ring."

"Interesting," he said.

"Money."

"Not essential."

My mouth dropped open. "Because you have a printing press in your basement?" I asked.

Albert was playing pirates with his new friend, wielding an imaginary sword and demanding to know where the treasure was buried. "I don't crave money," said Peter, watching the little boys as he spoke. "Sure I have to have it for bills and life, but I'm not itching to become rich."

My shoulders stiffened. Shouldn't everyone be trying to become ridiculously wealthy? I thought so, and it was one of the reasons I found Griffin worth dating. No one was gunning for millionaire status harder than him. "So you want to be poor?" I asked, sounding a little defensive.

"Of course not," he said. "But you only have so much time on this planet, Sophia. I don't want to miss out on birthday parties and baseball games because I'm so focused on amassing wealth."

My future daughter's words rang in my ears. *I want a father, not a hedge fund manager!* But I shoved them aside and said, "Life is expensive, Peter. You have to plan for the future, for preschool and summer camps and trips to the mall, doctor visits and orthodontia, not to mention college and weddings, and the occasional trip without the kids to recharge the battery." The thought of it all left me feeling exhausted, like I'd just taken the stairs to the top of a skyscraper.

"But you're forgetting something, Sophia."

"The swimming pool?" I asked

"Not the swimming pool, although I'm not against the idea as long as it comes with a safety gate. No, what you're forgetting is that all those things don't have to be paid for at once."

"True, but—" I started, ready to persuade further that babies triggered an avalanche of expenses that only careful planning and a Kilimanjaro-size pile of cash could contend with when he playfully ruffled my hair.

"And where's your faith, Sophia?" he asked, his lips curling into an easy smile. "I'm newer to the gospel than you, but come on, blessings come to the obedient," he said, bumping my knee with his. "We both know we're here to have a family."

I gulped. I knew he meant *we* in the general sense, but still, I gulped, and then our eyes locked, and I gulped again, and it was as if someone somewhere hit the mute button and everything—Albert playing, Imogene cooing, the leaves rustling in the wind—it all fell away until the only sound left was the beating of my heart. Fear and courage flashed in Peter's eyes, both vying for dominance. He opened his mouth, ready to say something, and then—

"So how about that Santa guy?" said the father of Albert's new friend as he and his wife walked hand in hand toward us. "We do all the work, and he takes all the credit. Sort of reminds me of my boss. We're Braeden and Brinley," he said.

Peter stood and extended his hand. It was a little more formal than the situation required, and let me catch a glimpse of Peter as a boy, homesick and lonely in boarding school, and trying hard not to get a toe out of line. "And we're Peter and Sophia," he said, not bothering to explain further.

Peter and Braeden shook hands. "Nice to meet you," said Brinley, bouncing to keep the newborn strapped to her front asleep. "Are you both as sleep deprived as we are?" she asked, sounding and looking far too perky for someone claiming fatigue.

"I'm telling you," said Peter, his glance telling me to not blow our parent cover.

"But it's all worth it when they see what Santa's left under the tree," she said, her eyes crinkling with a smile.

"Absolutely," I said, going along. "Albert mostly wanted furniture from IKEA. It took forever to put together."

Braeden raised an eyebrow. "That's unusual," he said.

I smiled. "He's a funny one, but he's ours," I said, beaming at Peter, who beamed back, trying to look every bit the father of a four-year-old furniture lover.

Just then our "funny one" tapped me on the leg, making me jump. "I think Baby Imi has a stinky," he said, sniffing the air.

"That's impossible!" I cried, a note of unmistakable terror in my voice. Imogene lay awake in the stroller, legs kicking, arms swatting, happy, but suspiciously smelly. I lifted her enough to check her backside and saw a brownish ooze seeping out of her diaper and soaking her onesie almost to her neck.

"Yep," said Albert. "She's got a stinky."

Peter put his face in his hands. "This cannot be happening," he said, sounding like we just got in a fender bender.

Imogene laughed and kicked, like there was nothing more fun than grossing people out. "You change it," I mumbled, leaning into Peter.

Peter took a deep breath. "I can't. I think I'm going to be sick."

"Well, someone's got to change it," said Albert.

I stood up, throwing my hands in the air. "That's it. I can't handle this," I said, gesturing at adorable, happy, stinky Imogene. "We're going to have to go home and figure this out."

"Nice to meet you," said Braeden, but the way he said it, it sounded more like a question.

"Yes," said Brinley, determined to sound perky. "Huxley had fun playing. Merry Christmas to you." I could tell Brinley liked her life to be one happy Facebook post after another, and meeting us had been a disappointment.

"Merry Christmas," Peter and I said.

And just in case Braeden and Brinley didn't think we were the weirdest people on the planet, Albert said as we left the park, "Hey, do you think we have time to go play at the cement factory?"

"Another time," said Peter. "Another time."

chapter 15

SOMETIMES IN LIFE, it's better not to look. Like, for instance, when you're getting blood drawn, or if you're me, riding shotgun and your mother's behind the wheel. Scary parts of movies, a home video of your friend's appendectomy—sometimes the best you can do is block your view and try to think of something else. Griffin and I, of course, needed to talk about what had happened, and Griffin being Griffin, I knew he'd want to do so right away, but I didn't want that. I didn't want to spend Christmas hashing out in texts where our relationship stood, so I did what had always worked for me in the past—I chose not to look.

According to Barry, a know-it-all intern in our office who can't remember that I don't drink coffee (no lie, every morning he offers me a cup), there is no difference between people who *need* their phones and babies who need pacifiers. "For the weak, a phone is more comforter than communicator," he had said, standing by the copier, tugging on his wispy goatee. "A baby's binky, if you will, pacifying the pathetic masses with its connectivity."

I had rolled my eyes and mumbled, "Yeah, whatever," before walking away texting. But while getting dressed upstairs Christmas morning, Barry's words popped into my mind, and I grabbed my phone from my purse and turned it off, partly to prove to myself I could, and partly to give myself a break from Griffin. I didn't mind a day away from my phone. Yes, I'd been accused of having it super-glued to my hand, but that was because of the demands of my job, not some sort of neediness on my part. (Take that, Barry!) But assuming that powering down would keep Griffin from reaching me was naive. The same doggedness that had made him a prince on Wall Street would certainly make figuring out a way to reach me a piece of cake. And it did. When I didn't answer my phone, he tried my parent's house phone, and when my mom (happily) blocked him from speaking to me, he just relayed messages to me through Peter instead.

"He says he's still thinking about how pretty your eyes looked when you were angry," said Peter, reading Griffin's latest text.

"Tell him I'll call him tomorrow."

"He says that's a long time."

"Tell him it's not."

"He says it is."

"He makes me want to pull my hair out!"

"You want me to text that?"

"No!"

With Peter acting as our carrier pigeon, Griffin and I communicated so much on Christmas that when I looked at my phone before going to bed, all I was thinking about was the certainty of seeing texts and calls from my boyfriend. It hadn't occurred to me that my boss might have been trying to reach me as well.

Horrified, my hand flew to my mouth as I saw that two of the seven texts waiting for me were from Mr. Dilwooten. "Oh no, oh no, oh no," I breathed, opening the first one. *Powwow with Luxe Air exec, Neal Crosby. Our office tomorrow at 5 p.m. Are you in?* I groaned knowing my boss had been waiting for my answer all day. Fingers twitching, I opened his next message. *If you're in, see you at five. If not, Merry Christmas.*

I'll be there, I texted back, not considering until after that short message was sent what it would cost me, and I'm not talking about the price of a last-minute ticket from Phoenix to New York. I would miss going to the zoo. Going was Gram's idea. She wanted to try the zoo's new motorized scooters her friends had been raving about, since, according to her, the old ones moved slower than a crawling baby. The whole family was going, including my mother, which usually would have meant me seizing any excuse (let alone a legitimate one!) to beg off. But Peter was coming too.

Peter. It seemed strange, all that had happened since seeing him at Hanno's wedding. Yes, I was being shoved into his arms by a bossy preteen, and my mother and grandmother were definitely in the cheering section, but all that pressuring aside, I liked Peter, and in the past few days we had laughed and talked too much for us to simply part ways. We were friends now, and I hated to leave so suddenly, especially when we had big plans to eat funnel cake and ride the ancient camel that had been giving rides since I was a child. *Don't be ridiculous*, New York Sophie scolded. *You can't miss this meeting to wander past zebras and eat carnival food. Be realistic. An opportunity this amazing doesn't come around more than once. Don't let it slip away. And besides, you're only leaving a day earlier than scheduled. Yes, Peter is nice, but what could possibly happen between the two of you in a day?*

I sighed. "I'll be there," I said, and with silly tears pricking my eyes, I began to pack.

The only flight that could get me to New York in time left at seven, and the only seats available were in first class. "There goes my new sofa," I mumbled as I punched in the numbers of my debit card and bought the ticket. Maybe I could convince Mr. Dilwooten to expense the cost. I was, after all, flying to a meeting with a client who operated a luxury airliner. Traveling first class was practically research. But for a guy who kept a car in the city and owned a house in the south of France, Mr. Dilwooten hated to spend money. Who was I kidding? He'd talk himself into keeping my flight off the company books, unless, that is, I came up with a campaign idea the people at Luxe Air loved.

I needed to be sharp, at the top of my game. If I showed up to that meeting articulate and fresh-faced as a zombie, then I might as well have just splurged on a sofa. There was no question that my future daughter was going to have A LOT to say about the choice I'd made, and though I wanted to see her again, I needed my rest. No more Mrs. Nice Future Mom; it was time for a preemptive strike. Buried somewhere in my toiletry bag was an expired bottle of Tylenol PM that I had bought after arriving in Japan a few years ago with a migraine. I found the bottle, took two tablets, and, after setting my alarm, went to bed. What I had hoped for was deep, restorative sleep. What I got was another all-night conversation with my future daughter, only now underwater.

We sat, legs crisscrossed, at the bottom of the shallow end of a pool. I'm a wimp when it comes to water temperature, so though the water wasn't cold, it wasn't warm enough either, and to make matters even more uncomfortable, my swimsuit was too small and the straps were digging into my shoulders. I wanted to jump out of the pool and head for a hot shower. It all seemed so real to me, except that as if weighed down by an anchor, I was stuck there, arguing underwater with my future daughter, unable to even claim that I needed to head to the surface to catch my breath, since at the moment, breathing wasn't necessary.

"Why are you leaving?" she shouted, her words slowed and garbled by the water.

"I have an important meeting!" I shouted back, frustrated by how the water took the umph out of what I'd said.

"More important than me!" she challenged.

"No."

"Then stay! My dad's here!"

My hair wandered in front of my eyes. I pushed it aside. "He's not your dad!"

"I want Peter!"

"You don't get to choose—"

"And I want Sarah to be my name."

I opened my mouth to object, to tell her I hadn't yet made up my mind, but all that came out were bubbles. Who was I kidding? She was Sarah, not because she was demanding it, or because of Peter's grandmother, but simply because the name fit her. And besides, it was exhausting arguing underwater.

"And to get my ears pierced."

"What?"

"I want my ears pierced!"

"Absolutely not," I said, because wearying though it was to speak, you had to take a stand on some things.

"Why?" she screamed.

"You're too young."

"Babies get their ears pierced all the time!"

"Not my babies."

"You're so mean!"

"You'll thank me later when you don't have sagging ear holes," I said, tugging at my ear for emphasis.

"I won't get that!"

"Enough heavy earrings and you would."

"But all I want to wear are little peace signs!" she cried, her honey-colored hair hovering above her like a halo, and her eyes wide as harvest moons. She was so beautiful, too beautiful to have a stupid hippie symbol pinned to her ears.

"No, no peace signs," I said.

"Then panda bears!"

All night we argued, our words dog-paddling between us, the one bright spot being that underwater Sarah couldn't play the clarinet or cymbals, not that she didn't try. When my alarm sounded, I awoke coughing and spluttering, and could smell a whiff of chlorine in the air.

"Good heavens!" my mother cried when I stepped into the kitchen early in the next morning. "You look absolutely terrible."

"Thanks for your honesty," I said, trying to make light of her observation.

My mother eyed my suitcase. "Where are you going so early?" she asked.

"I have to head back to New York," I said. "There's a meeting this afternoon with a new client, and I can't miss it." My delivery was perfect, not the least defensive. I could have given myself a pat on the back.

Mom tutted. "It's advertising, not heart surgery, Sophie. They can get along without you for a day."

And just like that my back was up. What made her think that just saying I didn't need to be at a meeting would make it so? "Mr. Dilwooten wants me there," I snapped, though to my credit, quietly.

"Well, your mother wants you here! We're going to the zoo!" she snapped back, not trying for quiet at all.

I pointed at the screened porch. "Ssh! You're going to wake Peter."

"He's not here," she said. "He and George left to watch the sunrise at Pinnacle Peak. George wanted to wake you, but Peter wouldn't let him. He said you needed your sleep," she said, arching an eyebrow as if my being awake was a betrayal. "And I suppose you intended to march out of here without saying good-bye to them or anyone else!" I ignored the hurt in her voice.

"It can't be helped," I said, tightly gripping my purse and suitcase, just in case she tried to snatch one to keep me from leaving.

Mom folded her arms and jutted her chin, which somehow made her look both strong and vulnerable. "I suppose we're used to your abandonment," Mom said with a contemptuous sniff, "but what about Peter?"

My mouth fell open. "Abandonment, are you kidding me?" I cried, taking advantage of Peter's absence by raising my voice. "You're not six, Mom, and I'm not enrolling you in a summer-long camp so I can travel through Europe with my husband!"

"Your brother was with you!"

"And ten-year-old boys are excellent at comforting sobbing little girls. 'Don't worry, Sophie. Planes run out of gas and crash into the ocean only some of the time. They're probably fine.'"

"Camp Watoosie had a five-star rating! You were at the best of places," she shouted.

"I was lonely!" I shouted back even louder as tears stung my eyes.

Mom waved a hand in the air as if doing so would shoo away the unpleasantness and the hurt. "Well, I can't help it if Gram planned a trip to Canada that summer without consulting us."

Of course no "I'm sorry," or "I wish things would have worked out differently." Right on cue, she passed the blame to someone else. I looked at my watch through watery eyes. "I don't have time for this," I said and started for the garage door.

"You never have time for anything, except your work and Griffin!" she cried, saying his name like it was a hated thing. Her eyes shot upward. "How you put up with that insufferable hobby of his, I'll never know."

If I were guilty of abandoning anything, it was the resolve to leave without having a major fight with my mother. I stepped toward her. The gloves were coming off. "Sorry you don't like what Griffin chooses to do in his spare time, but unlike you, I don't try to turn people into my little puppets."

"What on earth are you talking about?" shrieked Mom. A piece of her perfectly coiffed hair had fallen in front of her eyes, but she was too angry to bother moving it.

Tears slid down my face now, taking with them the heavy coating of Princess Marguerite I'd applied under my eyes. "I'm talking about the way you treat Dad!" I shouted. "Christmas morning he was so excited to give you those cooking classes, he could hardly stand it." I watched as guilt flitted across my mother's face. "But his gift wasn't what you'd asked for, wasn't one of the 'items'"—I made quotes in the air—"on your official wish list. Dad gave you something *he* thought you'd enjoy, and were you nice about it? Did you even fake a gracious smile? No, you totally shut him down."

Mom took a deep breath, giving herself a moment to calm down. "Sophie," she said, "the only people who truly understand a marriage are the two who are in it."

I didn't bother taking a deep breath. Instead I let go of my suitcase and balled my fists. "That may be, but I understand you," I spat. "You want to control the people in your life. Their choices need to make sense to you, or they just need to make other choices."

"You're being ridiculous!" she cried. "I don't expect that from anyone. When have I told your brother he needs to leave London and move back to Mesa?"

"Yesterday!" I screamed back, smacking her on the cheek with my spit.

"That was just wishful thinking! I know he needs to be there for his career. It's not what I'd prefer, but I accept it. And as far as you're concerned, sometimes a mother's job is to say what needs to be said!" She yelled louder than I'd ever heard her, and it occurred to me that we were in it—our worst mother/daughter fight, but did that make me back down? No, and the shouting continued.

"Say what needs to be said," I parroted. "Yes, there's always that day when you have to warn your growing daughter to not let her feet get any bigger or no boy will want to date her."

"I don't remember telling you that!"

"How convenient!"

"Enough of the past! Do you expect me to stand by and watch you ruin your life?"

"By not going to the zoo," I scoffed.

"No, by pursuing a man who when you finally wake up you're going to despise, especially when you consider who you gave up!"

"Who am I giving up?" I asked, shouting just as loud as she was.

"Peter!"

I rolled my eyes. "I don't remember him being offered up to me like a cookie on a platter."

"It's obvious he cares for you!" she cried, her voice cracking with emotion.

This softened me a little, but I didn't show it. "You realize he leaves tomorrow. What do you expect to happen between us in one day?"

"Nothing, if you're apart," she said, and all at once she looked frail to me. My indomitable mother looked frail.

I could almost hear Sarah shout, *You tell her, Grandma!*

"You forget that I have a boyfriend."

"The one you threw a rock at. No, I haven't forgotten about him."

"Honestly, Mom, I think growing up I would have preferred a hurled rock to your barbed words and disappointed looks."

Mom shook her head. "Here you go again, bringing up things that I don't remember and that no longer matter."

"They matter to me. How dare you expect to have a say in what I do with my life after all the times you've hurt my feelings!"

Mom clucked her tongue. "Your feelings!" she cried. "Has it ever occurred to you that you're easily offended?"

Yes, it had occurred to me. I knew I tended to be hypersensitive, but there was no way I was admitting it, not when she had so much to admit herself. "Opinionated, interfering, demeaning. Has any of that occurred to you?"

Mom narrowed her eyes into menacing slits. "Insult me if you want, but you need to hear the truth. Griffin is a buffoon, and for you to rush off to New York to be in his arms—"

"My going to New York has nothing to do with Griffin. I have a meeting!" I screamed.

From upstairs I could hear footfall. We had awakened Dad.

"But he will be there, and he'll worm his way into your heart—"

"So I'm defenseless as an apple. Give me some credit, Mom."

"You're wasting time!"

"It's my time to waste!"

"It's time for you to get married, Sophie!"

"What does it matter to you?" I asked, my voice cold. "As if I'd allow you anywhere near the most important day of my life! Whoever I marry, you're not invited!"

My mother did her best not to crumble, but my words had stung like a slap to the face.

"Hey, hey, what's going on?" asked Dad, his voice pleasant, like he hadn't just heard us screaming at each other.

Dad put his arm around Mom and she slumped on his shoulder, defeated. I grabbed my suitcase and kissed Dad on the cheek. "Nothing's going on," I said. "I have to get back to New York. Mom and I were just saying good-bye." *Forever!* That's how I wanted to end that sentence, but I didn't.

Dad opened his mouth, like he was about to delve further, to ask why had he heard shouting, and what was it that had upset his wife. But if there is one thing Dad doesn't like, it's confrontation, and so instead, he held my mother and said, "Well, I suppose if it can't be helped."

"It can't," I said.

He patted me on the shoulder. "Then good-bye, sweetheart," he said, sounding tired and looking sad. Mom wouldn't look at me. "Bye," I said, and left, waiting until I was halfway to the airport before I let myself cry again.

chapter 16

$\mathscr{I}$ TRIED TO TELL myself that it didn't matter, fighting with my mother and having such a terrible relationship with her that I never wanted to see her again, but that didn't stop the tears from falling. They spilled from my eyes and slid down my face as I checked my bag, boarded the plane, stored my carry-on, and requested an extra pillow. They fell as I said hello to the businessman sitting next to me, sipped ginger ale, and flipped through a magazine. And when I thought of Peter, they turned from quiet tears into sobs. Chest-heaving, nose-blowing sobs that made the businessman pat my hand and ask me if my pet turtle had died. Apparently a few years back he'd sobbed uncontrollably on a nonstop from St. Louis to Cincinnati after learning his dear Mr. Toodles had gotten out and been snapped up by a Japanese chef driving past. Talking about it made his eyes mist up, and interestingly enough stemmed the flow of mine.

Sleep, of course, wasn't an option. The second I closed my eyes, there was Sarah, eyes swollen from crying, begging me to turn the plane around or, worse yet, playing "One Is the Loneliest Number" on her clarinet. My flight from Atlanta to JFK was delayed two hours, so by the time I landed in New York, there wasn't time to head to my apartment for a hot shower. As the taxi crawled toward Percy Dilwooten Foster, I did what I could to spruce up my appearance, applying makeup, fluffing my hair, but when I opened the conference room door, my boss took one look at me and said, "Yowza!" which I know could be taken as a compliment, but trust me, he didn't mean it that way.

I was about to apologize, to explain my situation, the sleepless nights, family drama, and long day of travel, but before I could start, a small man with rimless glasses and clean-shaven head rubbed his hands together and said, "I love it."

I may have been so exhausted I was seeing random starbursts, but I still knew without being told that this was our client, Neal Crosby of Luxe Air. He was around forty, which was younger than I was expecting and lean as a long-distance runner.

"You love it," said Mr. Dilwooten, not masking his surprise.

Mr. Crosby hooked a thumb on the neck of his gray cashmere sweater and walked around me as if studying a work of art. "She's the perfect visual," he said, jutting a hand in my direction.

"She is," said Mr. Dilwooten, agreeing with his client, though furrowing his brow in confusion.

"This is what we're offering—freedom from arriving looking and feeling like this."

I smiled like I didn't mind being crowned Miss Travel Worn, and only then did it occur to me that maybe I should have parked my suitcase and carry-on at my desk instead of bringing them inside the conference room with me.

"She's haggard, she's drained." Mr. Crosby cupped his hand to his chin. "This is what flying on your typical airline will do to you. They may as well tag your ear because you get treated like livestock."

Mr. Dilwooten was now up to speed. "Exactly," he said, sounding his usual confident self. "Why don't we have a seat?"

"No need," said Crosby, checking his watch. "Just looking at her I know we're on the same page."

Mr. Dilwooten shrugged. "I'm all for short meetings, Crosby, but since we're all here, wouldn't it be wise to discuss—"

Mr. Crosby put his hand up and shook his head, like he was saying no to an appetizer. "The sooner I get to Paris the better," he said, then struck by a sudden burst of inspiration, he fixed his eyes on the ceiling and said, "Luxe Air passengers want to experience . . ." He took a deep breath, as if the words he sought were floating in the air, and when they eluded him he exhaled hard, making his lips flap. "I don't know how to say it, which doesn't matter, because that's your firm's job, but this," he said, pointing at me, "this is what they don't want! And they're willing to pay more because of it. They want shiatsu massaging chairs that convert into beds, foot baths, aromatherapy, chef-crafted meals made from only the finest ingredients, and they want it all at the right price point. It's all in the packet of information I sent you."

"Of course," said Dilwooten.

Mr. Crosby took a step toward the conference room door and then turned to us. "It's not about arriving. Anyone can get you there. It's about how you feel once you've arrived." Mr. Crosby turned to me. "What did the carrier you flew with today do wrong?"

I could have told him the many things they did right. How kind the flight attendants had been and quick to hand me more tissue as I cried my eyes out. But Mr. Crosby was interested in hearing what they did wrong. "Well," I said, rubbing my forehead, "they ran out of peanuts."

"And how do you feel now?" he asked.

I decided to be honest. "Like I want to toss my phone in the toilet, fall on my bed, and bawl my eyes out."

"Wow," said Mr. Crosby. "That's a girl who likes her peanuts."

Mr. Dilwooten gestured toward me. "This is Miss Sophia Stark. She will be taking the first stab at your campaign, flying solo, if you will."

"Really," said Mr. Crosby, shaking my hand.

"When it comes to creativity," said Dilwooten, "teamwork early on is stifling."

His index fingers peaked, Mr. Crosby pressed them to his lips and thought. "Interesting," he said. "We'll see if it works, and if it doesn't, we'll know who to blame." There was no smile, no light-hearted delivery to soften his statement. Gulp. "But I like your work ethic, Miss Stark. Your commitment to research."

"You can be assured, Mr. Crosby, I won't rest," I said, deciding not to elaborate.

"As well you shouldn't," said Mr. Crosby. "You're under the gun, Miss Stark. We want visibility during polo season which kicks off in January, so ASAP's NSE, as the saying goes." Then, to make sure we understood, said, "As soon as possible's not soon enough."

"I don't think I've heard that expression before," I said, aware that I was blinking slower than usual.

"That's because I just made it up," he said, grabbing his briefcase and coat. "Maybe there's something to this working alone thing, Dilwooten. I'm off, but I'm glad we had this talk. Good to know we're on the same page."

The door to the conference room swung open, and in walked Barry the intern, carrying a tray. "Coffee," he said. It was a demand, not a question, and it was directed at me.

Mr. Crosby caught the door, keeping it from closing. "You better get her a thermos of it," he said. "She's going to need it. I'll expect your presentation in three days."

Mr. Dilwooten hurried, following Mr. Crosby to the elevator, leaving me alone with Barry. "Coffee," he said again, taking a step toward me.

"Have there been any late-breaking changes to the Word of Wisdom?" I asked

Barry smiled, his little teeth reminding me of confetti. Coffee-stained confetti. "Since I don't know what you're talking about, I'm going to have to say no," he said.

"Then back off with the coffee, Barry!" I snapped, making him flinch, sending the coffee slopping onto the tray. I walked to the conference room door. "By the way," I said, turning to look at him, "cell phones are not for the weak. Coffee's for the weak, Barry. Coffee!" Barry's eyes grew wide and his shoulders shrank. He looked as confident as a substitute lion tamer, but did I take pity on him and try to be nice? No. I was tired and stressed out, and his goatee annoyed me. "Fear has a smell, Barry," I said as I opened the door, "and it smells like a triple mocha cappuccino!" It would have been a dramatic exit, except my carry-on slipped off my shoulder and as I fixed it, the door shut on my suitcase

"Miss Stark!" called Barry just as I was about to close the door behind me.

"Yes, Barry," I said, assuming that what was coming next was an "I'm sorry" or "Good luck with the Luxe Air campaign." Silly me.

Barry pressed his lips together as if deliberating whether to say it. "Would you consider . . . decaf?" he asked.

"Go away, Barry," I said. "Go away."

My phone vibrated, announcing the arrival of another text. Since leaving Arizona, I'd received several. A few from my brother and Gram, both chastising me for leaving without saying good-bye, a few from Mr. Dilwooten, prepping me for the meeting, and more than a few from my super serious boyfriend. I hadn't bothered to open any of Griffin's, but walking to my office/broom closet (think ridiculously small) I glanced at my phone and saw that the text I'd just received was from him. Curiosity getting the better of me, I clicked on my screen to see what he had to say.

HEARD YOU WERE IN TOWN. CAN YOU MEET ME AT MANHATTAN RACQUETBALL CLUB AT SIX!!! URGENT!!!

Griffin liked to use all caps and exclamation points the way my father liked to use salt—liberally. In other words, whatever he had to say probably wasn't going to be earth shattering. Still, he did say it was urgent. And besides, it was nearly six and the Manhattan Racquetball Club was just a few blocks from work. I decided to text back: *I just finished a meeting at work.*

FANTASTIC!!! he texted. *COURT 2!!! SEE YOU SOON!!!*

To which I texted: *If you want to see me, you can come here,* but I didn't send it, because when you get right down to it, all caps and exclamation points are fairly persuasive. *Fine,* I texted. *See you there.*

Racquetball was a new love for Griffin, and one that I'd encouraged, mainly because his games often made it necessary for him to cancel his weekly didgeridoo lesson. "There is no I in team racquetball," he'd say, furrowing his brow, when a scheduling conflict arose. I was always the understanding girlfriend at such a time, though deep down I wanted to say, *Blek. Who cares? You don't sound any better and your teacher sleeps through your lesson.* Or at least he looked like he did. The great didgeridoo teacher, Quantu, liked to shut his eyes when he spoke, or listened, or drove on the interstate. Well, I'm not sure about the last one. But seriously, I doubted he even noticed Griffin's absence.

The echo of balls thwacking against walls greeted me as I stepped inside the Manhattan Racquetball Club. All the courts were fronted by glass, which made it easy for me to see Griffin in Court 2 jump and swing at the ball too late. He turned to see where the elusive ball had gone and saw me standing there. Griffin's face lit up, his eyes sparkling with happiness behind his goggles. Telling the other player he'd be right back, he wiped the sweat off his forehead with his electric blue wristband since the electric yellow headband he was wearing was already drenched and not doing its job.

Still wearing his goggles, he rushed toward me, arms out-stretched, ready for a hug. "Sophie!" he cried.

I put up a hand, stopping him. "Griffin, you are super sweaty."

"I know," he said, pleased. "It's such a great workout." He wiped his forehead again with his wristband and leaned in for a peck on my cheek, but I wasn't having it.

He looked like someone had found a bucket full of sweat and decided to pour it over him. "I really just need my space right now," I said, letting go of my suitcase and carry-on, and taking a giant step backward.

Griffin straightened up but was in too good of a mood to mind being denied. Flipping his drenched bangs off his goggles, he sent a few beads of sweat sailing into my face. "Griffin!" I cried.

"Sorry about that," he said, patting my shoulder and leaving a sweaty handprint on my coat.

I glared at the handprint and then at him. "Look," I said, "I came because you said there was something urgent you needed to tell me."

Griffin clapped his hands together, sending more sweat flying, and one disgusting drip in particular landed on my hand. "Griffin!" I cried again.

"Sorry again," he said, "but I'm just so excited to tell you what I have to say!"

I pulled out the small bottle of hand sanitizer I kept in my coat pocket and squirted some into my palm, making the air around us smell like Christmas cookies. Well, slightly sweaty Christmas cookies. Still, it was an improvement. "Then go ahead and say it," I said, rubbing my hands together, "but could you do me a favor and take off your goggles first?"

Griffin winced. It was the trademark look he gave before telling someone no. "To be honest, Sophe, I'd rather not," he said.

I folded my arms. "To be honest, Griffin, it's hard to take you seriously while you're wearing them. They make you look goofy."

"But I have perfect adhesion right now," he said, cupping the rim of his goggles and nodding, as if doing so would make me agree with him.

I guess it worked. I let out a breath. "Fine," I said. "Keep them on. Just get on with it."

"Right," he said, and all at once I noticed how tall he was. So tall that had he any skills, the NBA would have been interested. So tall our daughters wouldn't have a fighting chance of one day wearing stilettos. Not that it mattered. There were more important things. But still. "Since Christmas Eve, I've been doing a lot of thinking, and well, you know how when you're dating you generally have a contingency plan."

"A what?"

Sweat continued to pour off Griffin; he sniffed. "A contingency plan, a running list ranked according to your level of interest of who you'd date if the relationship you're in goes south."

"Oh," I said, "a contingency plan," like the idea wasn't completely foreign to me, and offensive.

Griffin smiled and tilted his head toward me. "Sophie," he said.

"Get to your point, Griffin," I said, not angry, just tired.

"All right then," he said, so excited he bounced on his heels. "I think we," he pointed back and forth between us, "should take our relationship to the next level."

I turned around, scanning the area for friends hiding behind benches or garbage cans, waiting for the signal to jump out and shout "Congratulations!" No one was there (thank heavens), but what else could "take our relationship to the next level" mean other than he was about to propose to me? It didn't matter, because when it came to Griffin I was done jumping to conclusions. "And what does that mean, taking our relationship to next level?" I asked, all business, like I was talking dishwashers with an appliance salesman.

Griffin mopped up the sweat from his face with the sleeve of his already soaked T-shirt and smiled. "What it means is I'm ready to crumple it."

"Crumple what?"

"The list, silly," he said, like it was so obvious. "I'm ready to crumple the list."

As if doing so would keep my head from feeling like it wanted to explode, I pressed my fingers to my temples. "So for the past eight months you've been shuffling and reshuffling a list of people you'd like to date," I said to clarify.

"Well, not every week, but that doesn't matter," he said. "It's as good as crumpled now, Sophe, and I want to move forward—"

"I didn't have one," I said, cutting him off.

"You didn't have what?"

"A contingency list."

He reached for my hand. I let him take it, but it was a dead fish. "And I don't now either."

"I thought it was just us."

"It is just us."

"No, it's not," I said, taking my hand back. "I can't date you anymore, Griffin."

Griffin raised a quizzical eyebrow and laughed. "What?" he asked, like I'd said something preposterous. "Why can't you date me anymore?"

I hoisted my carry-on back on my tired shoulder and grabbed my suitcase. "Because, Griffin, right now I'm lumping you with fruitcake."

"Fruitcake?"

"And misty cottage paintings."

"Misty what?

"Liverwurst and onions."

"Sophe, come on. You're not making any sense," he said as I turned and started walking away.

"Overalls," I said, pulling my suitcase behind me.

"Sophe! Come on, I'm in the middle of winning a game here! I can't leave!"

I didn't turn around, slow down, or speed up. I just kept heading for the exit. "Toddler pageants and game shows."

"Sophie!"

A man walking in held the door for me. I should have said thank you, but instead as I left the Manhattan Racquetball Club, I shouted one last nonessential. "Griffin Overland Oscar Ploof the third!"

"What!"

I let the door shut behind me, let the sounds of the city envelope me, and an eager taxi driver take my suitcase. "Good-bye, Griffin," I said, and as we drove away, I didn't look back.

chapter **17**

$\mathcal{I}$F POSSIBLE, I would have rented a drill sergeant, someone to get in my face, and shout that I needed to get my head together, because a deadline was looming. A DEADLINE! Someone to mock cry, call me a baby, and tell me to quit dwelling on my personal life, and focus, for Pete's sake, on the fact that if I managed to wow Neal Crosby, it would change everything—my job, my office, my income, my life! There was no one but me, however, to shake me by the shoulders, so I sobbed into my pillow a little longer, then sat up, sighed deeply, and got to work. Now was not the time for falling apart or falling asleep (as if Sarah would let me sleep anyway). No, now was the time to hit it hard. "There's too much at stake," I told myself after hanging up with Doña Redonda Mexican Grill. I'd ordered their trash heap nachos with extra hot peppers because if crunchy didn't keep me awake, hot would.

What Neal Crosby was looking for was the vibe of the campaign, the slogan, the genius. A rough sketch of the commercials for both print and video, but not the finished products. That part would be a team effort. Right now was all about harnessing a winner idea. "This is going to be a piece of cake," I told myself, jumping up and down and throwing punches like a boxer because the nachos hadn't arrived yet. "I have so many ideas! Too many ideas, all charging at me like stampeding horses! The hardest part is going to be deciding which one to lasso." From punching I switched to twirling an imaginary rope above my head and throwing it around the neck of a wild mustang. "I'll be done in an hour, two tops. Mozart wrote a sonata in twenty minutes," I said, pacing back and forth. "Well, maybe. You can't believe everything you read on Pinterest, but you can be on a roll, in the zone! And when that happens, things move fast, pieces fall into place, mountains move!" I shouted triumphantly.

My doorbell buzzed. "Doña Redonda," said a voice from just outside my door.

"Oh," I said, my hands still thrust heavenward, "just a second." And I rushed to find my wallet.

The aroma of trash heap nachos wafted into my apartment before I'd opened the door, making my mouth water. Money in hand, I undid the door's several locks and jerked it open.

"That'll be twenty," said the guy standing in front of me as I stared at his bluish black hair. It was missing the slightest peppering of gray, but other than that it was Peter's color, and seeing it made my heart flip.

"Huh?" I asked, rubbing my forehead.

"Twenty," he said again. Other than the hair, he looked nothing like Peter. He was short, stocky, and a good ten years younger, but that hair, that mop of hair. Looking at it, my knees buckled, and the hardwood floor beneath my feet seemed to give like a trampoline. I leaned against the door frame to steady myself and handed the guy with Peter's hair the money as he handed me a brown shopping bag filled with still-steaming nachos. "It sounded good, by the way," he said, folding the bills and putting them in his front pocket.

A stab of hunger hit me as the smell of grilled chicken and onions, taco meat and cheddar cheese, sweet pork and bell peppers rose from the bag and enveloped me. "I'm sorry. What sounded good?" I asked.

He ran a hand through his hair and I shivered. "The play you're working on," he said. "I could hear you practicing your lines through the door."

"Oh, right. The play," I said and cleared my throat to mask my blushing cheeks—the sort of thing that makes perfect sense when you're sleep deprived.

"Are you in a leading role?" he asked.

"You could say that."

"Is this your big break?"

"I hope so."

"So what's it called?"

Tears pricked my eyes, but I forced them not to fall. "It's called 'Sophie Misses Peter.'"

He nodded and started for the elevator. "I'll be looking for it," he said.

"Thanks." I shut the door, pressed my back against it, and slid to the floor where I shoveled nachos, one after another, into my mouth and thought of nothing but Peter.

❧

"Mom!" cried Sarah. She rushed toward me and threw her skinny arms around my neck. "You did it, you did it!"

I rubbed my eyes and enjoyed for a moment the smell of her apple-scented hair. "Did what?" I asked.

She pulled back and looked at me, her eyes sparkling with happiness. "You broke up with your dorky boyfriend!" She was so happy she threw her arms around me again. "Mom, you were awesome," she said, squeezing me tight, "the way you left without looking back! He was calling your name, but you just kept on going! I loved it, Mom. If I ever break up with Flynn, I'm going to do it just like that!"

I patted her arm, letting her know I wanted her to sit back. She did, and I looked into her eyes. "Excuse me," I said, "but who's Flynn?"

She was all a sparkle with joy. "We have social studies together," she gushed. "He holds my lunch box on the way to the cafeteria."

I brushed the nacho crumbs from my lap and sat up taller. "What am I packing for you, an entire watermelon? Surely you can hold your own lunch box."

"Duh, Mom," she said, her head wobbling in a happy way. "He does it because we're *hanging out*."

"No, you're not," I said, flatly. "You're too young to be hanging out with a boy."

And just like that, her joy was snuffed out. Sarah's eyes shot to the ceiling and she let out an angry sigh. "Everyone is doing it, Mom!" she cried.

My first thought was to go with the time-honored parental retort "If everyone were jumping off a bridge would you do it too?" But then I remembered how much that question had annoyed me growing up, especially when my mother substituted "wearing clashing colors" for "jumping off a bridge." And besides, I was tired—tired of a lot of things, but mostly, tired of fighting with the people I loved. And yes, for the record, that included my mother. I put up a hand, motioning for her to calm down. "Why don't you tell me about Flynn?" I asked, and just like that, the sparkle returned.

"Well," she said, tucking her feet beneath her, "he has red hair, but he doesn't have red hair. Does that make sense?" She scrunched up her nose, and I was zapped by a jolt of love for her. She was just so sincere, so beautiful.

"Do you mean brownish red?" I asked.

"That's it!" she said, smiling wide. "And he has brown eyes and plays soccer. He's really, really good at soccer." Sarah had a faraway look, like she was watching Flynn running down a field, passing a ball between his feet. Her admiration made me nervous.

I gulped. "Has he tried to hold your hand?" I asked.

"Mom!" she cried, her cheeks burning with embarrassment.

I touched her arm to reassure her. "Just trying to get to know Flynn, so . . . has he?"

"No, of course not," she said, her cheeks still aflame. Then, appearing to consider something, she bit her lip. "He did hold my rabbit's foot though," she said. "It's attached to the zipper on my lunch box."

"That's good to know," I said, the importance of this little confession not lost on me—my daughter trusted me enough to confide in me. I swallowed hard and blinked back tears from falling. How many times growing up had I wanted to confide in my mother, but knew I couldn't? In her eyes, your children's secrets were something you shared with your friends during lunch, like cheesecake.

"And he stares at me from across the cafeteria at the fifth grade dances," she continued.

I tucked a strand of her honey hair behind her ear. "Does he ask you to dance?" I asked.

She rolled her eyes at my ignorance. "No one dances at the dances, Mom."

"Well, what does he like to talk about?"

"We don't talk to each other. Mom, you're so weird."

"So essentially 'hanging out' in the fifth grade means he's your lunch box Sherpa."

"My what?"

"Never mind, but I'm okay with Flynn, for now." She smiled. I loved it when she smiled. "But no hand holding," I added.

"I would die."

"And no kissing."

She covered her eyes, mortified. "Oh my gosh, Mom. Gross!"

I laughed. "Excuse me, but aren't you the one demanding I kiss Peter?"

"That's different," she said.

"How is it different?"

"Because I want him to be my dad," she said, and the idea no longer sounded absurd to me, only beyond reach.

I held her hand. It felt warm and small in mine. "Let's not get started on that right now," I said, a hint of pleading in my voice. "I need to spend the next few days working, and then after I'm done, I promise, I'll text him."

"Text him? Mom, you need to chase after him!"

I let out a deep breath. It was draining being at odds with my daughter, going round and round in arguments, the two of us not seeing eye to eye. Something needed to change, and maybe that something was me. Maybe it was time I opened up and confided in her. I took another deep breath and went for it. "Sweetie," I said, "I'm not going to lie. I think Peter is cute." Sarah lunged forward and hugged me. "He's funny and sweet." She tightened her grip on me and swayed a little. "And I miss him." The hug was beginning to strangle me. "I miss him a lot."

"You love him!" she cried.

"Well, I don't know about that, but I like him very much."

She mouthed the word *love*, correcting me.

"But here's the thing, Sarah. I'm a grown-up, and grown-ups can't drop everything to chase after someone they like."

"Why not?"

"Besides being a bit stalker-ish, it's because we have responsibilities. The people at Luxe Air are counting on me. They have deadlines they're trying to meet. So you see, I've got to do this first, and then—"

"Why can't you do both?"

The question surprised me. "Chase Peter and work on the campaign at the same time? That's just not possible, honey. This campaign demands my full attention."

"The last few hours you gave it your full attention and all it got you were salsa stains on your T-shirt."

This was true. While brainstorming, I hadn't gotten anywhere, despite the number of times I hit the side of my head and shouted "Think!" Still, the statement struck me as disrespectful, and it was, of course, my duty as her mother to point this out. "Sarah," I said.

She smiled. "I like hearing you say my name, Mom."

I smiled too, but less so, to let her know a reprimand was coming. "Sweetie, I'm your future mother and when you talk to me, you need to be respectful," I said, hypocrisy settling on my shoulders like a weight. I wasn't respectful with my mother. If anything, I was short and dismissive.

"I know, I know," she sing-songed, "but you're selling yourself short, Mom. You can do two things at once!"

"This isn't running on the treadmill and listening to an audio book. Getting to know Peter and getting this ad done are two colossal things, Sarah."

"Two doable colossal things, especially when you have help."

"Help?"

"We're on the same team, Mom. I want you to succeed, especially at marrying Peter, but also with this ad assignment. If it's important to you, it's important to me, and I promise if you try and do both at once, I won't keep you up all night. I'll let you sleep, but you have to actually chase after him—go where ever he is, and pursue him."

I rolled my eyes. "Pursue him! Sarah, if I do what you're asking, he'll file a restraining order."

"No, he won't."

"How can you be so sure?" I asked, and there was something in my voice that reminded me of my awkward, unsure preteen years. I looked at Sarah. She was so much more confident at her age then I had been, and it made me swell with pride.

She shook me softly by the shoulders. "He loves you, Mom. Trust me on this. Find Peter!" She shook me again, only this time harder.

I sighed deeply. "He might be at the South Pole already," I groaned.

Sarah shrugged. "Maybe, or maybe not," she said. "It's worth a try. Besides, do you really want to be thinking of ads after a night of listening to this," and she pulled out her clarinet.

I scowled.

"I'm joking, Mom!"

I breathed a sigh of relief. "Sarah, there's a fine line between—" And then an idea hit me. "Hang on a minute," I said, jotting something down on the paper in front of me. "A fine line, a fine line. That might actually work for the Luxe Air campaign."

Sarah clapped, then lunged forward and gave me a hug. "You see," she said, "together we can do this!" She was still hugging me when my phone rang. Sarah pulled back. "You're going to have to get that, since I'm not born yet and all," she said. "Not that I'm not bitter. Not anymore anyway, because we're a team! My mom and I are a team!"

The ringing grew louder and the room unexpectedly brighter. With great effort, I pried open my eyes and checked the clock. It was nine in the morning. "Oh no," I moaned, and then moaned again when I looked at my phone and saw it was the office calling.

"Hello?" I said, groggily.

"Hello," said someone sounding even groggier. "This is Barry from the office, and I wanted to tell you that you were right. Coffee is for the weak. I didn't drop by Starbucks this morning and it's all I can do to keep from smashing my head inside the copier and just let it print page after page. For some reason that bright light whizzing past seems like fair substitute for a caffeine buzz. So yeah, going without is brutal."

I cleared my throat. "Well, thanks for saying that, Barry," I said, remembering slowly the conversation he was referring to.

"And there's something else. Yesterday I had to run some papers down to Neal Crosby, and as he was getting into his limo I heard him say that teleconferencing leaves him cold, and whatever happened to the good old days when someone went to the effort of meeting you face-to-face."

I rubbed my forehead and thought for a moment. "But where's he going to be?"

"Paris," said Barry with a yawn. "He'll be in Europe through New Year's Eve, working at the Luxe Air offices in Paris. Mr. Dilwooten was invited to join him for fireworks at the Eiffel Tower, but it's his year to spend New Year's playing pinochle with his wife's family."

My phone vibrated, letting me know I'd received a text. "Hang on a second, Barry," I said and flipped to the text. It was from my brother, George. *Hey, Sis*, it read, *no hard feelings about you leaving early. We're at JFK waiting to take off. Nice to be traveling with Peter. He's great at distracting the kids. We'll be ringing in the New Year together in London and will think of you. Take care. Big Bro*. A surge of adrenaline shot through me. "Peter's going to be in London," I said though no one was there to hear it, and it felt like I was close, super close, to the final twist of a Rubik's Cube. I flipped back to Barry. "Sorry for the wait," I said.

"No problem. It gave me some time for a cat nap."

"Look, I've got to catch a plane today for London. I'll text you the address where I can be reached if Mr. Dilwooten needs to Fed Ex anything to me."

"Hey, wait a minute," said Barry, sounding like he was beginning to wake up. "If you're in London, you could—"

"Make my presentation in person," I said, finishing his sentence.

"It will be the cherry on top," he said. "And as my public relations professor likes to say, more often than you'd think, people buy the whole sundae just for the cherry."

"Thanks, Barry," I said.

"Go, Sophie," he cheered, and somewhere in the background I thought I heard Sarah cheering too.

chapter 18

HEY THERE,

It's me again—Sophie, your wife. In an hour I'll be landing in London and thought I'd take a break from work to write you. If your name turns out not to be Peter De Boom, boy, am I going to have a crazy story to tell you one day. But, for the sake of this letter, let's assume that you are Peter. I just flipped through the letters in this book and the last time I wrote to someone by name it was Hanno. I still want to die when I think of how stupid I was to let him take me to his apartment in Prato, but in all fairness to the people seated near me, I shouldn't have just groaned out loud. Now they think I'm five seconds from needing a barf bag, and the thought has a few of them looking like they might need one too. Oops.

Ten years is a long time, yet the look on your face when you opened the door and saw me kissing Hanno still haunts me. I don't mean to sound dramatic, but it's true. Before that moment we'd never met, and yet I felt like I'd betrayed you, and the thought of you lumping me together in your mind with whoever else Hanno had brought home was almost unbearable. There's no denying it; I felt connected to you, which, as I told myself that night, was completely absurd. I mean, talk about rebounds. I kiss Hanno, he breaks my heart, and bingo, there *you are, and even accidentally bumping into you has the power to give me goose bumps. You can understand, I'm sure, why I decided I couldn't trust myself. Why I felt that the whole night had to be pushed aside, forgotten. It was just too much. So fast, so intense. One minute we were strangers, the next you were telling me you loved me.*

While apologizing to Gram about the gratitude rock I put through her window, she talked about my grandfather, and how meeting him felt like finding what'd belonged to her all along but had been lost. Because of this, the parable of the lost coin has grown to have special significance for her, and since my scripture study has been spotty lately, I decided to go ahead and memorize that parable. I don't know that it means as much to me as it does to Gram, but I do admire the lady in it. She's no loafer. Until she finds what she's searching for, she keeps sweeping. Over the past ten years, when it comes to finding my future husband, you could say I've done a lot of sweeping, and I'll be honest, I'm tired—tired of dinner and a movie, bowling, picnics, lunch, long walks on the beach, and, it must be said, didgeridoo concerts. I'm ready to put the proverbial broom away and announce that the sweeping is done. But if, Peter, you turn out to not be my future husband, then just like the woman in the parable, I will keep sweeping, until I find him, the one who was mine all along.

I guess we'll just have to see what happens.

With love,

Sophie

"George," I said, as my brother, opened his front door. It was past ten at night and George was dressed in reindeer-covered flannel pajama bottoms and an old 5K T-shirt.

"Sophie?" he said, folding his arms against the cold. "You're here?"

"I'm here," I said, feeling a twinge of guilt for landing on their doorstep so late and without warning, but just a twinge. Maybe it was silly, but I hadn't wanted Peter to know I was on my way.

George looked up and down the empty street. "So how'd you get here? Mary Poppins's umbrella?" he asked.

"More like an airport taxi driven by a guy with a lead foot. He took off like a bullet as soon as I paid him. I hope it's okay that I'm here, so late and unannounced." A solitary snowflake landed on my cheek, and my breath hung about me like the little match girl's.

George opened the door wide and motioned for me to come in. "Of course it's okay you're here," he said, looking around their flat, crammed with the debris of their growing family. "Our manor is your manor. We'll just put you in the east wing, also known as the children's room/exercise room/sewing room/office. Imi's in our bed tonight (big surprise), but Albert's asleep in there, and his bed has a trundle. You don't mind, do you?"

"Of course not," I said, rolling my suitcase inside. George shut the door. After a busy day of travel through cold, slushy weather, the apartment's warmth and quiet felt luxurious.

"I'd put you in the west wing, but that's where we house all the servants," he said with an apologetic shrug. "The bone china, suits of armor, and Peter. He's in there too." George gave me a knowing look. "You usually stay at the Hilton when you're in town," he said.

I cleared my throat. "They're cutting costs at work. You know how it is; this economy's a tough one."

"So this has nothing to do with Peter," he said, his hands turning at the wrists, encouraging me to say more, but I wasn't ready for that, so I just stood there, silent. George kissed me on the head. "Not that it matters, but I'm hoping it does have something to do with Peter, and not just because my wife's a terrible matchmaker. He's a good guy, Sophie."

"I know," I said, quietly.

"Just be careful," he said. "We like to think of our home as a broken heart–free zone."

I kissed him on the cheek. "I'll be careful," I said, then crept into the east wing and went to bed. Or tried to. Eyes open, I lay awake listening to Albert breathe, my mind racing from one thought to another. An hour went by, and through the wall I heard Imogene fuss and Margaret soothe her. A hole like the kind that open up and swallow houses in Florida seemed to be growing in my heart. I wanted to touch Sarah, hungered to see her standing in front of me smiling, her braces joined here and there by neon pink rubber bands. I shut my eyes and tried to will myself to sleep. It didn't work. Adrenaline was bursting inside me like water from a fire hydrant, forcing fatigue to the back burner. *She must be bouncing off the walls that I'm here*, I thought. *If I could see her right now she would rush toward me, fling her skinny arms around my neck, and hug me for all she's worth. Way too close to my ear, she would scream like a fan of the latest boy band, and declare that she knew it—she knew I could find him. Then on a dime, her face would turn serious and she would say, "Mom, now it's time to fall madly in love with him, marry him, and have me."*

I sat up in bed and cradled my head in my hands. What was I doing? This was crazy. Maybe I was crazy. Who has conversations with their future daughter? And who lets a ten-year-old play matchmaker? I liked Peter, but what could really happen between us in a few days, especially when I had so much work to do? I didn't have time for riding the London Eye with him or ogling the crown jewels. Even squeezing in dinner and a movie would be hard to pull off. This ad proposal was going to be huge for my career, assuming Neal Crosby loved it. And he would. Of course he would. Ads were what I did, and I did them well. Just last year my ad for Vivify Skin Care had created considerable industry buzz.

The essence of the ad had come to me while jogging through Central Park and seeing a mother chasing after her two-year-old. I noticed that she was beautiful, not twenty-something beautiful, but beautiful. She had taken good care of herself but didn't appear to be obsessed with her looks, which added to her allure. She wasn't chasing her youth; she was chasing her kid. And from that observation sprung the "chase" campaign: a beautiful, happy mother saying, "I don't want to chase my youth. I want to chase my kids, but I want to look good doing it." This was followed by a series of print ads of women from different walks of life saying what it was they were "chasing." Under the picture of the surfer, the line read "I chase the perfect wave"; for the photographer, "I chase the perfect shot"; the farmer, "I chase a bountiful harvest"; and the ballerina, "I chase perfection." At the top of each ad was the company name and tagline: Vivify—Whatever You Do, Look Good Doing It.

Having a gut that can read a client is a valuable commodity in the fast-paced, cutthroat world of advertising. I liked to tell myself I possessed such a gut, that my instincts were never wrong, but the truth was, clients could be fickle creatures. You'd present to them an idea that was innovative, incorporated their wish list, and tested well with focus groups, and sometimes they'd shrug their shoulders and say it didn't grab them. Still, there were times when my gut seemed to double as a crystal ball and I'd know the client was going to love what we'd done, long before the presentation. I wanted to believe this was one of those times. That the idea that had come to me while talking to Sarah was going to wow Neal Crosby, and I was practically convinced it would, until I talked to Peter.

Tired of staring at the ceiling, I grabbed my robe, crept out of the east wing, and headed down the hall to the kitchen. A soft glow was spilling from the kitchen into the hallway, the weak kind of light a night-light provides to keep you from bumping into things. So that was what I was expecting—a night-light, not Peter standing in front of the open refrigerator, looking for something to eat. Peter's back was toward me, so he didn't see me jerk back like I'd just spotted an enormous spider, and since I didn't make a sound, he didn't hear me either. I'm not going to lie. It crossed my mind to poke him in the sides and watch how high he'd jump. But that wouldn't have been very nice. Funny, yes. Nice, not so much. No, the right thing to do, I decided, was to clear my throat. It would let him know I was there, without alarming him. Or that was the game plan. I cleared my throat and Peter jumped like I'd just fired a cannon.

Peter turned around and whacked his hand on the fridge. "AAWW!" he cried, partly from shock, partly from pain.

"So sorry I scared you," I whispered, trying to sound concerned, but then a fit giggles overtook me, which sort of killed it.

Peter cupped his hand to my cheek, drew me into a hug, and

kissed my head. "You're here!" he said, all astonishment, but to his credit, quiet astonishment. If we didn't keep it down, Margaret would flip. "One minute I'm staring at a carton of milk thinking of you, and the next you're here!" He hugged me again, this time tighter. Any tighter and I could have cancelled my upcoming chiropractic appointment.

Silence passed between us, not the awkward kind that gets me talking about the latest headlines, but the kind that happens when you need a moment to soak in something, something so good you can scarcely believe it. Still in his arms, I wanted to open up and tell him that since we'd been apart it had felt like someone wearing work boots was stepping on my heart. That I'd listened to "Muskrat Love" more than once in the past twenty-four hours, and—one more teensy thing—that Sarah, my future daughter, was demanding that he be her father. I wanted to tell him all of it, but doing so would have made me feel as exposed as a shaved lamb, and if there was one thing more than a decade of dating had taught me, it was the importance of keeping my heart bubble wrapped, so I cleared my throat (this time he didn't jump), and I said, "So how was the zoo?"

Peter pulled back, and in the half-light from the open refrigerator, he gave me a look that said, *You seriously want to talk about the zoo?*

That was my story and I was sticking to it. "Did you, um, see the elephants?" I asked, twisting a bit of my hair around my finger.

Peter quietly shut the kitchen door, turned on the light, and closed the refrigerator. We squinted in the brightness. "Elephants, monkeys, we saw it all," he said as he pulled out a chair at the table for me. A shadow of scruff had grown on his face during the night, and as he looked at me, he scratched it. "By the way, the flamingos send their love."

"Thanks for the message, Dr. Dolittle," I said, wishing I had the nerve to reach across the table and hold his hand. Not because Sarah wanted me to, but because *I* wanted to.

Peter leaned forward and slid his hands across the table until they were just a few inches from mine. "I thought it was generous of them, considering . . ."

My fingers twitched but stayed put, because, the truth was, I wanted him to make the first move. "Considering what?" I asked.

"That they agreed with your mother—you shouldn't have left early."

I clucked my tongue in annoyance and put my hands in my lap.

"They also said not to shoot the messenger or anything with feathers."

Peter was about to see my sassy side. "Well, you can tell the flamingoes—" I started.

"I can't," he interjected, shaking his head slowly. "I can't get reception in this part of London."

"Then when you get a chance, let them know that I didn't leave because I wanted to. My boss wanted me to be at a meeting."

"You could have told him no," he said, his gaze fixed on me. "At least that's the flamingos' opinion."

"You don't say no to the chance of a lifetime!" I said, raising my voice so high Peter made calming shushing noises.

"Don't worry about what the flamingos think. Not only are they opinionated, but they have a brain the size of a Tic Tac. Tell me about this chance of a lifetime you've been given," he said, and then he smiled, sending my sass to go sit in the corner.

No question about it, Peter had a knack for calming me down. As I told him about the opportunity I'd been handed, I could feel the tension draining from me. Unlike my mother who viewed listening as a chance to catch her breath before hammering her point further, Peter really listened, and it let me know that if the ad campaign was important to me, it was important to him.

"So what have you got so far?" he asked, getting up from the table to make us hot chocolate.

"I like to come up with the slogan first and let it influence the other choices that need to be made about the ad," I said, bringing my feet up on the chair and wrapping my arms around my legs.

Peter poured milk into a saucepan and turned on the stove. "So you've got the slogan figured out."

"Thank heaven," I said, resting my chin on my knees, feeling my strength wane by the thought of all I had to do by the thirtieth.

"So let's hear it," he said, stirring chocolate powder into the bubbling milk.

I bit my lip. "I don't know if I'm ready to share. It's still a little rough."

"Come on," he said. Peter poured the hot chocolate into two mugs and placed them on the table. "I promise I'll love it."

The kitchen was chilly. I wrapped my hands around a mug, enjoying its warmth. "I don't want you to promise you'll love it," I said.

"Then I promise I'll hate it."

"Just tell me the truth!"

"Fine," he said.

We drank our hot chocolate in silence as I mulled things over. On the one hand, feedback was helpful, but on the other, new ideas were like incubated babies. You had to be careful with them, because they were fragile. *You mean your ego's fragile,* said my mother's voice inside my head. *It is not!* I argued back, marveling that even when we weren't on speaking terms, we didn't get along. In my mind's eye, I could see her arch her heavily penciled eyebrow. *Prove it,* she said. *I will!* I shouted back.

"Is everything okay?" asked Peter before taking another sip of hot chocolate. "Your nostrils are flaring."

"Everything's fine," I said, shaking my head a little to clear it of my mother and lingering self-doubt, "and I'm ready to tell you the slogan."

Peter rubbed his hands together. "Lay it on me," he said.

I put my feet on the ground and leaned forward. "Our client, Luxe Air, is a new airline for travelers who want their flight from New York to London to be restorative."

"Sort of like a spa in the sky."

I shook my head. "Too frivolous, that's definitely not the image they want to present. The majority of Luxe Air's passengers will be business travelers who need to hit the ground running when they arrive at their destination. So, travel time needs to not be draining. No cramped seating, no coffin-sized bathrooms."

"Where do I sign?" asked Peter.

"Of course, Luxe Air travelers do pay more, but in comparison to first-class travelers on other carriers, they're actually—if they use the reward system—paying less. And they get so much more at that price point."

"So then go with the more bang for your buck angle."

"Maybe later in the campaign, but not to start. Luxe Air's image has to be established first, that this airline is for the successful, the affluent, and for those who just want to experience the ultimate in transatlantic travel."

"I'm with you," he said, his hands moving like he was helping me pull forward into a parking spot.

"They are passengers who are accustomed to the finer things in life," I said, stalling.

"And so . . ."

"And so the slogan is . . ." I looked just above Peter's head, trying to visualize my idea lit up in Times Square on an enormous billboard, and then I took a deep breath and went for it. "Luxe Air," I said, my voice as sophisticated as I could make it, "the fine line between heaven and earth."

Peter folded his arms and shoved his lips to one side, and though I'm no body language expert, I knew that wasn't a good sign.

"You don't like it," I said as stupid tears welled in my eyes. "I was so convinced I had a winning idea, but you don't like it."

He rubbed the scruff on his chin and thought for a moment. "Sophia," he said, his voice gentle, "I need to be honest with you. Your slogan makes me think of death."

I felt as strong as a house of cards shuddering in the breeze, but somehow I managed to hold it together. "Why is that?" I asked.

Peter pushed his mug of hot chocolate to the side, leaned forward, and placed his hand on my wrist. It felt warm and comforting, but that didn't stop a cold blanket of desolation from wrapping itself around me. "I understand that by 'the fine line between heaven and earth' you're describing a luxury airline," he said, "but I get it only after I've already thought of people flatlining in the hospital. Maybe it's just the physician assistant in me, Sophia," he said, "but that phrase brings to mind how tenuous life is, and I don't think that's something you want to remind people of when they're about to soar through the sky in an aluminum tube held together by rivets."

I didn't defend my idea, didn't fight for it at all. Instead, I put my head on the table and sobbed.

"Hey, hey," said Peter, bending close to me and patting my arm. He said more, but it was drowned out by the sound of my misery.

I lifted my head, remembering as I did that I'd forgotten to take off my mascara. No doubt Raven's Wing Lustre was streaking down my face, making me look hideous. I tried to speak, tried to tell him he was right, the slogan was all wrong, and thank him for his honesty and for not wincing at my train wreck of a face, but an invisible hand seemed to be gripping my throat, making speech impossible, so I put my head back down and sobbed some more.

Peter tapped my arm. "All right," he said, his voice firm but still gentle, "that's enough."

I sat up, wiping my eyes (and nose) with my sleeve. "You don't understand," I wailed. "Tomorrow's the deadline, and I have nothing else. My mind is completely blank."

Peter picked up my empty mug, filled it with more steaming hot chocolate, and placed it in front of me. "Then we'd better get to work."

"We?"

"Sure."

I shook my head. "No, I couldn't do that to you. And besides, this campaign is supposed to showcase my genius." Struck by the realization that I didn't seem to have any, I burst into tears again.

"It will showcase your genius. We'll make sure of it."

"But—"

"Shh." Peter held his index finger in front of my lips. "A wise person once said that true genius is accepting help when you're frazzled."

I tilted my head and stared at him. "What wise person said that?"

Peter pointed at himself. "And I'm telling you, I'm up there with Plato," he said. I laughed though I was on the brink of crying, and doing so weakened my resolve to stay the course and go it alone. "Come on, Sophia," he said, nudging me. "Let's team up, or are you concerned Griffin wouldn't like it?"

I wiped my eyes again on my sleeve, smearing it black. "No," I said. "I think it's safe to say that I've attended my last didgeridoo concert."

Peter tried not to smile. "Are you upset?" he asked.

"Only that I attended so many," I said, making us both laugh. "But seriously, Peter. Don't feel like you need to help me. I mean, you've got a lot going on, right?" I asked, hoping as I did to hear him tell me that his schedule was wide open . . . forever, which probably had to do with me being jet lagged. International travel makes me loopy.

"I leave for the research center in two days, but until then all I've got is one teensy"—he put his fingers close together—"babysitting gig for George and Margaret."

"How long will they be gone?"

"They're just taking a jaunt over to Bath to celebrate their anniversary."

"For a few hours?"

"More like overnight," he said, wincing.

I covered my eyes with my hands and (quietly) groaned. "This will never work," I said.

"They're taking Imogene with them; it'll just be Albert."

My hands fell to the table and I gave him an incredulous look. "Albert," I said.

"Think of it as take-your-rambunctious-nephew-to-work day," he said with an impish smile. I sighed, doubtful that we could pull it off—put together a million-dollar campaign Neal Crosby would love *and* keep track of Albert. Peter took my hand in his, making my heart sprint. "Look, he's got a birthday party to go to in the afternoon, and between that, computer games, TV, and the occasional pillow fight, we'll hardly know he's there." He raised our clasped hands, placing our elbows on the table. "What do you say?" he asked, gripping my hand like he was waiting for the chance to force it to the table. "Will it be Team Sophia?"

I tried not to smile. "If we're on the same team, why are we about to arm wrestle?" I asked.

"Answer the question, ma'am. Team Sophia, yes or no?" he said, his jaw set and his eyes fixed on our joined hands.

I let out a deep breath. "Fine, Team Sophia," I said, and his arm fell to the table as if overpowered by mine.

"Wow, those spaghetti arms pack a punch."

"You let me win."

He let out a puff of air. "What are you talking about?" he said, his thumb moving sweetly across my palm. "I'm on Team Sophia. A win for you is a win for me."

You should kiss him! I thought I heard Sarah say in my head, but it wasn't Sarah at all. It was me. Of course, there was no way I was going to do it. I wasn't the kind of girl who reached across kitchen tables to kiss boys, and besides, my breath was terrible. But most important, it was time to focus. Time for Team Sophia, an idea I'd agreed to not because I thought we'd succeed, or because I was trying to score points with Sarah, but because of the growing realization inside me that when it came to Peter, I didn't like to say good-bye.

chapter 19

OKAY, I'M JUST going to throw stuff out there and you tell me what you think," said Peter as he tossed a foam football back and forth with Albert.

I sat on the couch next to a Lego monster Peter and Albert had put together. So far, Albert wasn't much interested in making himself scarce. He wanted to sit between us, chime in on our conversations, and have us (Peter in particular) play with him. "All right, go for it," I said, stifling a yawn.

Peter tossed the football to Albert, who gave it a karate chop. "Luxe Air—Welcome to the AIRistocracy," he said.

"No," I said, resting my head against the couch's arm.

Albert picked up the ball and threw it. "Cowabunga!" he said as the ball swung left of Peter and hit the china cabinet, rattling its contents.

"Be careful, bud," Peter said, picking up the ball, "and remember to aim." Ball in hand, Peter pointed at me. "Luxe Air—An Air of Privilege."

"Still off," I said.

Peter tossed the ball to Albert, who, trying to give it a roundhouse kick, fell on a mound of throw pillows. "An air of sophistication," said Peter.

I closed my eyes for a second. "Nope," I said.

"Air to the throne."

I shook my head.

"Luxe Air—For People Who Are Loaded."

"Yeah, that'll work," I said, giving him a withering look.

Albert threw Peter the football, missing him by a mile. "Why do you guys keep saying Luxe Air?" he asked.

I propped up my head with my hands. "Because there's an airplane by that name and we're trying to think of what to say to get people to fly it," I said.

"Just tell them to fly on it or you'll punch them in the face," he said, his little fists clenched.

"Interesting suggestion, big guy," said Peter, tucking the ball under one arm and Albert under the other, "and one that makes me think that you've spent too much time today playing Tough Tomatoes on my iPad."

"That game is awesome!" said Albert, punching the air.

Peter hoisted him higher under his arm. "What do you say we leave now for the birthday party so we have some time to run around the park first," he said.

"Yes!" cried Albert, kicking his legs like he was in swim class.

I laid my head back down and curled up on the couch. "I'll wait for you here," I said.

Peter headed for the foyer where all the coats and boots were kept. "Don't finish the puzzle without me," he said. According to Peter, there was but one perfect ad for Luxe Air and together, piece by piece, he was certain we'd figure it out.

I yawned. "I promise I'll wait to be clever until you get back." It was two in the afternoon and since forming Team Sophia early in the morning, neither of us had slept. We had been hard at it, bouncing ideas off each other, doing research on the Internet, and occasionally stepping outside, barefoot and coatless, into the cold to wake up. Just before lunch, George and Margaret had announced that they were ready to leave for their anniversary getaway, and as I curled up on the couch, I thought about how, for Margaret, doing so had been easier said than done.

"Are you sure you don't mind?" Margaret asked, biting her lip.

"They don't mind," said George, motioning with his head toward the door since his hands were full. In one he held the diaper bag and in the other the car seat where Imogene lay sleeping. Anxious for the car's rumble to extend their baby's nap as long as possible, George was in a hurry to leave. "Let's go, let's go," he said.

Margaret picked up her purse and pointed to the bulletin board in the hallway. "I've left you our contact info."

George took a few steps toward the door, then, turning to us, he said, "So if you want to call us, just wait until the feeling passes."

"George!"

My brother put the diaper bag's floral strap across his body like a messenger bag. "Just bear in mind that we're trying to get away . . . and enjoy some peace and quiet with our teething infant."

"I feel so bad leaving, right when the two of you are working so hard on that ad," said Margaret, sounding like she was contemplating getting the luggage out of the car and unpacking.

"We're practically finished," I said, casually hiding my fingers behind my back and crossing them, something I hadn't done since I was a child.

Peter gave me a quick wink. "Seriously, guys, we got this," he said, and walked over to the door and opened it for them.

Margaret gave us each a hug. "Thank you so much," she said. "Let us know if you need anything. And, Peter, I gave Celestina your number and told her you were staying with us for the next little bit, so don't be surprised if she gives you a call." She sang the last few words, a giddy, pitchy soprano.

George looked at his friend and slowly shook his head. "Caller ID, bro," he said before following Margaret out to the street. "This is the reason it was invented."

And then, after George dashed back in a few times to grab some things for Margaret, they were off.

"Oh my gosh, Mom!" cried Sarah, shaking me by the shoulders. "You're in London with Dad! I can't believe it! This is so awesome!"

I rubbed my eyes and the blurry image of my future daughter shifted into focus. "Hi there," I said, sitting up.

Sarah was jumping up and down. "You're together!"

"Geographically, yes, we're together."

"And you're working together on that ad thingy!"

Sarah's hair flew around her as she jumped up and down, a honey-colored halo that I longed to touch. I patted the spot next to me on the couch. "Come here," I said. She sat on her feet, still bouncing with excitement as I gathered her hair and smoothed it with my fingers. "That's right. We're working together on that ad thingy," I said.

Happy yet exasperated, Sarah's eyes shot to the ceiling. "So why haven't you kissed him yet?"

"Oh boy, here we go again," I said, separating her hair into three sections and braiding it.

"Mom, you've got to just lay one on him. Please, Mom . . . for my sake."

Her hair was thick, silky, and easy to work with. "I'll tell you what. Let me finish this ad and then I'll see what I can do," I said.

"You promise?"

"I promise," I said, slipping a neon-green elastic off her tiny wrist and tying off her braid.

"Do you want me to help? I can totally help! Like, I was thinking you could go with 'Luxe Air—We're Super Awesome!' "

I scrunched my eyebrows together and cupped my hand to my chin, like I was mulling over what she'd said rather than trying not to laugh. "That's a thought," I said, "though for some, it might come across as boastful."

"Then what about 'Luxe Air—We're Awesome'?" she said, pushing me over the edge.

I coughed to cover a burst of laughter I couldn't hold back. "Pardon me, um, yes, that does have potential. We'll keep it in mind."

"Do you want me to come up with more?" asked Sarah, her eyes wide and earnest. "I could totally come up with more."

I put my hand on her skinny arm. "That's all right," I said as a wave of love for her crashed over me. "But thanks."

"And you promise to kiss him as soon as you're finished," she said as somewhere nearby a buzzer sounded.

"I promise." The buzzer buzzed again.

"Because, Mom, he's heading to the South Pole soon." The buzzer was relentless.

"I know," I said, scanning the apartment. "Where is that sound coming from?"

"It's the doorbell."

"I'd better get it."

"No, Mom, don't do anything but finish the ad and kiss Dad."

"Sweetie, I will, but I think I can also squeeze in answering the door."

"Mom, no-o-o-o!" she cried, her voice trailing off like she was slipping away from me, down a long and winding slide.

The doorbell buzzed again and my eyes blinked open. Disoriented, it took me a moment to get off the couch and answer the door, and as soon as I did, I realized Sarah was right—I should have stuck to finishing the ad and kissing Peter.

"Hi," squeaked a diminutive blonde with a pixie haircut, "I'm Celestina, Margaret's friend." I'm sure Celestina was a lovely person. Certainly Margaret thought so, but beneath her unzipped jacket she wore a black T-shirt that said: LIFE—NO ONE GETS OUT ALIVE! PREPAY FOR YOUR COFFIN TODAY! And so I wrote her off as a weirdo.

I gave a little wave. "Hi, I'm Sophie, her sister-in-law," I said, unintentionally mimicking the sing-songiness of her voice.

Celestina jutted a thumb over her shoulder. "I'm working a Funeral Expo just up Tottenham Court and thought I'd see if Peter would like to pop out for a cup of tea."

I resisted (barely) the impulse to slam the door in her face. "He wouldn't," I said abruptly, and Celestina pressed her lips into a thin line of annoyance, which was perfectly fine with me. Still, I explained further. "What I mean is, he isn't here, and he doesn't drink tea."

Celestina smacked her lips together and smiled. "I see," she said. "Well, it doesn't have to be tea, does it? We could step out for a glass of wine. Everybody likes a glass of—" Shocked to see me shake my head and mouth the word *no*, Celestina was momentarily speechless. "Doesn't like wine?" she said with wonder. "What is he, a priest?"

"Actually, he is," I said, not bothering to elaborate.

Celestina's mouth fell open. "Margaret left out that little detail."

"Well, what can I say? She's a mother of two, and sometimes paints in broad strokes." Celestina's brow furrowed with disappointment, but I wasn't satisfied. Hoping to make him sound even less datable, I said, "And I should probably tell you he doesn't smoke."

"As he shouldn't," said Celestina, unwrapping a piece of gum she'd pulled from her coat pocket and shoving it in her mouth. "Those things will kill you." She smacked, *smacked*, then said with a wink, "Trust me on that one."

"I guess I'll take forming a smoking habit off my list of things to do today," I said, obviously joking, except to Celestina.

Smack, smack, smack. "Good for you," she said, "but if you change your mind"—*smack, smack*—"here's my card."

I took the card and shoved it in my pocket, wondering as I did, where George and Margaret kept their matches. "Thanks," I said, my nerves jangled from the sound of her gum chewing, "I'll keep that in mind."

SMACK, SMACK, SMACK. "Would it be all right if I came in and waited until he comes back?"

"NO," I said, maybe a bit too emphatically, so I tried again. "I mean, no, but I will be sure and let him know you came by, Cecily."

SMACK, SMACK. "Celestina," she said with a tense smile.

"I'm sure I'll get it right when the time comes," I said. "Anyway, hate to rush, but I've got to get back to work."

SMACK, SMACK, SMACK, SMACK. Celestina put her hands on her hips. "Work? I saw you through the window sleeping."

"Like I said, I'll tell him you came by."

SMACK. "Be sure you do." SMACK, SMACK. "I've sent him seven texts and he hasn't responded."

"Reception in this town can be spotty. Gotta go. Bye," I said and slammed the door shut. *You could have been nicer*, I told myself as I headed into the kitchen to make a mug of hot chocolate. *But then again, you could have kicked her in the shins, so good for you—way to keep it nonviolent.* And then, even though it was a silly thing to do, I high-fived myself.

⌒⌒⌒

"Anything interesting happen while I was gone?" asked Peter when he returned from dropping Albert off at the birthday party.

"Other than a small fire in the kitchen, nothing much," I said as guilt lapped at my ankles. Celestina was all wrong for Peter, that much I was sure about. Still, I should have told him that she'd stopped by.

Peter wiped the back of his hand across his forehead. "Whew!" he said. "Glad you made it out alive. Now, how about we get back to work?"

"Yes," I said, grabbing an apple off the table and sitting in front of my laptop. It was time to focus, time to make things happen, *not* time for the doorbell to buzz.

"Were you expecting someone?" Peter asked as he headed to the entry.

The apple was wedged between my teeth like a roasted pig. "Uh-uh," I said, shaking my head.

"Huh," said Peter, his hand on the doorknob.

Biting off a chunk, I mumbled softly, "It couldn't be. She wouldn't dare." I was almost convinced it was just the FedEx guy and not a perky undertaker when I heard a syrupy sweet, "'Ello!"

"Hello," said Peter, kindly gesturing for her to come inside after she'd already barged in. "You must be—"

"Celestine-ur," she said, pronouncing the A in her name as an R, and then giggling just long enough to make me want to tackle her like a linebacker. "And you must be Peter," she squeaked, wiggling her gloved fingers in his direction.

"And I must be ready to vomit," I whispered, taking another bite.

"Celestina—" Peter said.

"Celestine-ur," I corrected, which they both ignored.

"This is Sophia." Peter's eyes were smiling and friendly, encouraging me to be the same, but I batted the suggestion away like Imogene when offered a spoonful of mashed peas.

"Yes," said Celestina, "we've met." She smiled, though her voice was suddenly cold. "I came by a bit ago. Left my card with *this one.*"

"Oh," said Peter, his eyes widening with surprise at this news.

I bit into my apple. "*That one* did leave her card," I said. "It's in a pile on the kitchen counter," and added under my breath, "a pile of ashes."

"Well, I'm sure you're busy—" said Celestina.

"We're swamped, actually. And don't you have a body to bury?" I asked, tilting my head in the direction of the front door.

"*This one's* got a sense of humor," Celestina said, her voice sweet, but her eyes daggers.

I took another bite. "*That one's* got a pimple," I said as I chewed.

Peter's eyes were wide, imploring me to be nice, and mine were telling him that was impossible.

Celestina sighed pleasantly like I wasn't bothering her at all. "I won't stay long," she said, pulling off her gloves.

"We wouldn't dream of it," I said, smiling.

And then she smiled, pretending she didn't want to punch me.

And then I smiled like I didn't want to put her in a headlock.

And then she smiled.

And then I smiled.

We were at war, a smile war, and only Peter suggesting we both needed to floss was able to bring about a cease fire.

"Look," said Celestina to Peter, "I'm a bit of a Modern Millie when it comes to dating, so I wanted to see if I could take you to dinner tonight."

I tossed what was left of my apple into the trash. "I can answer that," I said, raising my hand.

"No!" he said, his hands flaring like he was trying to stop traffic. "Let me do it." I shrugged and he turned to Celestina. "Unfortunately, I have to pass. That would have been nice, but Sophia and I are working tonight."

"On what?" she asked.

"An ad campaign."

"Ooh, sounds fun. Can I help?"

"Sure, if we keel over." I smiled.

Celestina smiled.

Peter suggested we use whitening strips. "That's truly kind of you, Celestina."

"—Er," I corrected.

"What's the ad for?" she asked.

"A new airline," Peter said.

Celestina frowned. "We don't work much with the airline industry. Very safe way to travel."

"Double darn," I said.

"Thank you for stopping by and for the dinner invitation," said Peter, taking a step toward the door.

"It was my pleasure, Peter," she said, swooping in and kissing him on the cheek.

My fists clenched and my cheeks burned with anger. *Who did she think she was, kissing my, er, kissing Peter! I thought. This isn't Italy! And it's flu season!*

Peter opened the front door. Celestina turned to Peter before walking out, ready to steal another kiss. Not on my watch.

"GOOD LUCK FINDING KILLER DEALS AT THE FUNERAL EXPO!" I yelled, and then we really went at it, smiling at each other like beauty contestants, until Peter shut the door. "That's five minutes of my life I'll never get back," I said.

Peter bit his lip and gave me a puzzled look. "What happened to you back there?" he asked.

I cleared my throat. I'm a fan of throat clearing when there's not much I can say to defend myself. Truth was, I hadn't been that possessive since preschool when a kid named Hedge (what were his parents thinking?) tried to take my shovel during recess. "I didn't like her," I said, shrugging. "But here's the good news. I think the feeling was mutual."

chapter 20

ANYONE WHO TELLS you that each hour is comprised of the exact same number of minutes has never stood in line at the DMV. However, the same way time drags when you're trying to enjoy a didgeridoo concert, it flies when you're working with someone who makes you laugh, and then the next thing you know, your sister-in-law's friend Gemma is dropping off your little nephew and letting you know that at the birthday party the silly boy drank an entire can of Pepsi.

"So sorry," she said, scrunching up her nose. "There were so many children and I'm afraid I lost him for a bit." Albert zoomed around the front room like an airplane. "It was only one can, though, I'm pretty sure of that, and some sweets, but other than that, he just ate pizza and a slice of birthday cake . . . er, well, two slices."

Later, Peter would tell me that I looked like I wanted to go a few rounds with Gemma in a mixed martial arts ring, but at the moment, all I knew was that he was taking over. "Thank you so much for bringing Albert home," he said, opening the door, "and for keeping a general eye on him at the party."

"I didn't do much," she said.

"Truer words were never spoken," I grumbled, but Gemma didn't hear me, thanks to Peter shepherding her quickly out the door.

"Have a great night. Happy New Year to you," he said, and then after one last wave good-bye, he shut the door.

"We'll never be able to do this now," I moaned as Albert zoomed around the room.

"Of course we will."

"Peter, be realistic."

"We're almost there," he said. "We've made so much progress. All the edges are in place."

"The edges? Oh," I said, rolling my eyes, "your puzzle metaphor."

"That's right," he said. "My *brilliant* puzzle metaphor. We've thrown out all the pieces that didn't belong and are closer than ever to fitting together what does."

Albert jumped up and down in front of Peter tugging at his shirt. "Can I play Tough Tomatoes on your iPad?" he asked. "Can I? Can I? Can I?"

Without a moment's hesitation, Peter handed over his iPad to Albert, who then climbed on the couch and started to play.

I looked at Albert, already absorbed in the game, his little feet dangling off the couch's edge, wiggling nonstop. "He should be getting ready for bed," I said, giving Peter a disapproving look.

Peter ran a hand through his bluish-black hair. "Sophia," he said, dragging out the last syllable of my name in a playful way. "He drank a can of Pepsi. He's not going to be tired for a while."

I laid my head on the table. "Which is why we're doomed," I moaned.

"Sophia, I've come to realize you're an optimist."

I sat up. "I just said we're doomed."

"In training," he said.

Tears welled in my eyes. "Peter, we have so much work to do."

He pulled me to my feet. "And we're doing it."

"But what about that Mexican jumping bean over there?" I asked, motioning toward Albert. "What's he going to do?"

"Basically anything he wants," he said. I opened my mouth to protest, but since pulling me up he hadn't let go of my hand, rendering me momentarily speechless. "Within reason, of course," he added, a smile hiding in the corners of his mouth. "Relax, Sophia," he said. "Everything will work out."

I took a deep breath. What was there to say in the face of such positive thinking except "You're wrong!"

Peter tapped his chest. "I'm right."

"Wrong."

"Right!"

"Hey," said Albert, his eyes fixed on the screen, "could you guys keep it down? I'm trying to do something here."

We looked at each other, both of us stifling laughs, and suddenly there was no longer room in that tiny apartment for my gloomy outlook.

"Let's do this, Stark," said Peter, pulling me toward the dining room table where our computers were set up.

"He's so into that game," I said, marveling at my nephew's tenacity. "Can you even remember the last time you played a computer game?"

"Sure, like twenty minutes ago," said Peter.

"I thought you were doing research," I said, pretending to be shocked.

Peter pulled out a chair for me. "I was, but there's something about being transported to the tough streets of the Bronx that clears my head."

I didn't sit down, didn't even come close. Bouncing on the balls of my feet, I flapped my hands like I was in a hurry to dry my nail polish. "That's it!" I cried. "That's it!"

"I don't know," he said. "Computer games can also be a way of running from your problems."

"I'm not talking about playing games. I'm talking about the word you just said!"

"Bronx?"

"No! All day we've been fishing for the right word to build this ad around, and you just hooked it!"

"Sophia, whatever you do, do not forget that word," he said, approaching me like I was holding a bomb.

"It's *transport*, Peter! The word is *transport*! Luxe Air passengers aren't interested in just flying, they want to be *transported*—moved emotionally."

Peter pressed his lips together and thought for a moment. "That actually might work," he said, "but how do you want to use it? Luxe Air—Let Us Transport You."

"That's close."

"Transporting you?"

"Interesting," I said as the two of us began to pace though space near the dining room table was limited.

"What about this," I said, passing Peter, "a wide interior shot of a random airline's economy class. One traveler among the many stands out, because he's miserable and the only one looking toward the camera." I wheeled around and found myself face-to-face with Peter. "Sorry," I said, stepping out of his way, but not before deciding he was the perfect height for me—tall enough to be officially taller than me, but not so much that kissing him involved getting on my toes. I closed my eyes tight then opened them, forcing myself to focus. Now wasn't the time to be thinking about kisses!

"I like it," said Peter. "What's next?"

I cleared my throat. "A voice," I said, passing him again.

"A little girl?"

"Too scary."

"How is that scary?"

"Stringy haired little girls in long white nightgowns pop up in horror movies."

Peter's mouth pulled down at the edges as he thought. "Fair enough," he said. "Then use a man's voice, stately and gentlemanly. You can even throw in a British accent for added gravitas."

"Not alluring enough," I said as he stepped aside so I could pass by. "It has to be a woman's voice."

"A lunch lady."

"Be serious," I said, turning to look at him.

He smiled. "That's the first thing that came to mind; you need to specify."

I smiled back. If he wanted specifics, I'd give him specifics. "Fine," I said, "a woman's voice that exudes beauty, intelligence, and serenity."

He nodded in approval as we passed again.

"Not a hippie-commune sort of serenity, but a peacefulness borne from inner happiness—a happiness with who she is and the direction her life has taken. Oh, and it has a slightly breathy quality, which has nothing to do with a former Nicotine habit."

"You mean your voice," he said.

I snorted with laughter, expecting him to the do the same. "Oh, please."

Peter wasn't laughing. "You have a beautiful voice, Sophia," he said, making me blush. "And if you need to sound breathy, you can run up the stairs in this building."

I stopped pacing. "You really think I have a pretty voice?" I asked.

Peter stopped in front of me. "Absolutely," he said.

What was I doing? Where was I? What the heck was my name? For a moment, everything vanished from memory as I looked into Peter's eyes. In them, there was kindness. I hadn't noticed it when we first met so long ago, but it was easy for me to spot now. And they were such a beautiful, almost exotic brown, they reminded me of spices transported by camels in caravans. *It is, however, totally unfair how long his lashes are, but with a bit of luck maybe Sarah will end up with them*, I thought just as Peter nudged me.

"So it should be your voice, but what are you going to say?" he asked.

I whacked my palm against the side of my head, forcing myself to think. "Right!" I said. "Okay, where was I?"

Peter summed up. "An interior shot of a crowded plane with one passenger in particular looking miserable, and then, you, Miss Stark, say . . ."

I didn't need time to mull it over. The finished product was already unfolding in my mind. "Then I say, 'Don't just fly.' I mean, 'Don't *just* fly,'" I said again, the second time trying to make my voice glamorous, but it didn't sound glamorous. In fact, it sounded like I was doing voice work for the Muppets, but that didn't slow us down.

"Okay, so it's 'Don't just fly' with an up close shot of a beleaguered traveler, and then what?" asked Peter.

"The beleaguered traveler is no longer beleaguered. He's smiling and the shot opens up, revealing the reason why. It's because he is now on Luxe Air, sitting in one of their spacious and beautifully appointed seats."

"I'm telling you I'd smile if I could travel that way."

"You smile all the time anyway."

"That's because you only see me when I'm with you."

"Focus, Peter," I said, like his flirting was tiresome.

"Why do I suddenly feel like I'm at the optometrist?"

I raised an eyebrow. "You're going to make me forget—"

"No," he said, curling two fingers through the belt loops on my jeans, "you're unforgettable."

I gulped. "That doesn't even make sense."

"It does to me," he said, gently pulling us a little closer together. "This has taken us a while."

"Talk about your long hauls," he said, his eyes fixed on me.

"But we're almost there," I said, wondering if we were still talking about the ad.

Peter pulled me closer still. "Patience pays off in the end," he said, leaning in toward me.

I was certain—more certain than I had ever been about anything—that we were going to kiss. Our lips were just inches away from each other; we had done it before. Sure, it was ten years ago, but that still had to count as some sort of icebreaker. Then at the moment when I was about to close my eyes and just let it happen, Albert wedged between us. "JUICE BOX!!" he shouted. "I WANT A JUICE BOX!!"

And the moment was broken, snapped in two by a thirsty four-year-old.

"How about the word *please*?" said Peter, ruffling his hair.

"Puh," said Albert, not finishing the word, just to be a stinker.

"Good enough," said Peter, heading to the kitchen. "So tell me," he shouted as he opened the refrigerator. "What comes next?"

"Hopefully you taking me in your arms," I said, too softly for him to hear.

"What?" he asked.

"Nothing!"

He walked out of the kitchen with Albert, both of them sipping juice boxes. "Please don't tell me you can't remember how the ad ends," he said, offering me his juice box.

I took it and sipped, something I never would have done with Griffin, because, first of all, he never would have offered, and second, if I would have asked, no doubt, he first would have given me regurgitation statistics. I handed Peter his drink. "There's no way I'm forgetting how the ad ends. It's right in here," I said, tapping the side of my head.

"So let's hear it."

Albert sat between us at the dining room table, sipping and playing his game, which was a good thing, at least for me. It made it easier for me to get back to work. "After the traveler is seen to be happily on board Luxe Air, then I—are you sure it should be my voice?" I asked.

"No question."

"All right, so I've said, 'Don't just fly,' and then I say, 'Be transported.'"

"Don't just fly, be transported," Peter said, then bit his lip and thought. I wasn't sure if that was a good sign, but I decided to go ahead and tell him the rest.

"The shot pulls farther away, showing more of the plane's interior, back even more to show the plane in flight, and then just as all that can be heard is the sound of clouds moving in the sky, I say, 'Luxe Air' and their logo appears in the heavens."

Peter tapped a knuckle on the table. "And that, my friends, is how it's done."

"You like it?"

"I really like it."

"I don't know. It feels like it's missing something. You're sure you like it? You're not just saying that because we're running out of time and you're afraid I'll fall apart?"

"Let me put it to you this way: I tell people they're fat all the time."

"Huh?"

"It's the classic question that people answer with a lie. But not me. I'm a physician assistant, and if you ask me if you're fat, I'm going to tell you the truth. So, yeah, I really like the ad. And if I didn't I'd tell you."

"But you don't think I'm fat, do you?" I asked, just as my phone lit up, letting me know I'd received a message.

"I don't know. Let me check," he said, poking me in the side, which I knew was his way of letting me know it was a ridiculous question.

I burst out with laughter and a cry of protest.

Albert looked up from his game. "Uncle Pete," he said, his raspy voice serious, "we're not supposed to tickle girls. Mom says it's inappropriate."

"Okay, and by the way, that is a big word," said Peter, his hands in the air to make it clear he was done tickling girls.

I grabbed my phone off the dining room table. "Yeah, Uncle Pete, inappropriate," I said as I opened the text and read it. "Well, it's a good thing you like the ad, because that was Barry."

"Who's Barry?" he asked, the hint of jealousy in his voice making me absurdly happy.

"He's an intern at our office who's helping me finagle face time with Neal Crosby, the Luxe Air executive I'm pitching to." Peter nodded. "Anyway, he's managed to get me a meeting with him tomorrow at ten in the morning and has booked me on the five-forty train to Paris."

Peter looked at his watch. It was eight o'clock. "Then it looks like Team Sophia had better get busy bringing this ad to life."

Albert rubbed his nose with the back of his hand. "Can I have a bunch of cereal and eat it in one of the big spaghetti bowls like my dad does?"

"Sure," said Peter, albeit a little warily.

"And sit on the couch?"

It was time to put my foot down. "If you're going to eat a vat of Cheerios, you're going to do it at the table, young man," I said.

"Fine," he grumbled.

Peter pointed at me. "You get cereal, and I'll start looking for images we can use?"

"Sounds like a plan."

And as a show of solidarity, Albert burped.

chapter 21

As a chaperone, Albert was no slouch. There was no falling asleep on the job, no letting us wander from sight, and he had a zero tolerance policy for shoulder rubs that he strictly enforced. Not since stake dances had I felt so closely monitored. There was no question about it, Albert ran a tight ship, but it seemed inevitable that at some point my little nephew's watchfulness would wane, and he would rub his eyes, let the iPad slip from his fingers, and drift to sleep. It seemed inevitable, but that's not what happened next, not even close. So—a word to the wise: Unless you like pulling all nighters with preschoolers, treat Pepsi like you would toilet bowl cleaner, and keep it out of the reach of children.

Albert was indefatigable. As we worked on the ad, he worked alongside us, ridding the world of tomatoes bent on a life of crime.

"Albert," I said, getting up from the dining room table and stretching, "aren't you tired of playing that game yet?"

"Nope," he said, keeping his glassy eyes fixed on the screen. "I could play this game forever."

I looked at Peter who was putting the finishing touches on the mock-up we'd created for my meeting with Neal Crosby. "While I'm away," I said, "the two of you should probably spend the day unplugged."

"So you don't want us to use the toaster," said Peter, feigning ignorance.

I pressed my lips into a thin line, like he was trying my patience. "I'm not talking about the toaster."

"Good, because I have bagel plans."

"Try and steer clear of—"

"Please don't say the refrigerator."

"You're killing me."

"Uncle Pete," said Albert as he swiped his little finger across the screen, "quit killing Aunt Sophie."

"Sorry, little man," he said before looking at me and smiling. "You were saying . . ."

"Do something together that doesn't involve a TV, iPad, or computer," I said.

"I'll take him to the park."

"Isn't it too cold?"

"You're asking the guy who works at the South Pole if it's too cold."

"Maybe not for you, but what about El Frito Bandito," I said, pointing at Albert.

"He'll be fine," said Peter, squinting as he scrutinized our work. "It'll be colder this morning when we go with you to the train station." He said this matter-of-factly, like the two of them going with me was a given.

I shook my head. "No, no, no, you don't need to do that."

Peter rubbed his eyes and then looked at me. "Sophia, you're not going there by yourself at four thirty in the morning."

"I live in Manhattan, Peter. I know how to navigate my way around dog poop and unsavory characters," I said, my voice rising the way it does when I argue.

"Which is great," said Peter, his voice softer than before, "but doesn't change that we're going with you."

This isn't traffic court, Sophie, I told myself. *Quit trying to get your way! And remember what your mother says, even if she does annoy you: Never kick a knight in shining armor; they topple too easily.* I took a deep breath. "Fine," I said, looking at my watch, "I don't have time to argue. We'll just make sure he's bundled up like nobody's business."

"Trust me," said Peter, "I know how to bundle."

As I put on my makeup in the apartment's sole bathroom, I wondered if Peter's protectiveness bugged me. Griffin had certainly never fretted over me like that. And hadn't I liked it, the way he seldom walked me out when I left his apartment? And why should he have? I was a confident city girl who didn't need an escort. Over time, wouldn't I feel suffocated by such concern for my safety? *Don't be silly*, I said, as my conversation with myself continued. *It's nice to have someone looking out for me.*

I frowned, staring at my reflection. Maybe there was something wrong with me. My girlfriends had often teased me, telling me that I was a bit of a cat the way I liked to wander the city alone and drink saucers of milk. Okay, so I'm joking about the milk, but they did make a valid point—I liked alone time, and from what I could tell, that didn't seem to be a priority for Peter. He was a bit more like a dog—always glad to see you. Could two such people ever fall in love?

And what was love anyway? If it was what my parents shared, I wasn't sure I wanted any part of it. Sure they'd weathered life's storms together, raised a family in the gospel, but Dad was always having to acquiesce, be the bigger person, the kinder person, the walked-on person. If Mom was angry, it was Dad's job to calm her down, and if she made a decision, that was final, no matter how stupid. There was no talking her out of anything, no coming to an agreement. I knew they cared for each other, but I wondered sometimes if my dad had moments when he wished he had married someone else. At thirty, my search for my husband had been fairly exhaustive, but during all those years of dating, had I ever felt true love? I wasn't sure. And that was at the heart of what troubled me: Would I know it when I was in love? I thought of Hanno and my shoulders slumped. I had certainly gotten that one wrong, thinking I loved him. Ugh. The thought made me want to take a shower, the kind for people who've been exposed to hazardous material.

I rolled on lip gloss and pressed my lips together. There was no time for lamenting past mistakes. Between pitching the ad we'd created and figuring out if I loved Peter, my schedule was packed. I snapped shut my mirror compact. "You can do this," I whispered to my reflection. "You can do this."

At the train station, Peter turned to me and brushed the rain off the shoulders of my coat. "You're sure you have everything?" he asked.

"I've got everything," I said as a call for boarding sounded. It echoed through the great brick arches, but Albert didn't notice. He sat in the stroller, head lolling to one side, at last fast asleep.

Dark circles had formed under Peter's eyes from our all-nighter, but he was far from sluggish. "Don't let Neal Crosby intimidate you," he said, taking my hands in his.

A businessman dashed by us and boarded the train. "I won't," I said, my heart flipping and flopping like a caught fish.

There wasn't time to pause, but we paused anyway, and since we were too lost in each other's eyes to speak, we kissed. During that kiss, there should have been steam engulfing us, stacks of leather strapped trunks lying about, waiting for porters to stow, and corseted ladies with parasols strolling by—it was that romantic. Instead, the speaker blared, telling us they weren't kidding this time—the train was really leaving the station.

"I've got to go," I said, in between kisses.

Peter pulled back, his brow wrinkled with concern. "Text me when you get there."

I smiled and rolled my eyes. "Okay, Dad."

"I want to know you're safe."

Like a Boy Scout taking a pledge, I held up three fingers. "I'll text you," I said, then picked up my briefcase and forced myself to start walking.

Peter curled his fingers around my ring finger, touching me one last time before we parted. "But don't text me what they think of it," he said, as I stepped on the train. "I want to hear it from you in person."

"All right," I said as the door slid closed and the train began to pull from the station, making me lurch forward as if something bound us together and refused to snap. I could have taken a seat or rifled through my purse for a stick of gum. I could have done a lot of things, but I didn't. Instead, I stayed where I was, locked in a gaze with Peter, until the train gained speed, snaked around the corner, and he vanished from sight.

Those kisses we'd shared right before I boarded the train were my personal brand of Pepsi. Too buzzed with happiness to nap, I worked all the way to Paris, fine-tuning my presentation, and thinking, whenever I took a break, about those kisses. Sarah was going to scream with happiness. After all her cajoling, it had finally happened—I had kissed Peter. Or he had kissed me. At any rate, we had kissed each other, and that moment had softened me like butter in the sun, and though Near-Liquid-State Sophie still cared about wowing Neal Crosby, she cared about Peter more—a lot more. There was something freeing about that shift in priorities. It made striding into Neal Crosby's office with confidence effortless, and kept stress and anxiety from clamping down my creativity, so that at key moments in the presentation I was witty, insightful, and, more important, persuasive.

"Be transported?" said Neal Crosby, his brow furrowed after viewing the video Peter and I had put together. "I don't know, Miss Stark. We're talking about passengers here, not crates of salmon."

Crosby was lukewarm. I leaned back in my chair in Luxe Air's glass-walled conference room and stretched. Not because I was panicking and needed to buy time. I just needed to stretch, plus it gave me a moment to take in the room's incredible view of the Eiffel Tower. Team Sophie hadn't nailed it, but it wasn't over. I was still here, sitting across a polished conference table from a man who had the power to green light a multimillion dollar deal. He just needed the right idea, and ad ideas were what I did. They were my thing. There was no crystal ball when it came to advertising—or to life, for that matter—but I knew what I was doing. It was time to trust myself that I could make the right choice. I sat forward, resting my hands on the table. "Mr. Crosby," I said, "at Percy Dilwooten Foster we understand that Luxe Air is more than an airline. It is the art of conveyance—for the discriminating traveler it is the fine *line* between heaven and earth.

Mr. Crosby's eyes opened wide and he smiled approvingly. "I like that. Why didn't you say that from the beginning?"

"Because physician assistants see death at every turn."

"I don't follow, but I like it: 'the fine line between heaven and earth.' And what's more, I like the way you say it. Honestly, your voice was the best part of your presentation."

"Really?" I asked. What was it about my voice lately that people were drawn to?

"Yes, there's a quality to your voice, and it's the perfect yin to your haggard traveler yang that I saw in New York. How can I describe it? I suppose the closest I can come is to say that it possesses . . . radiance, like you're in love. Are you in love, Miss Stark?"

It occurred to me that Mr. Crosby might be flirting with me, which on top of being icky would have been awkward. Blek. But I was firing on all pistons and so almost instantly discerned that wasn't his intention. He was just making an observation. "Possibly," I said.

"Possibly? You sound like my mother when I ask her if she wants to go to Aruba." He paused for a moment, his finger pointed at me. "You should know."

"I'm working on it."

"It's not your taxes, Miss Stark. How could you not know?"

Was I really discussing my love life with one of the richest men in the world? "It's a big decision," I said.

Neal Crosby folded his hands, resting them on the table. "So is deciding who will handle the advertising for Luxe Air, but I'm confident I can make the right choice. Thank you for coming."

I tore a page from a legal pad, wrote down *the art of conveyance* and *the fine line between heaven and earth,* and placed it on top of the of the other presentation materials we'd created. "Thank you, sir," I said. "And I assure you that we at Percy Dilwooten Foster are committed to doing whatever it takes to craft a message that encapsulates all that Luxe Air is and has to offer."

Neal Crosby stood, extending his hand to me. "We'll be in touch," he said, his tone unreadable, which typically would have driven me crazy. Did he like it? Was it a yes? Had I closed the deal? But there would be no anxiety fest today. I shook his hand, thanked him for his time, and walked out of that transparent building—out to a sunny winter's day, not wondering about the meeting or whether to take a gander at the Mona Lisa or Notre Dame Cathedral or any number of priceless things. All I wanted was to get on the next train to London.

I smiled thinking about how Peter would smile when I told him about the presentation, how calm I'd felt, and how I'd saved the meeting by pitching my first idea, the one he'd hated. He would blush with embarrassment and apologize for steering me in the wrong direction, but would be so happy for me that I was able to improvise. The fact that I didn't know if I had the account in the bag wouldn't faze him. He'd shrug his shoulders and tell me whatever happened would be fine, and then, hopefully, wrap his arms around me and kiss me again. Sigh. If those kisses had assured I wouldn't sleep on the way to Paris, the anticipation of more kisses made it impossible to sleep on the way back.

The journey home seemed interminable, but at last I exited the tube near George and Margaret's neighborhood, and walking—okay, running—made my way home. Turning the key and opening the door, I called out for Peter, then Albert, but there was no response. Evidence of their day lay everywhere, toys scattered about the living room as well as half-eaten bowls—large bowls—of cereal. Disappointment was soon replaced by the realization that their absence gave me a moment to enjoy a hot shower, and so after taking my things to the east wing, I headed to the bathroom.

There's a good reason I wasn't born in medieval times. My love of dental hygiene, for one, and second, my inability to live without hot water. For some, massages help them decompress, but for me nothing worked better than a hot shower. All the stress of the day rinsed away as I stood in that tiny stall with the water splashing against my back. I had pushed the limits of my last salon blowout.

My hair had appeared well coiffed for the meeting, but had Mr. Crosby tried to smell it, I would have had to deck him. It was past due, long past due, for me to wash it. I squirted a healthy glob of shampoo into my palm, working it into my hair until frothy suds dripped down my back.

I thought about Peter as I rinsed and repeated. I knew I wanted to see him again, and let's be honest, kiss him again, but did I love him? The question filled me with such angst that I looked upward in frustration, and just at that moment shampoo slid into my eyes. "Oi!" I shouted, doing the dumb thing and rubbing them. My eyes momentarily useless and searing with pain, I groped around, trying to remember where I'd placed my towel. I stepped out of the shower, feeling my way around the bathroom, trying to locate it when I heard the unmistakable sound of the doorknob turning. Shock made my throat as useless at that moment as my eyes. I wanted to shout out, "NO! DON'T OPEN THE DOOR!" But the words wouldn't come.

Dread for what was about to happen turned me numb, so numb that I just stood there waiting for the worst, but then, before the door could open, a hand thwacked hard against it, keeping it shut, and I heard Peter say, "No, Albert. A gentleman knocks before he opens a closed door."

Realization didn't dawn on me; it whooshed like water from a fire hydrant, and there was nothing more to ask. I loved Peter. I loved him completely. The search was over. This was the man I wanted to be with, and this was the man I wanted as the father of my children. I stood there, tears washing away all suds and doubts.

"Sophia, are you in there?" asked Peter as he gently knocked.

"Yes, it's me," I said, trying to not sound emotional. "Did you go to the park?"

"No," complained Albert, "we looked at dumb flowers."

"Shh," warned Peter. "Enjoy your shower. We'll talk later."

"Sounds good," I said, like I was ready to luxuriate, take all the time in the world, and stand under the hot water until it turned tepid. Ha! I wanted to run to him (fully dressed, of course) and tell him I loved him. And if I'd had a moment—even two uninterrupted minutes!—I would have. But, without fail, there was Albert. If he wasn't making some sort of demand (PLAY WITH ME! FEED ME! FEED ME SOME MORE!), he was wedging his way between us. You would have thought that bedtime would have been the answer, but the combination of staying up all night the night before and still recovering from jet lag proved to be a cantankerous concoction, and Albert was determined not to go down without a fight.

"I DON'T WANT TO GO TO BED!" he shouted as he put on his pajamas.

Too bad, so sad, was what I wanted to say, but as anxious as I was to talk to Peter, I didn't want to win the mean aunt award. This was just the sort of situation that when he was eighteen he'd bring up at family dinners. *And then she told me, "too bad, so sad," and threw me in my room. Can you believe it?* No, hard though it was, I needed to be patient and I needed to be nice. Ugh.

"Albert, you have to go to bed," I said, picking up toys in his room.

Albert jumped up on his bed. "READ ME ANOTHER STORY!"

"We've already read five."

"BUT I'M SCARED!" cried Albert

"Of what?" asked Peter, sitting on Albert's bed, holding a fluffy dinosaur.

"STUFF!" wailed Albert.

"Sounds reasonable," said Peter.

"Stay with me, Aunt Sophie! Don't leave!"

Frustrated, I let out a long breath.

Peter slapped his hand against the dinosaur like it was a football and then gently threw it to Albert. "I'll tell you what," said Peter, "I'll handle brushing teeth and saying prayers, and Aunt Sophie will keep you safe from scary stuff."

And so I stayed with Albert, until he stopped making rocket noises, his breathing grew heavy, and his little chest rose and fell slowly and deliberately, which, by the way, took FOREVER. But, at last, he was asleep, and I rushed from the room in search of Peter.

I found him near the front door, organizing the shoes and coats. He had been hard at it while I'd been on scary stuff duty and had already cleaned the front room and kitchen, which scored him some points for me, not that he needed them. I was already in love.

"Hey," I said, walking toward him as my heart tried to relocate itself into my throat.

"Hey," he said, turning to give me a smile. "You know, I was just thinking, and I don't think it's a bad sign that Crosby kept his cards close to his chest today." Peter bent down and placed a pair of wellies on the low shelf where the Stark family stored their shoes.

I swallowed hard. "I agree, but there's something else I—"

"If he hadn't liked what you'd put together, he would have told you outright. What would be the point in stringing you along—"

"I love you," I said, borderline shouted, and as Peter stood up I gathered my courage to barrel forward, and tell him the rest. "Look, I know we hardly know each other, but I know enough to say that you're kind and funny and good, and I never want to spend another day without you, if I can help it. Ten years ago I thought it was hasty when you told me you loved me, and you might think it's hasty for me to say it now, but it's the truth, Peter, and so it demands to be said." I swallowed hard. "I love you, Peter De Boom, and it's time, past time, for us to be together, and so I've got to ask you, will you marry me?"

Peter pushed his lips to one side, and my heart, which had traveled somewhere to the region of my tonsils plummeted like a faulty elevator. "Sophia," he whispered, his hands outstretched as he took a step toward me. "I can't. Just give me some time to explain—" Imogene's sobbing drowned out his words as she, in the arms of her mother, came through the front door.

"Hi, guys," said Margaret. "So sorry to come back with a screaming baby, but Imi's doctor doesn't want her falling asleep with her pacifier and we're trying to stick to our guns about it."

George walked in, suitcases in hand. "It's made for a lovely time," he said.

"You'll thank me later when she doesn't need braces," said Margaret, unfazed by her husband's little jab.

"I'll put her to bed," I said, careful to not make eye contact as I pulled Imogene from Margaret's arms. Tears were spilling down my face, and I didn't want to explain why.

"Are you sure?" asked Margaret as I walked toward the east wing and Imogene's crying turned to shrieking.

"Yes," I said.

"Sophia, wait!" said Peter, but I was already shutting the door and locking it, already telling myself that no matter how much he knocked (and, boy, did he knock) or gently pleaded, the door would stay shut. But it wasn't like it was made of steel.

"Just say whatever it is you have to say," I said, barely loud enough to be heard over Imi's wailing.

"Sophia, not like this. Not through a door."

"Please go," I said, my voice cracking with emotion.

The door bumped, like Peter was resting his head against it, and I thought I heard him sigh. "Whatever you do," he said to George and Margaret, "don't let her leave."

There was no need for someone to stand guard. I wasn't going anywhere. All I wanted to do was cry with my niece and let her wailing mask the sound of my own. And so we cried and cried and cried, until sleep finally overtook us both, and Sarah rushed into my arms, sobbing.

chapter 22

I STROKED HER HAIR, the chance to touch her like a sliver of sunshine on a stormy day. "Shh-shh-shh," I soothed, pretending to be strong though I felt like crumbling, but that's the thing about children, even future ones, they make you pull yourself together. "Shh-shh-shh," I soothed again. "There, there."

Sarah sat up, strands of her hair wet from tears and sticking to her face. "He said he didn't want to marry you, Mom"

I shrugged like that was a minor setback. "I'll change his mind," I said, smiling for Sarah's sake though tears slipped from my eyes.

"But he's leaving for his job at the South Pole tomorrow," sobbed Sarah.

"You make it sound like he'll be at the other end of the world," I said, making her lips curl briefly into a smile, which was for me another sliver of sunshine, even if it was quickly clouded over.

Sarah collapsed in my arms again as a new wave of sobs wracked her tiny body. "Shh-shh," I soothed, rocking her. "Shh-shh-shh." I wanted to turn her face toward mine, dry her tears, and tell her that everything would work out. That disappointment, sorrow, and heartache had nothing to do with being alive, and that she would see that once she was born, which, of course, would be soon. So soon. I wanted to tell her every story had a happy ending—every girl got her perfect guy, and every child their perfect mother and father. There was no reason for tears in this life, not ever—acne didn't exist, and it was never your night for dishes. But how could I paint such a picture when I knew that if she ever entered this world she'd do so crying? No, all I could do was comfort her, stroke her honey hair, and whisper again and again, "Shh-shh-shh "

Time blurred, and for however long she lay in my arms, I drank in the moment, happiness piercing my sorrow, like rays, not slivers, of sunshine, making me wonder if this could be enough—being her mother in my dreams.

Sarah wrapped her skinny arms around my neck, hugged me for all she was worth, and sat up.

"That ought to hold me for a while," I quipped.

She wiped her tears away with her hands, tucked her hair behind her ears, and looked at me with somber eyes. "I have to go," she said.

The storm clouds inside me thickened to a wretched gloom, engulfing me in despair and panic. "You have to go?" I asked, my voice cracking. How had I not seen this coming? Why had I assumed that even without Peter, Sarah would still rob me of sleep? And I didn't want sleep, not anymore. I'd learn to live without it, as long as I could be with her. "No, Sarah, don't go yet," I pleaded.

Her eyes glistened with new tears. "I have to, Mom," she said and took a step away from me.

"No!" I cried, trying to lunge for her, but in that dark and nameless place where we stood, something unseen held me back. "Please, stay! I'm not ready for this! Sarah!"

Sarah took another step into the darkness. "I love you, Mom," she said.

How did I still have the strength to stand, to cry out her name, to watch her turn, and walk away? "Sarah, please! There's something I need to know!" She stopped and turned to look at me. "Were there others . . . waiting for their chance to come after you?"

Sarah nodded almost imperceptibly.

Emotion like a vice clamped my throat, making it almost impossible to speak. "Tell them I love them," I said.

She nodded again and then turned and slipped into the darkness with my heart following after her, unraveling itself into a scarlet tendril of agony that took with it everything—Sarah's birth, learning to sit up, teething, wailing when in the arms of anyone other than mama, her tottering first steps, making friends, looking back one last time before walking into her first day of school, scraping her knees, getting baptized, her braids flying behind her while running, braces, her first date. Like a ribbon dancing in the breeze, my heart chased after her, and knowing I couldn't do the same, I dropped to the ground and wept until the darkness consumed me and I fell, tumbling down, down, down into a sleep so deep no dream could reach it.

And I stayed there until something soft and fragrant smacked me on the side of my face.

I opened my eyes, surprised to see the sun streaming through the window and Albert holding a white rose. "You've been asleep a super long time," he said, his voice raspy as usual.

"Albert!" cried Margaret from the living room, a note of happy hysteria in her voice. "You were not supposed to go in there!"

Albert tossed the rose on the bed. "But she's taking forever!"

"Which is fine, because I still need a minute!" Margaret said.

George rushed into the east wing, his guitar in hand, which struck me as odd. I hadn't heard him play in years. He took in the sight of me—sprawled on the bed, still in the jeans and T-shirt I'd worn the day before—and didn't even raise an eyebrow. "Hey, Sophe," he said, sounding a bit like he'd just sprinted down the street, "whatcha doin'?"

"Drooling," I said.

"Good! Do you mind giving us a minute before you come into the living room?"

"DO NOT COME OUT YET!!!" shouted a frantic Margaret.

I closed my eyes and smacked my lips. "Not a problem," I said. "I'll hang out here for a while."

"Stupid, dumb flowers," grumbled Albert as he left with his father.

"Albert!" warned George.

I rolled onto my back and stared at the ceiling. Wow. What a night I'd had. It had left me so emotionally spent that though I hadn't forgotten a thing, I didn't cry. A cocoon, protective and numbing, seemed to have wrapped itself around me, and for the moment anyway, I felt a calm acceptance about the way things had turned out. It was a new day, the sun was shining in, of all places, London, and somehow my heart had returned to its rightful place without missing a beat. Grabbing the rose Albert had discarded, I sat up and stretched. It was impossible to know what the future held, but whatever happened, I was certain about one thing—I could face it. The last few weeks had made me stronger. "Are you ready?" I asked.

"AAHHH!" cried Margaret.

"Is that a yes?" I asked as the sound of George playing "Hotel California" drifted into the east wing. There was no response to my question, which I took as a no, and that was fine with me. The Luxe Air pitch was over, I'd been denied by the man I loved—so basically, I was in no rush. My brother's clumsy playing of the old Eagles' song made me smile. It had been one of the few songs he had bothered to learn during eighth grade guitar class. Where had the time gone? I had been ten then, Sarah's age. Had I been as precious in my mother's eyes as she was in mine? I wasn't sure. But it didn't matter, the cocoon made nothing matter, but the sunshine and the happy memory of being little and listening to my brother playing the guitar.

"READY!" cried Margaret. "George, how do you press record?"

"Weird," I mumbled as I pushed my feet into my fluffy slippers and pulled on my robe. The cocoon made Margaret's rambling slide past me almost unnoticed. Almost. "All right, here I come," I said.

"WAIT!"

I waited a few seconds. "How about now?"

"OKAY, OKAY, NOW!"

I should have taken a deep breath before opening the door, because once I saw what was waiting for me I almost forgot how. The room was filled with white flowers of every kind—roses, tulips, hydrangeas, lilies, peonies, daisies—all white, all beautifully arranged near white candles, and in the center of it all stood Peter, wearing a tuxedo and a tired smile, waiting for me.

Waiting for me? I looked around the room, half expecting to find Celestina or some other lucky girl ready to walk down the rose petal–strewn path toward him. I spotted George sitting in a corner, playing the guitar; Margaret, Imogene strapped to her back and camcorder in hand, slowly circling the room; and Albert brooding on the couch, his lower lip jutting, but there was no Celestina, no one else at all—just me.

"Sophia," said Peter, a hand outstretched toward me, "could you come here, please?"

Thoughts flashed across my mind like a meteor shower: I hadn't brushed my teeth, I had bed head, the antiperspirant I'd bought that claimed to work for twenty-four hours had lied, my mascara was smudged into raccoon eyes, and my jeans were smeared with Imi's boogers (I hadn't felt like searching for a tissue). I was a train wreck, no question about it, yet Peter wanted me to come to him, which scored him some points, not that he needed them. I was already in love.

The room was thick with the fragrance of flowers, a scent as heady as the feeling of love and family that was there. Whatever Peter did, he had done with George and Margaret's help, and despite the half-baked guitar playing and directorial cues (look this way!) I was glad they were there. So glad.

As I stepped in front of him, Peter took my hands in his. "Sophia," he said, his eyes gazing into mine. "I've spent the last ten years searching for someone like you, but as it turns out there is no one more like you than you." The upshot of looking terrible is you don't have to worry about your makeup, and I didn't. I let the tears fall. "I'm sorry you misunderstood me last night, but I couldn't, after waiting so long, let you deny me this moment."

More tears and maybe a tad of ugly boohooing, but just a tad.

"Would you say your full name?" he asked.

My voice was wobbly with emotion. "Sophia Olivia Stark."

"Essential," said Peter as he got down on one knee. "Will you,

Sophia Olivia Stark, do me the honor of being my wife, the mother of my children, my companion through all my years into what awaits in the beyond?"

"Wait!" cried Margaret, fiddling with her camcorder. "Okay, I'm ready!"

I didn't mind the interruption. That Peter's proposal wasn't wedding magazine flawless made it all the more wonderful. "Yes," I said, and just to clarify, I said it again. "Yes."

And then as Margaret came in for a close up and Albert said, "That's disgusting," we kissed, and maybe would have kept kissing, had Peter not remembered. "The ring!" he cried, pulling away from me and slapping his forehead. "I can't believe I forgot to give you the ring! He fished into his pocket and pulled out a small box that was worn at the corners. "If you want, we can get something flashier, but I didn't want to do this without a ring." He opened the box, revealing a modest diamond flanked by several smaller ones in white gold that had been worked into an elaborate lattice design. "My mother gave this to me when I visited last. It belonged to Sarah."

I wouldn't have traded it for a five-karat honker from Tiffany and Co. "I love it," I said as he worked it onto my finger. "And it fits!"

"I had it sized. That's why I held your finger at the train station; I was taking measurements."

"Sneaky," I said and kissed him.

George came toward us, his face split into a grin. "Congratulations, guys," he said, hugging Peter first and then me. "Mom is going to faint from happiness."

"You mean she doesn't know?"

"Oh, the things Margaret threatened me with so I wouldn't make that call," he said with a playful wink.

Margaret, who had already scurried around the room blowing out candles, kissed her husband on the cheek and then gave us both a bouncy hug meant to keep Imogene from squalling, which it didn't. "We are so happy for you both!" she shrieked almost as loud as her baby girl. "And to think I didn't think of it! But you, Sophie, were dating Griffin, and I just assumed you wouldn't be interested in anyone else. You know what this means."

"You're giving up matchmaking," said George, sounding hopeful.

"Of course not. I'm widening my pool. Unless there's a ring on your finger and you've got a date set, you are fair game, that's all there is to it."

"Heaven help us," said George.

Imogene wailed again.

"We're going to give you two a moment to yourselves and retire to the solarium. Come on, Albert."

He followed behind his parents and baby sister. "Why didn't Uncle Pete fill the house with something awesome, like Legos!" he shouted, kicking at a bowl of hydrangeas as he walked, making a clump of petals fall.

George saw the flower abuse but didn't reprimand his son. "What can I say, son," he said, putting a hand on Albert's shoulder, "life is full of disappointments."

"But it's also full of joy," I said, and then as Imogene wailed in the other room, we kissed, and probably would have kept kissing had one sticky detail not been bothering me. "Peter," I said, pulling away, "can we do this without a lot of fanfare, maybe just elope to the temple. Your parents can't go inside, and I don't want mine inside, my mother anyway." I held his hands, certain his love for me would persuade him into giving me this simple request.

He leaned down (I loved that he was just tall enough to need to do that!) and kissed me on the cheek. "Sweet Sophia," he said, his voice soft. "I love you and that love will never be used as a weapon to wound anyone."

"I'm not wanting to hurt her. I just don't want her there," I said. Peter looked at me, saying with his eyes, *Are you kidding me? Of course it will hurt her.* "It's complicated, Peter. My relationship with her isn't easy."

He held my hands and took a moment to lick his lovely lips. "Remember when we were in Italy all those years ago, we helped a woman who had lost her wedding ring."

"Of course I remember it," I said.

"When I found her ring, do you remember how happy she was? She wanted to share that happiness with everyone, not just a few. And she did. She hugged everyone, those who'd helped her look, and those who were just walking by and heard about what had happened. Everyone, Sophia, *everyone* was invited to rejoice."

Like an old, wise friend whispering in my ear, the words of the parable I'd just memorized came to my mind. "Rejoice with me," I said, "for I have found the piece which I had lost." Peter tilted his head, looking at me with curiosity. "It's a verse Gram taught me, and you're right, even though—I'm not going to lie—a part of me hates to say it, we need to include everyone, even my mother." Peter kissed me again, but I had more to say, and I didn't need a moment to remember it. "But I don't want a long engagement. It's got to be absolutely as short as possible."

Humored by my emphatic tone, Peter kissed my forehead. "And why is that?"

I looked into the eyes of my future husband as a wave of happiness almost knocked me over. "Because, my love," I said, "there's someone I'd like you to meet."

acknowledgments

$\mathcal{T}$HERE IS ENOUGH to do in the course of a day without taking time to follow your dreams. This book has been a dream of mine, and there are those I wish to thank for helping it become a reality. Alissa Voss for being the first person (other than my husband) to say they loved it, Emma Parker for her keen editorial eye—*Letters* is a better book because of your input. Thanks to Michelle May for designing the cover, Melissa Caldwell, and the rest of the crew at Cedar Fort who contributed to bringing this book to life. And thanks to my husband, Rich. For a cheerleader, you have extremely hairy legs and terrible high kicks. Still, I'm glad you're always there, rooting for me.

About the Author

*L*ISA MCKENDRICK LIVES in Lakeland, Florida, where she divides her time between writing, carpools, and occasionally folding laundry. The mother of seven children (all accustomed to wearing unmatched socks), Lisa is author of other books for the LDS market, including *On a Whim*, and, thanks to her husband's support, has earned a master's degree in English from BYU. Lisa enjoys hearing from her readers and can be contacted at Utterance.org.